Rai Johnson
Lakeside

THE
APPLE

THE APPLE

by Devashish Sardana

The Apple
Copyright © Devashish Sardana, 2019

All rights reserved.

No part of this book may be reproduced or transmitted in any form or by any means, electronic or mechanical, including photocopying, recording, or by an information storage and retrieval system—except by a reviewer who may quote brief passages in a review to be printed in a magazine, newspaper, or on the Web—without permission in writing from the copyright owner.

Dedicated to

*Megha Kapoor,
my wife and best friend,
my Apple*

Part One
Finding Eden

Chapter 1
The Day It Is Stolen

Azura, the Queen of Sentinels, jolts straight up in bed, sleep abandoned, dream forgotten.

A lightning bolt illuminates the night sky outside. White light seeps through the veins of darkness, igniting life in the dead of night. Boom! Thunder tears through the white light, nipping its fairy wings before they spread.

Azura's chest heaves as she hauls broken chunks of air into her lungs. Her heart is on fire, like a piece of it has been ripped apart; grabbed, jerked, and yanked out. Unimaginable pain engulfs her. She has never felt this way. Never.

Am I having a stroke? No, can't be. I am too young to have a stroke.

She gasps. She remembers her mother's dying words. And she knows. She knows what the ripping means: for the first time in six thousand years, it has been plucked, stolen, gone.

How is it possible?

She clutches her chest and cries through gritted teeth. "Guards!"

Her voice fails against the ravaging duel between thunder and lightning. She draws a deep breath.

"GUARDS!"

Two men, dark of color and heavy of build, charge into the hut. They wear skirts made of pine needles. The loosely bunched pines waft in the breeze and crackle as the men dash into the room. Both carry tridents, three-pronged spears. Their sinewy, hairless chests shine brilliantly in the white light that dapples through the meshed window in the room.

Apart from the pine skirts, they wear nothing. No armor, no ornaments.

"My queen?" says one of the guards.

"Wake…" Azura pauses and bites her lower lip to wade through the burning in her heart. "…wake Commander Bani. Gather troops."

The guard glances at his comrade, who looks at him, equally confused. He considers asking 'Why?'. But one never questioned the queen. Instead, he asks, "*Now*, my queen?"

Azura glares at him. Her eyes ablaze, her countenance fierce.

"YES! NOW!"

"Umm…" The guard looks everywhere except directly at Azura. "…what should I tell the commander?"

"Tell her it has been stolen." Azura takes a deep breath. "An apple from the Garden of Eden has been stolen."

Chapter 2
I Dream Of Saraph

"Welcome to North Sentinel Island, the last untouched island on Earth!" pronounced the girl in exuberant delight.

The two-seater kayak splashed onto the beach and came to a sudden halt. Almost on cue, the half-crescent moon brushed aside wisps of dark clouds and revealed its glorious soft curves.

"Shhh! Keep your voice low!" he whispered.

"Relax, darling." Her tone was one usually reserved for a pet puppy. "Based on the drone surveillance report, the Sentinel guards never patrol this bay at night."

He knew this. He had read the surveillance report. Twice. After he wrote it. After manning the drone. Himself. But, if there was one thing he swore by, it was *caution*. Which was counter-intuitive to the profession he had chosen, that is if one could call treasure-hunting a profession. But, then, years before word got around about his treasure hunting ability, he was a ten-year-old swindler on the streets of war-torn Mogadishu (Somalia) in the early 1990s, helping resistance fighters kidnap spoilt rich brats of corrupt Somali politicians. He hadn't cared if the brats were grown men or his age. He needed the money to feed his baby sister and fend for himself. Especially after his parents had chosen to go grocery shopping the same day a suicide bomber visited the neighborhood market. Swindling was *just a job that put food in the stomach* – that's how he tried to convince himself always, never successfully. But it was a job that required above anything else, caution.

"I know, Michelle!" He couldn't help with undertones of exasperation in his voice. He wasn't sure if the annoyance was directed at Michelle or his past sins.

He sighed. "That's what scares me. What's so treacherous that they don't even bother to patrol this bay at night?"

Michelle ignored him. She raised her hand to check the time on her gaudy pink watch. He had gifted her the analog watch on their one-month dating anniversary. She wanted to celebrate the "big occasion". She'd asked – no, demanded – a gift. For his mental wellbeing, he kept the frivolous thoughts of protestation to himself, and carefully picked a gift with Michelle's favorite Disney character – Elsa, the Snow Queen from the movie *Frozen*. Now, sitting behind Michelle in the kayak, he saw Elsa glow in the dark, clamping both hands above her head at twelve. Midnight. Give or take a few seconds.

"Right on schedule!" Michelle announced. She unhooked her seat belt, grasped the strap of her cross-body satchel and jumped onto the beach. "Let's go! Let's go!"

The kayak wobbled in the squashy sand. He braced himself, still strapped in the seat. He shook his head. There was no point in asking her to keep the excitement levels down. Michelle was born that way.

"Wait!"

He unhooked the seat belt and stood. Cautiously, one foot at a time, he stepped onto the beach, trying to prevent his boots from sinking in the mushy sand. The boots were new, especially bought for the mission; carefully polished and shined an hour ago with such gusto that now he saw the silhouette of his reflection in the boots before they sank into the mush. He grimaced. All that effort. Wasted.

He unzipped the thigh pocket on his trousers and took out a compass. "Let me align our direction with true north."

The instructions from his rich client, Dr. Costello, the aging chairman of *the* biggest pharmaceutical company in the world, had been simple: "At Sentinel's end, let the true north guide you to the Garden."

Dr. Costello had elaborated between coughs that sounded like the old man's death knell (lung cancer?). Sentinel's end meant the North Sentinel Island. It was a speck off the southern coast of India in the Bay of Bengal. A quick Wikipedia search told him it was home to the last uncontacted tribe on Earth – the indigenous Sentinels, apparently among the first homo sapiens to walk the Earth. The Indian government had banned any contact with the Sentinels after peaceful anthropological missions to the island had turned ugly. The Sentinels had attacked the gift-bearing anthropologists with spears and arrows. As if the Sentinel's entire existence depended on protecting the island. They wanted no friends, no gifts. They wanted to be left alone. The Indian government had complied. What riches could they hope to claim by invading a tiny island of hunter-gatherers in the middle of the ocean?

True north, Dr. Costello had explained, meant the North Star. And the Garden – here was the kicker – was the lost Garden of Eden! He was drinking coffee (black, no cream) when Dr. Costello had made the revelation. He all but spewed the coffee on the expensive-looking Turkish carpet in the chairman's plush London office. "It is a myth!" he had protested. But Dr. Costello had convinced him. Not with logic, not with scientific research. With a signed blank check.

But, finding the Garden of Eden was only half the mission. Finding the Apple Tree of Immortality *inside* the Garden was the other half. The better half. Dr. Costello had promised, "Bring me an apple, ripe and uneaten. Prove its existence to me, and another check will be yours."

Now, he replayed the vague instructions to reach the Garden in his mind. He knew from past treasure-hunting expeditions: having instructions to reach the prize was one thing, successfully finding the actual prize was another. Who knew what dangers lay ahead?

He flicked open the compass and aligned it with a narrow path, the only path out of the bay.

Michelle walked over and cupped his face with her hands. Two green eyes, like oval emeralds floating in cream – an endowment from her Slavic heritage – gleamed at him from beneath her long, fake eyelashes. Her face was spotless – no freckles, no age spots. But without the usual touch of color cosmetics, her face reflected a pale, almost yellow, hue.

"Darling," she said softly. "You don't need a compass. At least not yet. There is one way out of this bay. And it follows the North Star. We did our research. We prepared for three months. We know this." She spoke like she was talking sense into a five-year-old. "Now let's go and get some action!"

"It's never a bad idea to double-check. But you are right," he said, closing his compass. "We know where to go from here."

She gave him a quick peck on the lips. They switched on their heavy-duty neon flashlights. She clutched his hand and led the way. The beach merged into a thick forest walled by tall, impenetrable trees. There was only one way into the forest; only one way that perfectly aligned with the North Star. It was a narrow forest trail, beaten down centuries ago with such force that not a shrub had dared to grow since.

"Is the dagger secure?" he asked.

She nodded and pointed to her right boot. Dr. Costello had given them the dagger. It was an ancient blade made of silver, short, wide with sharp serrated ends. On its handle was carved a seven-headed snake, a king cobra, its seven heads bunched together like a protective canopy overlooking the blade. According to Dr. Costello, it was "The key that unlocks the gateway in the tree." Which gateway and which tree he had no clue.

They entered the hallowed forest in a single file. Suddenly, wings fluttered, branches shook, and leaves fell. A raucous chirping of crows filled the air. Chirping that sounded more ominous than cheerful. They stood there, stunned.

"That was scaryyy!" She tittered.

"Well, seems like we are not welcome here," he said.

She let out an involuntary laugh. "Ha! What were you expecting? A bow-tie wearing concierge with a welcome drink in hand?"

They brushed aside the momentary scare and marched on. The path meandered like a lazy snake. It narrowed with every step. Occasionally, they had to walk sideways, shoulder to shoulder, to maneuver the tight path. No one spoke a word. He was enjoying the solemn serenity. She was scared.

They came to an abrupt halt thirty minutes into the trek. A gigantic redwood tree blocked their path forward. He flashed his torch from the bottom to the top of the tree. And then on either side. There was nowhere to go, except to trace their steps or cut through the dense foliage on the sides with a machete.

"Well, that's a quick anti-climax to our adventure." She still seemed nervous. "On the bright side though, now you know why Sentinel guards don't patrol this area. It's nothing but a dead end."

"No, this might be the tree with the gateway."

"Do you see any gateway in the tree? I don't."

He shook his head. "They beat this path for a reason."

"Yes, someone beat it for a reason. But later someone else planted a tree to secure the path. Just like our politicians," she snickered. "One does the work, and the successor overturns it."

He wasn't convinced. He hadn't prepared for months and come this far to turn back within half an hour. He moved closer to the redwood and flashed the light on its trunk. The trunk was massive, as wide as the red buses in London. It stood like a fifty-story skyscraper in the middle of the forest. He examined the trunk from its leftmost corner to its rightmost, scraping his hand over the bark, stopping at every contour that seemed out of place. But there was nothing out of the ordinary.

Till his hand reached the middle of the tree.

A paper-thin rectangular slit had been incised into the bark. He focused his flashlight on the slit. The wood had been shaved off. Right above the slit was a mark. He bent closer and squinted at the carving. It made his heart knock faster.

"What is it?" the girl asked.

"Show me the dagger."

"Why, what is it?"

He stepped away from the tree. "I think we found the gateway to Eden. Look."

She squinted at the spot illuminated by his torch and gasped. A coiled, seven-headed snake was carved on the tree. It was the same mark as on the head of the dagger.

She bent hastily, threw aside her smoky brown hair, and took out the dagger strapped inside her boot. She placed the blade next to the mark on the trunk. There was no denying it. The marks were identical.

"Wow!" She exhaled the breath she had been holding.

"There is also a slit below the mark," he said. "I bet the dagger goes there. The key to open the gateway."

"Then what are we waiting for?"

She stepped forward, located the slit, lined up the tip of the dagger, and thrust it into the redwood. She let go of the dagger.

They waited. Nothing happened for a few seconds. Then, suddenly, the dagger handle started to glow a bright crimson. The dagger itself started to quiver as if waking up from slumber after years. It was both frightening and fascinating.

"What's happening?" she said, her voice a blend of impatience and fear. "Should we run away?"

He shook his head, his gaze never leaving the enchanted dagger.

Slowly, the dagger started carving into the trunk, like a crimson laser beam cutting through wood. They watched in awe as the dagger traversed a full circle, steadily carving an oval door large enough for five people to walk through the tree together. Once the door was carved, the dagger fell to the ground. It lay motionless, no longer bursting with crimson hues, in deep slumber again.

They glanced at each other, unsure of what to do next.

She took a step toward the dagger and was about to pick it up when he said, "Wait! Don't use bare hands. It might be hot."

He took out a cotton handkerchief from his pocket and used it to pick up the dagger.

He chuckled. "Would you believe it's freezing cold!"
"Seriously?"
"Here you go." He offered her the dagger.
She gingerly touched the dagger with her finger, as if the carving was a real snake. The dagger was icy. She took it from him and secured it in her boot.

"Time to open the door," he said.

He gently pushed the door in the tree. The large block of cut wood fell into the doorway, revealing a huge dark hole in the tree and beyond. He waited, trying to hear the crashing sound of the falling door contacting the floor. There was no sound. No way of deducing the depth of the fall. It was as if there were an abyss beyond the opening.

He bent forward to inspect the deep black hole. He put his hand into the hole, one finger at a time, unsure of what lay beyond. For a moment, he imagined some black magic would transport him to their destination. Or worse, someone would grab his hand and drag him into the abyss. But nothing happened. It was just that – a large black hole of nothingness.

He turned and faced the girl. "What now?"

She shrugged her shoulders. "I do not-"

Suddenly, he saw her eyebrows contort as she focused on something behind him. Her pupils dilated, her mouth opened, and blood drained from her face as she forgot to breathe for a second. She looked shaken to the core.

"Welcome!" He heard a deep-throated voice behind him.

He twisted on his heels. Standing between him and the black hole stood a creature. A creature he had only seen once in his life - on the dagger handle.

A seven-headed snake!

Bright yellow eyes drilled him. At about twenty feet, as tall as a duplex house, the snake towered over him. Seven blood-red fork-like tongues stuck out from each head, hissing menacingly. The snake had emerald-green horns, each adorned with a diadem. Like a prince among snakes. He couldn't decide which part of its anatomy he dreaded most – the terrifying eyes, the hissing tongues, or the sharp horns.

While he contemplated in a frozen stupor, the snake opened its belly and out came two human-like hands. The hands were fire-engine red. Milky goo dripped from them. He grimaced and retched, both at the same time.

The snake joined its hands at the palms. "Welcome! I am Saraph, the gatekeeper of paradise, the Garden of Eden."

He finally blinked and moved his lips, "You can speak?"

Saraph laughed, a terrifying boom of noise interspersed with hissing.

"Usually that's not the first thing humans say when they see me."

"Then what do they say?"

"I don't know. I can't hear them."

"What do you mean you can't hear them? You can hear me fine right now." He realized his accusatory tone the moment the words left his mouth. He took a step back, fearing unthinkable repercussions from a giant snake.

Saraph lowered its seven heads close to his, the slippery tongues inches from his face. Saraph hissed, "I can't hear them because they are in my mouths by the time they open theirs to speak. After that I only hear the crushing of bones in my throats."

He cringed while Saraph hissed. It sounded like glee.

"Then why do you welcome us and not..." he looked askance at the girl before finishing the thought, "... and not kill us."

"I am the Gatekeeper of Eden. I respect the key. You used the key to unlock the door, so here I am welcoming you. If you had forced open the door, I would be having dinner right now."

He opened his mouth to speak, but no words came out.

Finally, Michelle spoke up with her usual exuberance. "Okay, great! Can we enter the Garden now?"

"Of course! All you need to do is leap into the hole in the tree," said Saraph. "Are you ready?"

Michelle hesitated. She looked at him, her face confused - should we trust this creature?

He shrugged and nodded. What else could they do? You obey a seven-headed snake or get eaten alive.

"Yes, we are ready," she finally replied.

"Very well." Saraph slithered away from the tree. It coiled its long, scaly body and sat behind them. "You may jump. One at a time."

They inched to the edge of the hole.

She whispered to him, "I feel like a cornered deer, forced to jump off a cliff." She forced a smile. "See you on the other side. Hopefully still alive!"

Before he could muster a reply, Michelle leaped into nothingness. He heard her shriek, a cry that dulled to nothing after a few moments. She was gone. Alive or dead, he had no clue.

He waited at the threshold where the earth met oblivion. His instincts told him not to jump. Every inch of his body told him that something was not right. Why would you fall into paradise? Don't you soar to paradise or heaven? You fly, you don't fall. You only fall into- He gasped at the realization. Hell!

He felt a cold shudder on his spine and a slimy tongue on his nape.

"Just having the key does not make you worthy of Eden," Saraph hissed in his ear. "First prove yourself worthy. Pass the three divine tests of body, mind, and soul. And you shall find Eden."

And two slimy hands pushed him into hell.

Chapter 3

Who Am I?

"No! Don't push me into hell!" My voice reverberates in my ears.

I fall through darkness; fall till my shoulder hits the ground hard, darkness till I open my eyes and bright sunshine blinds me. I blink rapidly. I am on the floor. I look around and find myself in a small, clean room. No Saraph. No girl. I brighten up at the realization - it was only a dream. Saraph and the girl were figments of my imagination. The reality is calming. Of course, seven-headed snakes with slimy red hands do not exist. Of course, the girl was imaginary. What was her name? Yes, Michelle. She felt so real, but I am sure I don't know her.

The room is cubical, maybe ten feet in all three dimensions. Big enough to comfortably hold two people my size. But nothing more. Right next to me is a bed of sorts, a rectangular block of stone covered with soft shrubbery. Must be the bed I fell from when Saraph pushed me in the nightmare. There are no windows in the room. It's completely airtight apart from the door. Is it a prison?

I suddenly realize that these are strange surroundings. I have never been here before. Where am I? Panic starts to grip me.

"Hello! Anybody there?" I shout.

Nothing happens. Then, after a few moments, I hear the door open. By the time I raise my head and look, the door is banged shut again.

I hear a muffled voice bark an order outside, "He is awake. Call the queen!"

The queen? Did he mean Queen Elizabeth of England? I look around the room again. Doesn't look like Buckingham Palace.

I shut my eyes. Suddenly, I hear a suppressed giggle. I open my eyes again. Instant pain ignites inside my head. It is unbearable. I press my head with my palms and clench my eyes shut. I start counting loudly, "One, two, three…"

Now I hear loud, unsuppressed giggling. I look up. The door is ajar. A little girl, maybe five years old, is peeking through the half-open door. The girl's laughter is infectious. It makes me smile. The smile works like magic and the throbbing in my head subsides.

"Hi there." I wave my hand sluggishly. "What's your name?" I ask.

The girl, still giggling, puts a hand on her mouth and runs away, banging the door shut behind her. Who was she?

I take a deep breath. I smell an instantly gratifying aroma - the smell of fresh rain. The room isn't as airtight as it seems. I hear the rain falling, the faint sound of pitter-patter on the roof. It calms me a little.

I push myself to sit up, but my whole body feels sore, as if I have not moved a muscle in years. As I rise, my head starts to spin again. What is the problem with my head? I stop trying to get up and lie down. "Calm yourself and rest," I tell myself loudly.

"Fallen to the ground, have you?"

I look up and glance at the strange girl—woman?—standing at the door. She is tall and lean, with petite yet muscular curls in her arms. Her skin tone is a darker shade of caramel and her face brims with youthful luminosity.

But everything else about the girl seems odd; odd because of her garb. She is wearing a flimsy skirt made of pine needles, strung around her waist with vines. Two immense pink flower petals cover her voluptuous breasts. Lavender orchids adorn her wrists. And, precariously balanced atop her mane of curly black locks, is a headdress, a crown of sorts, made of rainbow-colored flowers and twigs.

"You have finally woken up after many a day."

I keep staring, trying to search my memory for any recollection of her. Her tiny, beak-like nose is too peculiar to forget. The sharp bend in the middle makes her look like a cute flamingo, ready to nibble at me. I am certain I don't know her.

She looks around and notices a wooden stool in the far corner of the hut. She picks up the stool and sets it beside where I lay on the ground. She sits with a flair, a lady-like elegance. A circular locket made of metal, probably silver, dangles from her neck and glints in the light.

"Do you know what I am talking about?" she asks.

"Who are you?" I question back.

"I am Queen Azura. Who are you?"

"I am…"

Oh my God! Who am I? I cannot remember my name. I summon my thoughts to muster an answer. But no reply comes from my seemingly dead brain.

"What's my name?" I mutter.

"You don't know your name? Do you even have a name?"

I snap at her. "No, my parents thought how fun would it be not to give me a name."

"Calm down. People here would not take kindly to your tone."

"Calm down? How can I calm down? How can I possibly begin to calm down?" My tone intensifies with each question.

Azura sighs.

I continue the rampage. "I wake up in a bizarre place. I am talking to a strange girl. I cannot even remember my name. I don't know where I am or how I got here in the first place. And you want me to calm down?"

Azura raises her eyebrows as she picks up on something I said.

"So, you do not remember how you got here? Interesting," she says half smiling, half nodding, with a faraway look in her eyes, her fingers rubbing the locket around her neck absent-mindedly.

Nothing enrages me more than her distrustful half-smile. Does she think I am lying?

"I have had enough of your mysterious babbling. Tell me, where am I?"

My pointed remark brings her back from her momentary trance.

She looks at me sharply, weighs her thoughts and says, "You are on North Sentinel Island."

I have heard that before...where?

She continues, "It is the last land unexplored by your kind."

"My kind? What do you mean?"

"I mean outsiders. Like you. The curious outsiders who for centuries have tried to unravel the secrets of our land. The pathetic outsiders who have never been able to set foot on this island, lest we chopped their legs and left them on the beach to die."

Her outburst filled with both disdain and calm practicality leaves me speechless. I shift my gaze to check and ensure the wellbeing of my legs. Ah, still there. I heave a sigh of relief.

She stands up and speaks firmly, "We are the protectors of this island. We are the Sentinels."

"The Sentinels? I have never heard of you," I say.

She starts to laugh in my face. "You have never heard of us and still here you are. Care to enlighten me how you got here if you didn't even know we existed?"

"I don't know. I can't remember anything." A deep frustration churns inside me.

I press my temple to dampen the pain that is starting to grip me again. Azura notices my discomfort.

"Come, let's get you up from the ground."

She bends to help me up. Leaning on her shoulder, I manage to sit on the stone bed.

She rummages through a hidden pocket in her pine skirt and takes out three scarlet colored leaves. She hands them to me and says, "Chew these, you'll feel better."

I do as directed, and indeed the leaves prove magical. I feel instant relief.

"Thank you. I feel much better."

She moves closer, looks me straight in the eyes and whispers, "Do you know you are the first outsider who breached this island unnoticed? And the first to successfully steal what we have protected for centuries. Tell me, where is it?"

I know that being a first at something is usually a reason for celebration. Instead, I feel threatened. Her last sentence is ominous of the evils that may befall me, if I don't find the answer, and find it soon.

I tread with caution. "I would gladly tell you, but my memory won't agree. Leaving aside what I stole, I don't even remember how I got onto your island."

"How do I know you are not lying... you filthy outsider!" With that, she reaches for the inside of her right thigh and unveils a dagger.

"I have lived among your kind long enough to know your lies. You grimy beings are capable of killing your mothers with darts of lies."

She flashes the blade and looks me straight in the eyes. "If I tell you that I am going to take away your manhood, do you believe that I am lying?"

"I am telling you the truth, Azura. Believe me." Fear dries up my mouth.

She presses forward, grabs my balls, and says, "Believe you me. I tell the truth as well."

And she slits the string of the pine skirt I am wearing. It falls to the sides revealing my nakedness. I become numb. I want to stop her, even wrestle her, but my body becomes heavier with each passing moment. I try to lift my hand to push her away. But the best I can accomplish is to push the air with my finger.

She throws her head back and laughs. "What happened? I am sure you haven't forgotten how to fight. That is a primal human instinct and requires no memory."

I try to move with all the strength that is left in me. No success.

"You know why you feel numb? It's the scarlet leaves that you ate so eagerly. We call it the Truth Essence. It makes you numb and forces the truth out of you. Now, tell me where you have hidden it?"

"I told you I don't know." I whimper. "Please don't do this. I beg you."

"Then you are of no use to me anyway."

Pressing the blade against my bare skin, she whispers, "It's always cold before the warmth of blood shrouds it. Any last words as a man?"

I let out a deep breath and say, "I can't make you believe me, Azura. In God I trust, and I trust that He knows the truth. That is good enough for me."

I close my eyes and wait for the bloody turn that my life is about to take. There is pin-drop silence in the room; the calm before a blood-red storm.

"You tell the truth," Azura says finally. Her voice is as composed as I first heard it. "No one can escape the power of the Truth Essence for this long, especially when compounded by fear of life."

I open my eyes, dizzy in the aftereffects of the drug she gave me.

She puts the dagger away and shouts, "Guards!"

Two men charge in. They carry tridents and wear nothing but skirts made of pine leaves, just like the one I was wearing.

"Take him to the guest quarters," she orders.

Heavy hands lift my shoulders and my legs, and off I go, dangling in a tipsy world. I notice Azura walking beside my baggy body. But drowsiness clouds my vision. After a few moments, I can hardly see her. Or the guards clutching and carrying me. But before sleep engulfs me completely, a glistening metal on Azura's thigh catches my attention. It's the dagger with which she had threatened me. I find the seesawing motion of the dagger immensely intriguing; flapping this way and that, caressing her naked leg.

Before I completely close my eyes, it hits me where I have seen the seven-headed snake carved on the dagger before - in the dream.

Chapter 4

Spiders or Scorpions?

"Hey! Watch where you are going!" Michelle cried out as he rammed into her from behind.

He lay flat on stone-cold ground. He recalled being pushed into the dark chasm by Saraph. He remembered falling with a thud onto a slant, winding tunnel and sliding down till he crashed into the girl from behind.

"Sorry." He moaned. He raised his head a little, his eyes groping in the dark for a visual of Michelle. It was pitch black. She switched on her flashlight and pointed the light in his face.

"Hey! Move it away!" he yelled, covering his eyes with his hands.

She moved the torch away and laughed. "Serves you right, mister!"

He wasn't amused. He blinked several times as his eyes adjusted and managed to make out a silhouette of Michelle. He stood, dusting his clothes of dust he could feel but not see.

"What is this place?" said Michelle as she flicked her flashlight haphazardly around her. "Looks like an abandoned cave."

He clicked on his flashlight and shone it straight in front of him. There was a narrow, bumpy path that went deeper into the cave. Irregular rocks jutted out from both its sides. He flashed the light above him and followed the roof. It was rocky and crooked, rising above ten feet where they stood and plunging to three feet at the farthest point he could see. He groaned. He was six feet two inches. Traversing through three feet meant crawling on all fours in an old, dusty cave.

"AHHH!" Michelle suddenly shrieked.

"What happened?" He flashed the light in her direction. She stood a few yards away, staring directly at a rocky bulge on the right side of the wall.

She gulped. "There is a HUGE spider on the wall."

He ran to where she stood. On the wall, scampering away to safety, was a baby tarantula.

He forced hard not to laugh. "You call that HUGE?" he mimicked her.

Michelle nodded vigorously, her eyes bulging like a scared puppy.

He burst into laughter. Her expression was too cute not to laugh.

"Don't mock me!" she said sternly.

The reprimand made it worse. He guffawed, his shoulders shaking with glee.

"Get lost! I am not talking to you!" She stormed into the cave with long, angry strides. It took him a moment to come out of the outburst that had befallen him. He ran to catch up to her.

"I am sorry. I was messing around, babe," he said.

"I said I am not talking to you." She suddenly stopped. Jabbing a finger in his chest, she said, "And if you dare call me 'babe' again. I'll rip out that tongue of yours."

"I am sorry, Michelle. I really am." He cautiously put his hand on her shoulder to comfort her.

She flicked his hand away like an unwanted insect. "Don't touch me! Just. Stay. Away." He could not fight with such finality in her voice. It was best to stay quiet.

They walked in silence. Anger fueled her swift strides, and he barely managed to keep up, crouching and squeezing through rocky walls as the grotto narrowed further. His breathing became shallow as claustrophobia spread its roots in his heart. His mind went into overdrive, answering questions with more questions. *When are we going to get out of this* place? What if we don't get out of this place ever? Do we have enough food to last us a week? Oh no, we don't have enough food! Then, will we die here? Will Dr. Costello send reinforcements to find us?

Lost in thought, he barely registered Michelle's warning, "Quick, bend your head. Now!"

He was a second too late.

Expecting to hit a low hanging rock, he rammed full-face into something mushy. Relieved that he didn't break his nose, he embraced the caress of satin. But, he soon realized that the satin stuck to his face. He instinctively used his hand to tear it away. Just as immediately, his hand got stuck to his cheek. He tried to jerk his hand away, but in vain. He was stuck. In a moment of panic, he grasped what the sticky satin was – a cobweb.

"Help! I am stuck!"

Michelle arched her face, gave him a condescending smile, and said, "Now, who is laughing?"

"Michelle, we don't have time to play games! Help me out!"

Michelle crossed her arms. "No! First, say you are sorry."

"But I said I was sorry before!"

"Did you?" Michelle looked genuinely confused. "Then say it again."

Argh! He glowered but decided to play along. "OK! I am sorry. Really sorry! Happy?"

"Good. Now, say please get me out of here, babe."

He would have banged his head into the wall if he wasn't stuck. She was ready to rip his tongue out for calling her 'babe', and now she herself…argh!

He seethed. "Babe. Please. Please. Get me out."

"Good boy!"

Michelle reached for her boot and took out the dagger. She juggled the dagger in her hands and said, "Now stand still while I get you out of this mess."

The dagger cut sticky cobwebs like a knife cutting through air. In no time he was a free man, except his hand was still stuck to his face.

She giggled at his plight. "I am glad your hand is not stuck to your lips." She moved closer. "Otherwise, I wouldn't have been able to do this…" She leaned into him and pressed her soft lips to his. His pupils dilated, and a flutter ran from his head to toe. He clumsily put his free hand on the small of her back and pulled her closer. He kissed her. One deep kiss to satiate his core, one long kiss that left her breathless. He kissed her again. The second time it was rough, driven by raw hunger for her.

The urge to give in completely pecked between her thighs, but sanity prevailed as she remembered where they were. "Okay. Let's stop before I cannot say no."

"Well, then let me make it easier for you to not say no," his voice was a heavy whisper.

"Oh! No. No. No. You stay where you are. This is neither the place nor the time."

She gave him a quick peck on the lips and continued, "First, let's free your hand." With delicate hands and precision of a surgeon, she cut through sticky cobweb without scraping his cheeks.

"Terrific job, Michelle!" she exclaimed once his hand was free again. "Now, let's get out of this spider-hole."

His body tensed up all of a sudden.

"Oh God! Why did it not strike me earlier? We need to get out of here. NOW!" His voice was as strained as his body.

He grabbed the dagger from her, held the torch in front of him, and ran. "Follow me!" he shouted over his head.

"What's the sudden rush?" she called after him.

The dagger blade rattled as his hand hit the rock.

"Spiders!" he yelled. "If the strength of that cobweb is anything to go by, we might actually encounter a huge spider. And I am not talking about that baby tarantula!"

Fearful, she scrambled after him.

Slash! He cut through a cobweb with the dagger. The silence right after was uncanny, till it was marred by their hurried footsteps. It heightened his fear.

Slash! Another cobweb. Another cut with the dagger.

He knew they should be quieter. All the noise would seem like ruckus to any creature dwelling in the sinister cave. But walking with stealth would only delay the inevitable, not prevent it.

Slash!

He kept up the pace. He strained his ears for any sound other than their footsteps or…Slash!…the interspersed sound of steel slashing through spider webs. The spacing between webs became so predictable that he heard the slash in his head right before it actually happened. Slash! He just wanted to face the inescapable; the mystery was killing him.

And then, instead of hearing another slash, he heard his prayer being answered.

At first it was an imperceptible tap on the ceiling. He stopped. She stopped. Michelle had heard it too. Both looked up. There was nothing but emptiness, near and beyond.

But then they saw two red unblinking eyes, like large crimson globes. Each globe the size of their heads. A monstrous spider, as if the Mother of all spiders.

A flurry of taps followed, and he knew she was coming after them.

"Run!" He screamed and pushed Michelle onward.

Michelle broke into a mad scramble. She did not need to look. She knew what was upon them. He dashed after her and so did the giant red globes.

He chafed his arms at every turn. The spider was right behind him, following at a leisurely pace it seemed. It was a game for the spider, his precious life for him.

At a sharp corner, he banged shoulder-first into the rock and let out a sharp cry. But there was no time to stop. He clutched his bruised shoulder and kept his feet moving. It seemed like an interminable sprint, bound to end in their death. If it comes to that, he thought, I just need to buy Michelle enough time to escape. I must not let the beast hurt her.

"I see light!" Michelle let out a shrill cry.

He heaved a sense of relief. Just a little further, just a little more, he told himself.

And just when thoughts of freedom were on the cusp of reality, he rammed into a stationary Michelle from behind. Michelle hit the floor face-first as he tumbled on top of her. She screamed in pain as her jaw hit the rocky floor.

He rolled off her and tried to help her to her feet.

"Why did you stop, Michelle? Come on, get up! We can't stop."

She writhed in pain and tried to mumble an answer while massaging her jaw, "…the light."

He looked up to see the light at the end of the tunnel. What he saw both scared and flustered him. There was light, yes, faint buttermilk daylight streaming through an opening a hundred yards away. But, right in front of him, barely five yards away, were two giant red globes gleaming in near darkness. Exactly like the red globes behind him.

Another spider! A bead of sweat fell on the tip of his nose.

He understood why the first spider had moved at such a leisurely pace. It was waiting for its partner to close off their prey. Now, he and Michelle were trapped. She was hurt and scared. He reeked of fear himself.

But, fear can be a wonderful force. Once you understand you are in its grasp, you'll either run from it or fight it. Either is a struggle. The more you do it, the firmer the grip of fear in your heart. He understood that fear was clutching his heart. But he neither ran from it nor fought it. He embraced it. Fear flowed through his veins, but there was a difference - he was channeling the power of fear, and not the other way around. At that moment, he understood, fear can be a wonderful force.

He picked up the dagger and circled around Michelle. "Come on, you filthy creatures! You'll have to kill me before you can touch her!" he yelled.

As if accepting his challenge, the first spider lurched toward him. He slashed in the air, thwarting any advance that the spider had planned. It was a small victory, but he knew they wouldn't be able to survive for long if they remained holed up between two giant spiders. He had to trick them somehow. Or kill them.

He heard Michelle sobbing as she cradled her hurt jaw. The spiders, however, were in no mood for sympathy. The second spider made a cautious advance toward him. He slashed hard at the creature, but the spider parried his blow.

He was suddenly alarmed. What had parried his blow was not a spider leg but a pincer, like that of a scorpion. Was it a spider or a scorpion?

The second spider danced forward again. He raised his hand to hack. Except, this time the spiders were expecting this ploy. He heard pincers click behind him. Oh no! The first spider was on the move behind him. It caught his dagger-wielding hand in midair. He twisted his hand just in time and jerked it out of its razor-sharp pincer.

Luck eluded him. His thumb was a tad bit slow. It got caught in the pincer. And it got snipped off!

He remained stumped for a moment. And then came the incessant, painful shriek as his left thumb rolled away into darkness.

Chapter 5
Yoni, My Savior!

I wake up shrieking, or was it in the dream? I cannot tell for sure. The grating wailing still buzzes in my ears, and my mouth is dry from all the wailing. My mind is disoriented, lost between two worlds, till morning sunshine slaps me across the face and brings me back to reality. The cave is gone. Darkness replaced with daylight. I am in a hut, but a nicer and larger version of the "prison" I was in earlier.

Why am I having such wild nightmares? First a seven-headed snake and now a spider-scorpion couple? A sense of betrayal wafts over me, and I feel a sudden urge to lambaste my brain. It cannot even remember my name, but it can imagine freaks of nature with utmost ease.

I close my eyes, forget the dream, and breathe.

Crisp morning air enters my nostrils. Hmmm...wet grass. I sniff. And flowers. Lavender, definitely! My heart jumps with alacrity. The fragrance invigorates my every pore. My face relaxes into a smile, and I reach out to savor the whiff with my nose. Nice!

I open my eyes and arch my head to the right. Next to the stone bed is a flat wooden table, and on it is a clay pot with stalks of lavender flowers. Right next to it, in another pot, is a queer bulb-shaped plant with silver-green leaves. I do not recognize it. I extend my left hand and reach out for a stalk of lavender. How nice would it be to hold it and smell it up close?

But before my hand reaches the flowers, I stop. Something catches my eye. Rather, the lack of something. I gulp hard and swallow in the agony.

My left thumb is missing!

A lump grows in my throat. I cannot swallow. I cannot speak. I pull my hand closer to get a clearer look. I blink fervently, like a magician bewitching with his eyes. But reality doesn't change. No thumb appears. It had been a clean cut. There is a stump where the thumb had been. A fit of palpitation grips me. Fullness in the chest and throat make my breaths shorter and harder. I start massaging my chest and force myself to gulp more air into my lungs.

Was the dream true? Are my nightmares some sort of twisted reality?

And at that precise moment, it returns. Not my memory, but the unbearable pain in my head. A thousand tiny nails start pricking me from inside, each prick more excruciating than the last. The pain is more than I can tolerate. All semblance abandons me as I fall into a single, uncontrolled bawl of torture. I howl. I shout. I clench my eyes shut. Tears fall along my cheeks.

I hear hurried footsteps outside my room. I try to get a grip on myself, but I can still feel my facial muscles grimacing in unremitting pain.

"What happened? Are you okay?" an old woman asks as she bolts into the room.

Another bout of pain erupts, and so do my vocal cords. "Do I look okay?"

I toss around in the bed, clamp my head between my hands, and clench my teeth together.

She dashes to the side-table and plucks a few leaves off the bulb-shaped plant. She thrusts the leaves toward me. "Here, eat these. They'll help with the pain."

I don't ask; I don't say anything. I grab them all and shove them into my mouth, all at once. The woman opens her mouth in protest, but I am already halfway down to grinding the leaves into pulp. I munch hungrily and don't stop till I swallow the last shreds. Head buried in the soft shrubbery on the stone bed, I wait.

Soon a battle ensues, the pulp from the leaves flooding my head. The prickly nails fight back. Just when I am about to give up, I get a hit. A hit like no other. My head swims in an ocean of solace. I take to the sky, soaring into the clouds, wings spread. Serenity wraps me in a bubble and gently lays me on the bed. The pain is gone.

"Are you okay?" the old woman asks with a soothing gentleness in her voice.

I nod. "Thanks!" I say.

The crease on her forehead relaxes and color returns to her cheeks. There is a glint of relief in her deep brown eyes. She has an aura of a gracefully aging grandmother. A tiara of white shrub roses adorns her white locks. Like everybody else, she wears a pine skirt, but the color of her skirt is white not pine green. Apart from the white lilies covering her breasts, she is not wearing any ornate flower-accessories like Azura.

"Who are you?" I ask.

"I am Yoni, the Ayurvaid."

"Ayurvaid?"

Her wrinkled laugh lines around the lips broaden into a smile. "A doctor, in your language."

"Oh!" I say.

She says, "Queen Azura would want to know that you are awake. I'll get her. If the pain returns, take a few more leaves of this plant. Okay?"

"May I get some water first?"

"Of course, of course."

She rushes to the other side of the bed. There, sitting atop another wooden table is a spherical clay vessel covered with a lid. A cup rests upside down atop the lid. She picks up the cup, removes the lid off the vessel, and pours me a cupful.

I quaff three full cups of water before I let her go.

Alone again, a sense of tranquility engulfs me. In the stillness, I try to recall my name, my past. When nothing surfaces, my mind reverts to the dreams in search of answers. I now realize that the dreams have reality hidden behind fantasy veneer. When I first dreamed of Michelle and me, she said that we were on the North Sentinel Island. I didn't know such a place existed till Azura told me so.

And then, I saw Azura carrying the same dagger that Michelle carried with her. I'd dreamed of that dagger before I actually saw it. That cannot be a coincidence!

Moreover, I dreamed of my thumb getting chopped even before I saw it missing. Not a coincidence! Are my dreams a reflection of my past? Is my mind showing me glimpses of what happened in the past? I cannot for a moment accept that I encountered creatures like a seven-headed snake or a spider-scorpion. Those must be figments of my imagination. Or were they as real and true as the missing thumb on my left hand? I might never know, but I need to piece together the bits that appear true. It may be the only way to uncover my past. Or, find someone who knows what happened to me… Azura! Yes, I need to wrench more information from her. She knows more than she told me, I am sure.

With no more leads to discern my past and no great memories to reminisce about, I think of Michelle. My heart leaps, my neck arcs, and my shoulders release the tension they were holding. Even though Michelle was only an abstraction fluttering through the fantasies of my mind, I cannot stop brooding over her. Is she a real person? I have no idea. But, I am not ready to wave her away as a speck of creativity. I close my eyes. I feel the touch of her lips on mine as she had kissed me in the cave. I push my lips forward and relive that moment.

I am lost in the feeling when I hear Azura's voice. "I know those silver leaves give a hit, but not so much that you start kissing the air."

My eyes jerk open. Azura stands in the door, flashing her white teeth from ear to ear.

I sit up. "I am sorry…I was…it was only…"

She interrupts, "You don't have to apologize."

I purse my lips together in embarrassment and say nothing. She walks into the room, followed by Yoni and two guards. Yoni hastens to get a wooden stool, placed in the corner of the room, for the queen.

The Apple

Azura stops her and says, "Wait, Dai Ma! I'll get it myself."

Interesting, I think. The queen doing her own work. Or is it respect for the elderly?

She brings the stool and sets it beside the bed. She perches atop the stool with the flourish of a queen.

I still cannot forget the way Azura had tried to wrench the truth out of me. She had drugged me without my consent. Though come to think about it, I had treated myself to those scarlet leaves she calls Truth Essence.

"You remember anything?" She comes straight to the point.

For some reason, I find a natural appeal in sarcasm. "Well, good morning to you too, Azura. I am doing lovely, by the way. Woke up bawling like a child thanks to the sweet leaves you gave me." I look hard at her. "Sorry to disappoint you. You see, my brain has taken a particular dislike for that question. I am starting to think it's because of the 'leaf diet' you have put me on. A leaf for this, a leaf for that. Do you people even eat actual food of any kind?" As if on cue, a deep pang of hunger rumbles from my stomach.

Azura faces the guards and says, "Please bring him some food from the kitchen." One of the guards bows and scurries from the room.

"It's good evening, by the way," Azura says with the glint of a smile. "I hear your pain is getting worse. I understand you don't like it, but the leaves of that plant…" She points to the silver-green leaves. "…are your best friends till you recover completely. Trust me."

"Ha! Trust you? No, thank you."

"As it suits you. But I won't mince words when I say this – you are alive because we want to recover what you stole. We want you to remember where you hid it. I don't care if you must drug yourself with those leaves every night. All I care is the answer to that question. Answer right and you live. Answer wrong, and you are dead."

Threats and more threats. Why am I not surprised?

"What guarantee do I have that I'll live even if I remember and tell you the answer?" I ask.

"You don't. But we are not as inhuman as you outsiders. We will let you live if you help us recover it. However, I hope you understand that you'll never see the outside world again. You'll forever live here as our guest."

"As your guest or as your prisoner?" I retort.

"I think I have made myself clear enough. Remember and live. Else, we wouldn't hesitate to make an example of you to your governments in the outside world."

"You think I care about the governments? Or the outside world? I might be from there, but I have no link between that world and me. No memory, no emotion, no care." I shrug my shoulders. "And I equally don't care about whatever you say I stole. Which is why I'll tell you when it comes to me. There is no reason for me to hide the memories, as long as you promise to honor your word."

Azura affirms, "You have my word. No harm shall come to you. You are our guest, and in Sentinel culture, guests are afforded the same courtesy as our God."

And the deal is made.

I am unsure if I'll ever recall what she wants to know, but at least I wouldn't die for telling nothing, which for now is the only truth I know – nothing.

"Tell me something," I say. "You addressed Ayurvaid Yoni as *Dai Ma*. What does it mean? Is she your mother?"

Azura looks at Yoni and smiles. "She is everyone's mother. In our language, *Dai* means highest. Dai Ma is a respectful term for mother of the highest order."

I nod.

"My queen?" says the guard who has returned from the kitchen.

Azura waves an approval with her hand. The guard enters with two servant girls in tow. The girls lay out a spread of wild fruits, roast meat, and a steaming pot of stew. My mouth tingles at the sight. I cannot wait to dig into the hot stew. It looks scrumptious!

The Apple

"Thank you. You may leave us alone." Azura waves everyone away.

I don't ask for permission and help myself to the steaming stew. It burns my tongue, but I am too famished to care. I suppress the burn with a juicy pear and return to gulping the stew.

"You might want to take it slow, considering how long it has been since you have had solid food." Azura tries hard not to make it an order.

I ignore her and don't say a word till the stew and the meat are finished. Then, I take a golden apple and savor it.

"That was simply magnificent!" I finally let out the feelings in words.

"I am glad you liked the food. I would suggest that you rest now. The more rest for your brain, the easier for you to recall your past." She stretches to her right and breaks a couple of silver-green leaves. "Here, chew some more. For the pain and for sleep."

I don't argue and take the leaves. I don't want to suffer another bout of torment.

"Do you know what happened to me, Azura?" I blurt out the question that has been hammering me since I woke up.

"Now is not the time to divulge information that will worsen your mood. You are alive, and that's all that matters."

"Alive? Was I supposed to be dead?"

Azura bites her lips but doesn't answer.

"I was supposed to be dead, wasn't I? Come out with it, Azura. Tell me what happened?"

She curls her lips and fidgets with her index fingers. I can see her struggling to find the right answer.

Finally, she gets up, adjusts her headdress, and says, "That's enough talk for one day. I must leave as I need to attend to urgent matters. I suggest you sleep. It is paramount that you rest your brain after what it has gone through. Otherwise, those killing headaches will not go away." With that, she starts for the door.

"You haven't answered me. At least tell me why I am having these headaches? Does it have to do with me escaping death?"

Azura doesn't stop till she reaches the door. She pauses as if debating with herself. Finally, she turns around, steadies herself, and looks directly at me.

"You were shot in the head…"

What?

"…and you have finally woken up after two days. It's nothing short of a miracle."

She removes something from the vines around her waist and tosses it to me. I catch it with one hand and come face to face with a stub of metal.

"Here is the bullet that was removed from your brain. Had it not been for Ayurvaid Yoni, you'd be dead."

I have so many questions running through my mind, but not one reaches my mouth.

"Now, I must leave," she says. "Sleep well and sweet dreams."

Chapter 6
Pincer Vs Dagger

Boom! A gunshot cracked through the cave and roared in his ear.

"Hold my hand!" yelled Michelle. Her voice was unsteady and frantic. She held a flare gun in her hand.

Boom! He flinched and opened his eyes to red flares illuminating the cave. His head was whirling and his vision blurry. He kneeled on the rocky floor, clutching his left hand in his right armpit. He tightened the grip on the left hand, which sent a deep, grinding ripple of pain through him. It brought back the agonizing memory of his left thumb rolling away. He screamed, more from the tormenting memory than the physical pain. As if on cue, a musty, metallic smell enveloped him. The smell of blood. His blood.

Boom! A third shot ricocheted off the rocky walls of the cave, leaving behind smoky, red flares.

"Get up! I can't hold them for much longer," said Michelle.

What was she talking about? He ignored her. The blood on his thumb-stump had started to crust. He returned to caressing it with his other hand. But then an image bobbed into his head. Red globes, sharp pincers, slit thumb. The spiders! He scrambled onto his feet, the adrenaline sweeping away the cloud that blurred his mind.

Michelle grabbed him with one hand. Her other hand remained extended, holding the flare gun in front of her. She was shaking vigorously. She wouldn't be able to hold the bastards for much longer, he thought. A fresh spurt of adrenaline rushed through him as he cursed. So, he cursed again. It inflamed and infuriated him. It felt good!

Boom! The fourth shot elicited a gut-wrenching howl that filled the cave. He saw one red globe flitting in the direction of the clamorous noise. It was the second spider that had blocked their path forward. Only one dancing red eye. Where was the other one? And he understood that Michelle had hit her target. The light had gone out in one of the eyes. A bullet lodged in its place.

The creature bawled. The glow from the remaining eye jerked as it thrashed against the walls in the dark. The first spider rushed to its partner's aid. Its red globes blazed brighter than before.

"Now!" Michelle shouted.

She grabbed his forearm and ran. In two strides, she stopped as she remembered something. She dropped his forearm, ran back a few paces, and bent down. He saw the faint gleam of the dagger as Michelle picked it up from where it had fallen when his thumb got clipped.

He said, "There is no time. Run!"

Michelle ran to him. "There is always time," she said as she brushed past him, holding the dagger in one hand and the gun in the other. He scampered after her, barely keeping up. The creatures shrieked behind him. Loud, shrill wails. He increased his pace.

They dashed through the cave, toward muted, white daylight a hundred yards away. They reached the end of the path and realized that the exit wasn't straight ahead, but overhead at a forty-five-degree angle through a five-foot-wide slope. It was a long and steep climb. But, a life-saving climb. They ran for the exit. And slipped right back. The cave floor was moist and slippery. They tried again. Same result. Overgrown algae made it impossible to press ahead on the slimy slope. Their boots did not have enough traction to push themselves up.

So near, and yet so far.

Michelle half-smiled at him. "Don't worry. I know a way."

She gave the dagger and the flare gun to him. "Stand guard."

He pocketed the dagger and held the flare gun with both his hands. His grip was light. One thumb was no longer there to tighten his hold on the gun.

Michelle turned sideways and stood against the wall lining the narrow slope. She pressed both her hands against the wall. She lifted her legs, one at a time, and planted her feet on the opposite wall. She formed a perfect arched bridge atop the slithery passage. And slowly, she started to climb. One hand forward, one foot forward. Slowly, she hunched her way to the top.

She looked at him. "Easier for me, sweetie. Will be tough for you with your thumb…"

A loud screech tore through the stale air behind them. The spiders coming for revenge?

"No other way. I have to do it," he said with conviction.

He holstered the flare gun and propped his hands against the wall. His hurt hand screamed in pain. He clenched his jaw. He lifted his feet off the floor and planted them on the opposite wall. The sudden pressure jammed his thumb-stump against the wall. The crusted wound ruptured. Blood oozed out, bathing his hand red. It softened his grip. He dug his nails into the ragged wall in agony.

"You can do it, darling. You can do it!" Michelle cheered him from above.

He panted and perspired and bled, but slowly and steadily, he climbed behind Michelle. A dull, humming sound climbed with them. The farther they went, the louder the hum became. Till water vapor floated around them, and the hum became a pulsating rumble of water. Tiny water droplets caressed them as they made their way up.

"It's a waterfall!" exclaimed Michelle, nodding at the muted, white light ahead. The forty-five-degree slant culminated in an alcove, right behind a gushing waterfall.

The falling spray of water soothed his nerves. But he grew exhausted. Even without a mutilated thumb, the ordeal of maneuvering the climb was debilitating. The open gash made it worse. Every ounce of his body wanted to stop. Up ahead, he saw Michelle struggling as well. And they were not even halfway there!

Suddenly, he heard scraping behind him, like nails on a chalkboard. He turned his head. And there it was – the spider with two burning red eyes – trying to scrape through the narrow passage and exact revenge on them. But, it couldn't fit into the constricted corridor. In the white light, he saw the creature with vivid clarity. The arachnid had eight pencil-like, hairy legs. Two sharp, white fangs hung in front. Green, gooey venom dripped from its fangs. The oddity was the two pincers in front. The pincers scraped the wall as it tried to climb.

Michelle breathed a sigh of relief. "Thank God! It cannot fit into the passageway."

The spider clicked its pincers in frustration. And then it stopped moving. It watched them with red, unblinking eyes.

He knew it wasn't over. They still had to complete the climb. One misstep and they'd fall into the waiting pincers of the spider.

They continued, each step more measured than the last. Nothing could stop them now, except their own fall. Michelle reached the top of the slope, and cautiously entered the alcove.

He paused and huffed. Three more steps, he thought.

"Don't stop! Come on, keep moving!"

He nodded and moved forward. Just two steps now. He looked at the spider.

The spider suddenly burst into motion. It pranced on its legs, clicking the pincers in frustration. It could see the prey getting away. Never to be seen again.

"Don't look!" Michelle yelled at him.

The sudden alarm broke his concentration.

His hand slipped. His feet fumbled.

He fell.

He hit the slimy floor with a thud. His heart jumped into his mouth. He could taste its furious beating.

The Apple

"NOOO!" squealed Michelle.

His mouth was too dry for words. What came out was a puff of exhaustion. Or maybe it was fear.

Droplets from the waterfall splashed his face as he tumbled down the algae-ridden slope, toward the waiting fangs of the spider.

The spider clicked its pincers in anticipation. Apart from the fidgety pincers, the creature became still. No prancing. No dancing. Just patient waiting.

"NO…NO…NO!" cried Michelle. The sudden shock made her intone a single word – NO—and she kept going with it, chanting it like a mantra. Probably in the hope that it would wind back the clock. But, the moment had passed. He had fallen. Limp and weary. And he was seconds away from being torn into a hundred pieces.

His fall picked up speed, a pure function of gravity thrusting him downward on the slope. He squirmed, trying to latch onto the last shred of hope hanging in the path to his death.

The spider waited. Michelle cried.

He flailed his loose arm, trying to grab any jagged corner in the uneven wall. But the dank air, the moist wall, and a sweaty hand made it impossible to grip the wall. It was like his hand was painting the wall with butter. There was no traction. No hope.

He braced himself. For the fangs to rip into his flesh.

The spider braced itself. For avenging its partner.

And just as the spider opened its mouth for a bite, two things happened.

One, he instinctively went for the dagger in his boot. A natural reaction after years of human evolution. Fight or flight. There was no chance of flight. None. That realization focused all his energy on one thing only – fight. And nothing helps your chances more in close combat than a knife. Unless, of course, you are a giant spider with pincers for hands.

Two, he jammed the dagger in the ceiling of the spider's mouth. Right between the fangs. He twisted the blade and dark, gooey blood oozed from the mouth of the spider. He took out the blade and jammed it again. Quick and forceful. The spider squealed. Its pincers chattered haphazardly. He ducked underneath its belly, missing the bite of the pincers by a whisker, and jammed the dagger for a third time. This time into the soft, squashy belly. He twisted the blade. The spider screeched. Its legs wavered.

He went into a fury, jamming his blade in and out into the pulpy belly. In and out. In and out. He didn't care about the sticky, warm blood that bathed him or its foul smell. In and out went the dagger. The spider staggered, as if its eight legs were on roller-skates. It stumbled and fell on its side, the red globes burning faintly. Then, there was only darkness in those eyes. The spider lay slain, unmoving.

He lay there next to the spider, breathing hard and gulping air. The dagger trembled in his hand. The adrenaline still gushing through his veins.

"Oh, God! Oh, God! Are you okay?" Michelle called out from above. Her voice echoed in the narrow tunnel.

He moved his chin up and down. He was too exhausted for words. None came out.

"Hurry," she said. "The other spider might still be lurking there somewhere."

He did not care about the other spider. Not any longer. He got up and sheathed the dagger. He turned toward the slope and started his ascent to the waterfall. The same as before, painful and slow.

He reached the alcove at the top, panting furiously and a little dizzy. He threw himself on the floor, next to Michelle. His chest heaved. His breathing unsteady. He didn't have another ounce of energy to spend.

Michelle bent and stroked his hair. "Oh, sweetheart! Can't tell you how relieved I am. For a second, I thought I had lost you." She lowered her head and kissed him on the forehead. Tears fell on his cheeks. He opened his eyes. And smiled wryly.

"Oh, it'll take more than a giant spider for you to get rid of me."

She let her head fall onto his chest and hugged him.

"I never want to lose you. Ever."

He felt her nails dig into his skin.

"Ever," she repeated in his ear.

She slowly got up and helped him to his feet. He looked around. They were in a small alcove, just wide enough for the two of them. The tip of his head touched the ceiling of the nook. It looked like a water slide platform, culminating into a forty-five-degree slide on one end, and a misty curtain of the falling water on the other.

He bent a little and staggered the five yards separating the waterfall from the slide. He stopped as he came face to face with the thundering waterfall. Like shimmering white satin, it billowed with the wind. He was mesmerized. Huge water droplets pounded his face. Somehow, it soothed him. He stuck his right hand into the rapidly falling water, and the force nearly carried him downward. He flinched and stepped back.

"That's the only way out." His shout was nearly inaudible above the deafening roar of the waterfall.

"Where?" She looked around her, as if she missed a secret way out of the recess.

He said, "The waterfall. We need to jump."

Michelle gave him a blank-eyed look. "You got to be kidding me. We can die! What if there are rocks at the bottom and we fall on them?"

"What do you suggest? We stay here instead and bang our heads against the walls of this tiny nook?" He was tired and agitated. "Or better still, we return and meet the spider that just lost a mate and an eye. I am sure it would be delighted to welcome us with open pincers." He stood akimbo, and his eyes narrowed into a stare.

She raised her palms in defeat. "Okay. Whatever you say."

He let his hands fall on his sides and sighed heavily. He came and stood next to her. He held her hand and said softly, "We are not going to die."

She looked at him. "I am not afraid to die. But what if I lose you?" Her eyes reflected an intense sorrow burning deep inside her heart.

He took her hand in both of his, like cradling a fragile child.

"You are not going to lose me. Trust me."

She nodded, "Okay." She straightened herself and looked at the waterfall with renewed confidence. "Let's do it."

"Yes, let's." He gave her a sheepish smile.

But then a disturbing thought knocked on his head. "But..." He paused. "What if we get separated after we jump? What's our rendezvous point?"

Michelle pressed a finger to her lips and looked at the ground, thinking.

He continued, "We fall, and the gushing stream takes you someplace and takes me someplace else." He shuddered. "Not a rosy picture, is it?"

Michelle's face suddenly lit up as she picked up on something he said. "Yes, that's it!" she exclaimed.

His face crumpled into confusion. "What?"

"Rosy!" She looked at him with unbridled enthusiasm, as if she had cracked a tough puzzle.

"Rosy?"

"Yes! I know where to meet if we ever get separated on this trek...the Primrose!"

The Primrose? He was utterly befuddled.

She looped around him and cupped his hurt hand in her palm. "But we are not going to separate because I am not letting you get hurt again."

She leaned in and kissed him on the cheek. "Time to jump!" She pulled him forward, their faces inches away from the fierce waterfall.

She said, "On three, okay?"

His mind was racing. What was Primrose?

"One."

Where was Primrose?

"Two."

Forget Primrose. Just don't let go of her hand.

"Threee!"

And the next moment, water gurgled in his throat, in his eyes, and in his lungs. He couldn't breathe. He was falling. A heavy force pushed him down. He thrashed in desperation. And he didn't realize until it was too late… he had let go of Michelle's hand.

Chapter 7
The Do-Over

"Wake up, uncle. Wake up!"

I stir.

"Uncle!" Soft hands tug at my arm incessantly. "Uncle!"

I stir again and open my eyes.

A little girl, maybe five years old, beams at me with a toothy grin. One of her front teeth is missing. I recognize her. She is the same, shy girl who ran away giggling when I first woke up after two days asleep. She wears a tiny pine leaf skirt, like Azura, like everybody else I have seen on North Sentinel Island. Nothing else - no flowers on her head or wrists to hold her back from exploring the joys of unfettered childhood.

"Oh, uncle awake! Uncle awake!" She jumps in glee and claps her hands in merriment, rejoicing at the huge accomplishment of waking me up.

"Uncle, let's go!" She yanks my arm.

I look at the girl with her soft, brown eyes. Her long, curly hair runs amok, falling on her shoulders at the sides and on her dark caramel cheeks at the front. And flaring in the morning air is her petite beak-like nose, like Azura's.

"Hello, little flamingo!" I smile.

She turns around. Looks right. Looks left. And at me with confusion frayed across her creased forehead. "Who you talking to?"

I sit up and playfully poke her little pear-shaped nose. "I am talking to you, little flamingo."

She stamps one foot on the ground. "NOOO! My name is Aana, and I am not little. I am big." She stands on her toes, hoists herself up and cranes her neck. "See! See! Maa says I am a big girl."

I chuckle. "Oh! Maa says that? Who is Maa, Aana?"

She looks at me, puzzled by the question. "What you mean? Maa is Maa."

"No, I mean what do you call her?"

Aana tilts her head questioningly to the right and her curls swing over her left eye. "I call her Maa."

I bow my head and smile at my own stupidity.

I look up. "Sorry. I mean what do other people call your Maa?"

She stands upright and pushes away threads of hair from her face, as if getting ready to recite a poem in front of her class in school. "Queen Azuraaa," she pronounces her mother's name long and loud.

Azura? Isn't she too young to already have a five-year-old?

"Uncle, did you meet my Paa?" Aana tilts her head the other way. Her curls follow suit.

"Your Paa?"

"Yes, Paa went outside. You come from outside. So, you must have met him. Did Paa send a toy for me from outside?"

She must have noticed my blank face because the glint in her eyes dulls a bit. Her shoulders slump.

"Sorry, I didn't meet your Paa, kiddo. But I am sure the toy is on the way. Outside is far, far away. It will take a long time for a toy to arrive."

She perks up at the suggestion. The glint in her eyes returns.

She grabs my arm and pulls it with all her weight. "Now let's go, uncle. We are late. It will start."

I let myself get pulled up by her. "What will start?"

"I can't tell you. Maa said not to tell uncle. Maa said it is a secret."

I narrow my eyes.

Aana starts pulling me toward the door. "Uncle, do you like secrets?" Before I can respond, she says in the same breath,

"I like secrets! Should I tell you a secret?" She turns around to look at me. I catch the mischief in her eyes.

"Sure." I puff my chest and let out a loud yawn.

"But you cannot tell anyone because it is a secret. Okay?"

"Okay."

"You promise?"

I nod. "I promise. I wouldn't tell anyone."

"God promise?"

I sigh. "Yes, Aana. God promise."

"No, you have to pinch your throat!" she orders. Like mother, like daughter.

I pinch the front of my throat, as a gesture to not lie under the "God promise" oath.

She looks around like a scared rabbit, her ears tense. No one is around. No one is listening. She looks satisfied. She waves with vigor, gesturing me to come closer.

I bend a bit.

"Closer." Her voice is a bare whisper.

What is the big secret?

I sit on my toes and put one hand on the ground for balance. She walks to my right side, puts one hand on my shoulder, and hauls herself up. She cups the other hand around my ear, ready to spill the secret. I can feel her nose flicking my earlobe.

"Uncle…" I barely make out what she is saying. Her voice is too soft.

"Uncle…"

"Yes?" I whisper.

"BOOO!" she shouts in my ear. And takes off, giggling.

I recoil and rub my earlobe. Naughty kid! I run after her. "Come here, you naughty girl."

She hears me coming and screams in joy. The chase is on. I follow her giggles to the adjoining room. It's a spacious room with one long, knee-high community table sitting in the center. Nothing else. No chairs. No decorations. No rugs on the stone floor. The room seems like the central hub. Along its periphery are five connected rooms. Like the one I woke up in.

The Apple

I notice Aana's flowing curls as she takes a sharp left at the far end of the room and vanishes. She is fast. But I am taller. Five strides and I reach where I last saw her curls. I find myself at the end of a long, narrow corridor. Aana is standing at the other end of the corridor, waiting to dash out through the door behind her. Her face reflects sheer happiness. For her, it's a game, and she clearly finds the race amusing.

"I am going to get you, you naughty flamingo." I point to her and shout across the hallway.

She shrieks and giggles at the same time. She turns around, opens the wooden door and runs into the daylight.

I run across the corridor and burst through the half ajar door. But I come to a screeching halt as bright sunlight ambushes me. The glare blinds me. I shield my eyes with the palm of my hand. It is blazing. I cannot open my eyes. It feels as if someone poured hot acid in them. Staying indoors for days does that to you, I guess, especially if the room has no windows. I massage my eyes with the heel of my palms. I blink. Too bright. I blink again. And slowly, my vision returns. But my eyes still burn.

I look to my left and lock eyes with a huge guard standing at ease. He is a mammoth with a wobbly tummy that is pushing at the strings of his pine skirt. He holds a trident. The blunt end of the spear is resting on the ground next to his bare feet. He stares at me, ready to gobble me up whole. I swear I can hear the silent growls in his stomach. I avert my gaze and look to my right. Another guard stands there holding a trident. But this one is skinny with a thin, flowing beard at the chin. No other facial hair. Just a snaky beard hanging from the chin. Two sentries – Mammoth and Skinny – guarding the house. Or guarding me?

I turn and look at the house. Made of mud and wood, it appears more like a big hut than a house from outside. A temporary dwelling that one would burn down and move on. Except, it had not seemed temporary from the inside. It had seemed like a place where Azura might have grown up. Old and warm, not temporary and cold.

I forget about the house, use my hand to shade my eyes, and look around for the naughty girl. All I see is a clearing in the jungle. Around the circumference of the big hut are many smaller huts. All are identical – cubes wearing conical hats. Like circus jesters wearing bright mustard hats. All huts are arranged in concentric circles as if guarding the central hut from outside dangers.

"Why you stop? You are supposed to catch me, uncle."

I follow the familiar voice to my right but cannot see the girl.

"Where you looking? I am here." I feel the annoyance rising in her voice.

Finally, I see her. She is hiding behind a tree, barely ten yards from where I stand. I walk toward her, but she pushes away from the tree and breaks into a run. The game is still on.

I call behind her. "Aana, wait! Uncle is tired and can't run any longer." I lie. I bend, lower my head, and rest my palms on my knees. And make wheezing sounds for dramatic effects. As if one more step would kill me of exhaustion. She wouldn't listen unless I put on a show.

I see her from the corner of my eye. She is hesitant at first, expecting a ruse. But the more I wheeze and pant, the more believable she finds me. She walks toward me, a step at a time. Wariness gives way to concern. She runs the last few yards and puts a hand on my shoulder. "Are you okay?"

I shake my head.

She comes closer and pats my shoulder. "It's going to be okay." Her voice is serious and comforting. Like a mother would calm her child.

I smile to myself.

Now! I grasp her arms and roar with laughter, "Caught you! You naughty girl." I grin from ear to ear.

Her face hardens. She isn't impressed. Not even a bit.

"Cheater! You are a cheater. I am not playing with you."

My smile fades.

She twists, breaks free and runs toward the bushy woods, shouting, "Maa! Uncle is a cheater. Maa!"

Nice work, you idiot!

"I am sorry, Aana." I cry out after her. "Uncle is sorry!" I want to kick myself.

She runs along a narrow, beaten path that connects the huts. Like a linear line drawn across several concentric circles. I sprint behind her. And no sooner did I start, I hear dull, but heavy thuds behind me. I look back and find the two guards – Mammoth and Skinny – coming after me. I slow. They slow down too. I stop, expecting them to grab me and take me to Azura for upsetting her daughter. But they stop too. Ten yards from me. It perplexes me for a moment, but then I realize. They are just keeping the "prisoner" in sight at all times.

I push the thought away from my mind and turn around. I want to make amends with the little one. The least I can do is apologize to her. So, I survey the length of the beaten path, trying to track Aana. I see tiny legs broaching the end of the path, where it meets the dense forest beyond. But a moment later she is gone. Into the forest. Beyond the reach of my eyes.

I run as fast as I can. My breathing is shallow. I huff. But as I cross the circle of huts, I notice sharp, indignant stares from the few Sentinels out of their homes in the scorching heat. A mother carrying a baby on her hip squeezes the baby to her chest and runs inside her hut. As if afraid that I would take away her toddler. Three teenaged boys playing a game – of hitting and maneuvering a round stone with long wooden sticks – stop dead in their tracks as they see me. Their eyes flare. Their tongues shoot out. And they run away. Back to their mothers, I think. As if they saw a dead man walking. The same dead man their mothers warned them against, it seems.

Why is everyone afraid of me? If anything, I should be afraid of them. I am the prisoner here.

I look straight ahead and close my vision from distractions. I must find Aana. I reach the spot where the Sentinel huts end, and the linear path continues into the forest. But there is no sign of her. Where did she go?

"Keep going!"

I jump as a voice startles me from behind. I look and find the two guards, still ten yards out.

"What?" I ask.

"Keep going straight. Turn left when you hear water falling. You'll find them there." Skinny commands. Mammoth stares, trying to light me on fire with his eyes.

"Thanks. But why are you following me? I am not going to run away."

No answer. Mammoth tightens his brow and continues to stare.

I shrug my shoulders. "Okay. Suit yourself, boys. I don't mind two bodyguards at my service." A sly smile escapes my lips. But they catch it.

Mammoth slams his right fist into his left palm and takes a step toward me. I clearly struck a nerve there, but Skinny grabs his arm and stops him mid-step. Mammoth curses. He jerks his arm away from Skinny's grasp, but he does not argue with Skinny. I grin. He might be skinny, but he commands the mammoth.

I turn around and face the jungle. One step. That's all it takes me to cross the threshold where staid civilization gives way to thriving nature. One step and I am surrounded by overgrown trees on all sides.

"Come on, boys. Don't be shy now. You need to follow my ass around," I call out to the guards as I make my way deeper into the forest. I hear deriding grunts from Mammoth. I ignore him.

The beaten path narrows with every step. I put one foot right behind the other, like a tightrope walker, to stay on the path. I don't want to get lost in these woods. Heavy thuds pulsate behind me, and I know Mammoth is following me. I don't need to turn around and check for Skinny. If Skinny wasn't behind, Mammoth would be all over me by now – sitting on my chest and pounding my face into pulp.

I keep walking.

Soon the trees close on me. Animal growls and bird whistles fill the air. Fear crawls up my legs every time I lose the path, and relief flushes it down every time the path springs up again. For once, I am glad I have Mammoth and Skinny for company.

I hit an unexpected corner where the path divides itself into two, one continuing straight and one going uphill to the left. I stop. The pulsating thuds behind me stop as well. A steady rumble fills my ears. At first, it sounds like an undeviating gust of wind. But then I recognize it – the heavy, yet harmonious sound of falling water. I remember what Skinny had said. I turn left.

Each step magnifies the decibel level of the sound. Each step widens the circuitous path. In twenty paces, the sound booms in my ears. I continue to climb with the rising path. In fifty yards the path opens into a snug recess next to a white, smoky waterfall. A breeze of water droplets envelopes me and welcomes us to the secluded spot. It's a place you would come to for two reasons only – either to shut the outside world and ruminate over your private thoughts, or, to commit suicide by leaping into the gushing waterfall and crashing on the rocky basin below. It's a place you won't forget if you see it once. And that's exactly what my mind tells me. I have been here before. For what reason, I don't know. But I have been here before for sure.

This is where I find them. Mother and daughter. Azura and Aana. Azura is sitting on a knee-high rock cradling Aana, who is sitting upright in her mother's lap. They are only a few feet away from the thundering waterfall. They are too close. One misstep and they can fall with the gushing water. A pang of concern runs along my spine. I quicken my pace.

Aana sees me approaching first. She points a finger at me, shakes her head vigorously, and starts to speak animatedly to her mother. The waterfall is blasting. I can't hear her till I am within a few feet from them.

"No, Maa! Tell uncle to go away." I hear Aana complain to her mother. She shifts in her mother's lap and looks at me with bloodshot eyes. She has been crying. When she notices me looking at her, she immediately looks away and hugs her mother tightly.

You screwed up, you idiot! My conscience smacks me.

I bend on my knees. "I am very sorry, Aana."

No response.

I look at Azura. She smiles and prods me with her eyes to continue the apology. I force a smile.

"I should not have pretended to be tired to catch you. It was not fair."

No response.

I hold my ears. "Look, I am holding my ears because I am very sorry, Aana."

Suddenly, the little girl turns her head to look at me, maybe to ensure I am not lying about holding my ears. Once satisfied, she turns her head away. Still, no words are spoken.

Azura comes to my aid. "Aana, bad manners. When an elder speaks to you, you need to show respect and look at them. Come on. Enough drama."

Aana's face droops.

"I am very sorry, Aana. In fact, to show you that I mean it, I'll do anything you say."

I finally hit the mark. "Anything?" she asks.

I breathe a sigh of relief. "Yes, anything."

In an instant her furrowed brow lightens up. The mischievous glint in her eye comes rushing back. She jumps out of her mother's lap.

"You have to take me fishing in the reef! Now!"

The reef? I look at her puzzled.

Azura interrupts. "No, Aana. You know we have to go to the temple now."

Aana's shoulders slacken and her head droops a little. "But I want to go fishing in the reef. I don't want to go to the temple, Maa."

"I said no. We have to go to the temple now." Azura says sternly.

Aana's facial muscles contract, about to lever open the floodgate of tears. But before the tears start, I jump in.

"You know what, I'll take you fishing in the reef. But only after visiting the temple. How does that sound?"

This cheers her up. She looks at her mother with pleading eyes for a stamp of approval. Azura sighs and says, "Okay. I guess you can go fishing with uncle, but after visiting the temple."

"Yay! We'll go fishing in the reef!" Aana jumps in glee and claps her hands.

"Okay, Aana. Now you stand with the guards," Azura points to Skinny and Mammoth. "I need to talk to uncle here for few minutes. Then we'll go to the temple together."

"I don't like guard uncles, Maa. Why can't I stay here?"

Azura stands akimbo and towers over the little kid. "Aana, don't argue. Go."

Aana lowers her head and drags her feet to where the two guards are standing.

"Adorable kid," I say as the little girl trudges away.

Azura snorts. "She is a brat. Keeps the whole village on its toes." She then shakes her head and smiles. "But, yes, she is my brat, my adorable brat."

Azura sits on the rock and asks, "So, how do you feel?"

"Better, I guess. Woke up smiling for a change." I grin. "Thanks to your brat."

Azura chuckles. She points to a rock next to her and says, "Come, take a seat."

I nod and sit on the tiny, uncomfortable rock. I look at Azura and ask, "I am confused. What changed?"

She raises her brows. "What do you mean?"

"Yesterday, you didn't trust me. Today, you trust me enough to even let your little girl come close to a prisoner. What changed?"

Azura eyes me. Then, she looks up, thinking. Her long, thin neck stretches like that of a swan. Sunlight streams through the trees hovering above us and falls on the chiseled contours of her face. She looks at me and says, "Since my ancestors first settled on this island, we have classified outsiders into two categories - enemies and guests. That's it. No gray areas. You either come with malice, and we kill you, or you come with goodwill, and we go out of our way to accommodate you. The Truth Essence does the sorting; we do the rest."

She pauses, leans forward, and points a finger at me. "But you are a gray area. The first one. We know you came with malice." She straightens her spine. "But you are not that person anymore. The Truth Essence proved it. Custom demands that we treat you as a guest. And that's what we are going to do."

I nod at the two guards standing a few feet away. "Guards watching over makes me feel like a prisoner, not a guest."

Azura laughs. "Oh, dear." A huge smirk gets plastered on her face, a remnant of the hearty laugh. "You think the guards are there to watch over you? So that you don't escape?" She shakes her head, grinning. "We are not worried about you escaping. This island is covered with dense and treacherous forests. So dense that at most places light can't even penetrate the foliage of tall trees. Unthinkable creatures dwell in the forests. The forests have provided natural protection from our enemies for centuries. You won't last one day if you lose your way in them. And even if you manage to reach the beach, where would you go? How would you traverse the miles of ocean surrounding the island?"

"Then why are the guards following me around?" I ask.

"They are for your protection. You are new here, a guest. You don't know your way around the island. Like I said, you stray in the forest and get lost, you are as good as dead."

I remain silent, absorbing what Azura has said.

A bird breaks the silence with her melodious, sing-song call. I find solace in the cuckoo's singing. It soothes the incessant twitch in my head.

"But there is a reason I asked to see you here," says Azura. "I have thought long and hard, and decided to give you an opportunity."

"An opportunity?" I ask.

"Yes, an opportunity to start over with a clean slate. Forget the past and become one of us. Permanently."

"I need to remember my past before I can forget it. Why don't you tell me what happened? How did I end up here?"

Azura shakes her head. "I don't know how you ended up here. We just found you, left for dead. An item precious to us was stolen and we assumed you had taken it. We searched the entire island for other outsiders, accomplices, but found none."

Found none? I think. How about Michelle?

"That can't be it!" I shoot back. "What else do you know?"

Azura sighs. "I have told you what I know."

"You keep talking about this stolen item. What was it? Maybe if you tell me, it'll jog my memory."

Azura mulls it over. Finally, she says, "No. It is for you to remember and tell me. I can wait."

I frown. "I stole something precious to you and you are telling me that you can wait? You do realize that I might never remember it."

"Yes, I am aware of that possibility. But, I am not worried. Two reasons. One, it wasn't the only item of its kind. There are many more. It's precious, but not unique. Two, I am sure it's still on the island. You hid it somewhere because you never left the island and we didn't find it on you. You remember what you stole, great. You don't, that's fine too. The item remains hidden somewhere on the island."

She pauses, and looks at me closely. "I would have been worried, panicked even, had it been taken to the outside world. I am glad it hasn't." She smiled.

I remain silent, my mind in a state of tumult. Should I tell her about my dreams? About Michelle? They never found Michelle. Maybe she took the precious item to the outside world? A multitude of thoughts inundate my brain, but none reach my lips. No, I mustn't tell. I mustn't put Michelle in danger. Plus, there is that tiny possibility that my dreams are not real. I decide to wait and watch. I say something stupid, and it wouldn't take Azura long to change my status from "guest" to "enemy".

Azura says, "Look, I am giving you an opportunity to start afresh. A new life, a worthy life." She puts a hand on my shoulder and continues. "Stop fussing on who you were. You can choose to not be that person. Be who you want to be now."

"From where I stand, there is no choice. I don't know who I was. So, I can't be that person. I am who I am right now."

She smiles. "Good. Then there is only one thing left to do."

"What?"

"The initiation ceremony. To make you one of us. That's why we need to go to the temple. My people would never fully accept you till you formally become a Sentinel at the feet of our God."

I must be looking alarmed because Azura says, "Don't worry. Every toddler goes through it to become a Sentinel. It's not a test, only a religious ceremony."

I nod. And I keep nodding, trying to convince myself that it's the right decision. The word test echoes oddly in my mind.

"Wonderful!" Azura clasps her hands and stands. "Let's go to the temple."

I follow Azura to the guards. Aana stands in rapt attention in front of the guards, her arms folded, her lips pouted. The kid looks like a vexed army general, ready to blast off the enemy with her stare. The enemy, in this case, is her mother. Though unlucky for Aana, the enemy knows her weakness.

"Who wants to go fishing in the reef?" says Azura, pretending to pose the question to the guards.

Aana bites her lips. Her eyes dart this way and that. She looks at the guards, hoping they would answer on her behalf. They stay mum.

"Nobody wants to go fishing?" says Azura, her voice riddled with sham amusement.

"No, no! I want to go fishing, Maa!" Aana finally breaks her silence.

"Very well," says Azura. "We'll go to the temple first. And as uncle promised, he'll take you fishing afterward."

"Yay!" The little girl jumps in delight, completely oblivious that she got handed the same deal twice, in return for her smile.

"Okay, uncle doesn't know the way to the temple." Azura points at me. "But I told him that Aana knows. Can you show him the way?"

"Yes, I know the way!" The kid runs to me and grabs my hand. "Come fast, uncle. We go temple. Then we go fishing."

Aana jerks my hand forward, and we are soon on the trampled forest path that had led us to the waterfall. Azura walks behind us, followed by the guards, their footsteps soft thuds on the patchy path.

Aana remains tight-lipped. A sense of urgency comes from her. The earlier she reaches the temple, the earlier she can go fishing. So, she rushes us along, in silence. And as silence blossoms around me, I find myself deep in the spate of questions trying to drown me. All I want are answers.

How did I end up on this island?

Who tried to kill me?

But, one question bothers me most. The one piece of the puzzle that could answer them all – who am I?

We reach the point where the path diverges into two - one to the Sentinel dwelling and one that I have not yet seen. Aana turns left, onto the unexplored path. It meanders into the forest and in no time, we are surrounded by thick undergrowth. The farther we go, the tighter the foliage grows around us. Towering trees on either side of the path embrace each other to form a canopy above our heads. It darkens the path, eclipsing broad daylight.

"Are we there yet?" I ask Azura as restlessness grips me.

"Can you see anything that looks like a temple?" she says.

"No."

"Then we are not there yet."

My shoulders droop at the reply. I trudge along.

"Whose temple is it anyway?" I ask without looking at her.

"It's the Temple of Rebirth, the gateway to immortality." Azura answers.

The answer befuddles me. "How can you attain immortality via rebirth? You have to die to be born again, no?"

"The first Sentinels believed that immortality is not about never dying. It's about being reborn in a new skin, without letting go of your past or who you are."

"Huh!" I shrivel my nose. "How does it help if you are born again in a child's body, but with the past memory of an adult?"

Azura pauses before replying. "The term 'Rebirth' is only symbolic of the God that we worship. You won't be reborn as a child. You'll only shed your skin to be 'Reborn' into the new you. An adult you. It's like changing your clothes without changing your mind or soul, but with a new lease of life."

I see the temple shoot into sight in the distance. I stop in my tracks as my eyes fall upon an old friend. And suddenly, everything Azura just said starts to make sense. If the Temple of Rebirth is the gateway to immortality, then the God must be... A cold shudder rattles my spine as the answer hits me... the Gatekeeper!

I hesitate. "Erm... is your... erm... is your God by any chance a seven-headed snake?" I ask without taking my eyes off Saraph sitting in our path ahead.

Chapter 8
The Initiation

"Yes," says Azura. "We worship the God Saraph - a seven-headed snake. And right there is the Temple of God Saraph." She points to the twenty-foot tall Saraph ahead. It sits perfectly still.

It is Saraph. No doubt. The same seven heads. The same horns, each adorned with a diadem. The same hands protruding from its belly and joined at the palms in greeting.

But it isn't the real Saraph.

The horns are not emerald green. The diadems are not shining brilliantly. And the hands are not slimy red. The creature is charcoal black from head to tail. It's Saraph but made of stone. The stone deity just sits there, reveling in its unmoving glory. The seven forked-tongues stick out, some less and some more. Like the living creature was turned to stone mid-motion with the snap of fingers. As if it didn't have enough time to shut its tongues behind its many traps. Snap! And freeze.

The stone Saraph kindles in my heart the terror I experienced in the dream. I shiver but remind myself - it's not real.

Azura comes and stands next to me. She looks hard at me and asks, "How do you know of God Saraph?"

"Huh?" I mumble.

"I never told you the name of our God. How do you know his name?"

I mull for a second but decide to come clean. Half clean. "God Saraph came to me in a dream. He showed me the path to heaven."

Azura narrows her eyes. "What exactly did this 'heaven' look like?"

"No idea." I tell the truth. "I just remember Saraph in my…"

Azura raises her finger and cuts me mid-sentence. "Not Saraph. If you are to become one of us, he is God Saraph to you."

"Okay," I say nonchalantly, while rolling with laughter in my head. It's a stupid rule, but I know better than to make fun of it in Azura's face.

"Like I was saying, I just remember God Saraph pointing me toward the path to heaven. That's it." I cut out Saraph's savage push into the Spider-cave, but then Azura doesn't need to know it.

Azura's creased forehead relaxes. The tension subsides. Aana senses this and speaks up, "Maa, let's go!"

Azura nods. "Yes. Let's."

We resume the final stretch to the temple. The path curves abruptly to the left and narrows with each step. Crow chatter fills the air. The dense foliage thickens until I reach the stone effigy of Saraph. The path ends there. A dead end. It is blocked by a giant redwood tree right next to the sitting deity. I track the height of the redwood with my eyes. Bottom to top, it must be at least a hundred feet.

A crowd of maybe twenty people gathers around the redwood, each person holding a small basket of white flowers. They stand in two parallel lines, alongside a carpet of red roses that ends at the redwood. One line of men only and one line of only women. Men are bare-chested, while the women hide their womanhood behind flowers gracing their breasts. All are dressed in pine skirts. They seem to be waiting in anticipation for some guest of honor, who would walk the red carpet while they shower flowers from their baskets. I pump up my chest. Guess I am the guest of honor. My lips stretch into a smirk.

We stop short of the carpet of roses. The crowd stops murmuring suddenly.

"My queen!" says a deep baritone voice.

I expect a man from the deep-throated voice, but a woman steps out from behind the statue of Saraph. Two trident-bearing guards follow her. The woman looks as old as Saraph's statue. She is dressed exactly like the guards. In addition, two circular bands of pink flowers clasp her arms. A similar circlet sits snugly on her bald head. I would have marked her as "pretty", had it not been for her puffed-up physique and sharp, angular features, despite the old age.

"Commander Bani." Azura nods an acknowledgment.

Bani steps forward and bows. She takes Azura's right hand into both of hers and kisses it with her thin lips, not once taking her eyes off Azura. I get a sudden urge to push Bani aside and take Azura's hand in mine. I stop myself. Am I jealous? Why? I am starting to like Azura, but I don't like her that much. Or maybe I do? I check my thoughts before they tumble into a far-fetched fairyland.

Bani lets go of Azura's hand and straightens herself. She sends a vicious look at me, before speaking to Azura. "May I have a word with you, my queen?"

Azura says, "I know what's on your mind, commander. But as I told you before, my mind is made up."

"I urge you to reconsider, my queen." Bani locks eyes with me. "This man is the enemy. He belongs in God Saraph's belly, not in His temple."

Disdain drips from her lips. She spits on the ground in front of my feet and raises her voice, "He is an outsider. We are making a huge mistake by trusting him."

"Bani!" Azura's voice is threatening, yet calm. "I would not have you disrespect our guest. And in turn, disrespect the Sentinel culture."

Bani takes a breath to speak up, but Azura raises her hand. "Enough! The decision has been made. We will continue with the initiation as planned."

Bani looks hard at me. I am sure she would have murdered me had we been alone. I stiffen up.

"I want to be excused from the ceremony then…" She looks directly at Azura and pauses. "…my queen." She adds as an afterthought.

Azura nods once.

Bani bows to the queen and walks toward me. Her two guards follow her. She stops next to my shoulder and hisses, "Don't think this is over. You better watch your back."

And she storms off.

"Don't mind her," says Azura as I watch Bani walk away. "And there is no reason for you to be afraid," she says.

"I am not afraid." I look straight into Azura's eyes. "She enraged me more than she scared me."

Azura nods. "Okay. Then if you are ready, let's begin."

She walks to the head of the carpet of roses. Once there, she turns her head and calls out, "Aana! Come, stand with me."

Aana, who is standing next to me, immediately grasps my hand. She shakes her head vigorously. "No, Maa. No!"

"Aana. Don't behave like a silly little kid. You are a big girl now. Our next queen. Soon, you'll be standing here and doing the ritual instead of me."

As if the thought itself is too terrifying, Aana tightens her grip on my hand. Her fingers bite into the skin of my palm. Why is she so scared?

Azura eyes me. "You need to come and stand here too. It's your initiation. And please bring Aana with you."

But the child is like her mother. Unrelenting. Before Azura's fury falls on the little girl, I say, "Hey, Aana. You want to go fishing later, right? The faster we get this done, the sooner we…"

"Aana!" Azura says sternly.

Finally, the kid relents. We stand behind Azura, Aana dragging her feet the whole way. She keeps her head lowered and eyes fixed on the dull brown soil beneath her feet.

Satisfied, Azura raises her head to the apex branch of the redwood. She raises her hands in unison and says to the crowd of men and women, "Begin!"

The Apple

Suddenly, the silence is broken by the women. They chant: Sarp-Sarp-Sarp. Sarp-Sarp-Sarp. The men opposite the women chime in and start banging their thighs in tune with the incantation. Sarp-Sarp-Sarp. Bang! Sarp-Sarp-Sarp. Bang! The chorus rings in perfect harmony. The mantra booms, rebounds, and echoes through the forest. Such is the intensity that a tickle runs through my arms to the back of my neck, raising every tiny hair in its path. I tighten my grip on Aana's hand. Maybe, I am a little scared now.

Azura steps forward onto the sprawled red roses. With each step, the chorus ups the tempo. Sarp-Sarp-Sarp. Bang! At each "bang" of the thigh, the men and women sprinkle white flowers in Azura's path.

The chant grows louder and louder, like an alarm insistent on waking the Gods. It pierces through my head and kicks awake an old enemy – my headache. Terrible, stinging headache. The pain spreads its loathsome tentacles, as if mocking and saying, I am here! Did you miss me?

I clamp my eyes shut to rebuff the searing pain. It doesn't help. I massage my forehead with my fingers. It doesn't help. Sarp-Sarp-Sarp. Bang! It definitely doesn't help.

Azura reaches the base of the tall redwood and stops. But the chorus persists, providing enough momentum for the ache to run amok in my head. Azura raises her hands again and then joins them at the palms in greeting. Saraph's gesture. She starts with a mantra of her own, soft enough to sound like gibberish but loud enough for everyone to notice that she is talking to the tree.

The whole scene baffles me a little. Sure, it's some old ritual; a ceremony to please the Gods. But, isn't Saraph their God? Then why beseech the tree, and make the stone statue of Saraph feel left out?

Azura finishes her incantation. She bends, puts her hand inside her pine skirt, and pulls out the dagger strapped to her thigh. The dagger. The tiny snake-head glints as she moves it in her hand. Right at that moment, I feel a sharp twitch in my hand as Aana digs her fingernails into my palm. I look down.

I find Aana looking straight at her Maa. No longer afraid; chin up with a stoical expression on her face. But, her grip is hard, and her knuckles white; her innocence twitching and incriminating whatever ritual is unfolding before her eyes.

Azura nods to me. "Come here."

I hesitate for a moment. But then I recall Azura's words – "Every toddler goes through it to become a Sentinel." If toddlers can do it, I can do it. With renewed intent, I walk toward Azura. Aana releases my hand and remains behind. The crowd showers me with white flowers as I walk the bed of roses.

I stand a few feet from Azura. She faces me. Like a nimble fencer, she lunges forward and lightly taps the sharp tip of the dagger on my forehead.

It draws blood and stings. I bellow as I recoil, "Are you nuts?"

Before I can say anything else to vent my fury, she performs the same dagger tapping action on her forehead. Now I am baffled.

"Are you nuts?" I say again. This time my tone is soft, calmer, like that of a sympathetic fellow sufferer.

Azura says nothing.

Sarp-Sarp-Sarp. Bang!

And then starts the trip down memory lane.

Azura closely inspects the tree trunk with her fingers, searching for something. She stops as she finds her spot. Sarp-Sarp-Sarp. She thrusts the dagger into the tree trunk. Bang! She steps away. The blade remains stuck to the tree. It quivers and burns crimson red, like a welding torch. My breathing hastens, my heart hollers as my dream unravels right before my eyes. The blade tip etches a semi-circular door in the tree trunk, leaving in its wake the flaming orange remnants of the weld stitch. My mouth remains open in disbelief the whole time. Dreaming it is one thing, but how does a dagger move on its own in reality?

I shake my head to break through the incredulity and look around, hoping to find at least one expression of surprise.

At least one expression that empathizes with mine. At least one expression that says, "This is insane!" But all I find are calm, relaxed expressions that are at best unexcited. One of the women in the chorus yawns just as the dagger finishes off in style and bangs open the newly carved oval door in the tree. The door is twice as tall as any man in the crowd. And there is nothing but nothingness beyond.

The dream was real! The dream was real! The thought keeps jumping excitedly in my head, intensifying the unbearable headache.

"Bring the bali!" says Azura.

Both her guards, Mammoth and Skinny, bow and disappear into the forest.

Azura notices the confusion on my face and explains. "Bali means an offering to the Gods in Sentinel culture. Every ritual starts with a bali. We consider it auspicious."

Sarp-Sarp-Sarp. Bang! The choir hums in the background.

I imagine the guards bringing large bowls of exotic fruits, nuts, and other scrumptious eatables as bali. Soon, Skinny reappears with a large bowl in his hand. As he walks toward us, he sprinkles what looks like grass on the ground. He reaches the redwood and places the bowl in front of the gaping hole. I look closely. The bowl is filled with leafy forbs, juicy four-leafed clovers, and fresh grass. Is this what they offer Saraph, their God? Never knew a snake to be vegetarian!

But, nothing prepares me for what Mammoth brings back. I hear loud, piercing bleats in the direction where Mammoth had disappeared. With grim persistence and heavy steps, Mammoth plods out of the forest, pulling forward a thick leather leash slung over his shoulder. It's a rare sight to see Mammoth, a beast of a man, struggling at anything involving muscles. He gives a forceful tug to the leash and out comes a massive wild sheep, trudging on its thin thread-like legs. The sheep bleats louder as Mammoth pulls at the leash around its neck. But, in no time, the sheep smells the clovers and the grass strewn in its path, and it nearly runs Mammoth over as it chases its newfound fortune of food.

As the sheep munches over the treats, Mammoth walks gingerly from behind and unties the leash around its neck. The sheep is free. But, instead of running away, the dumb animal hungrily makes its way to the bowl of heavenly treats.

What is in the hole? My dream tells me - Saraph. But, seven-headed snakes do not exist. Dream is one thing, but reality is real. Either you exist, or you don't. And Saraph of my dream doesn't. I am sure, I tell myself.

Sarp-Sarp-Sarp. Bang! The tempo peaks. It's deafening.

My heart raps against my chest. Hard and unremitting. I hold my breath to arrest its charge.

Sarp-Sarp-Sarp. Bang! Headache ravages through my brain.

My mind races. I imagine something to pull the sheep inside the hole. One moment the sheep is there. And the next…whoosh!…it's gone! Swallowed by nothingness.

But, nothing happens. Just my mind playing tricks. Imagining the most dramatic moment. The sheep merrily rummages through the clovers.

I let out the breath. My heart eases a little.

Suddenly, the chorus stops. A wave of quietude sweeps through the forest. What a relief! My ears thank God Almighty, and so does my head, after the relentless battering of the past few minutes.

I close my eyes, savoring the relief.

The silence, however, is short-lived. Aana starts to scream - a shrill, persistent screech. I quickly turn toward her. The kid is staring at the redwood and howling uncontrollably.

I swing my head where I last saw the sheep standing. It isn't standing anymore. Its thin legs are in the air, jerking and flapping in desperation. Like a person twists, turns, and waggles in panic when drowning. Its fluttering feet hang in midair ten feet from the ground, swallowed waist-above by the dark, black hole. What the hell?

All men and women lower their heads and join their hands at the palms in greeting. Saraph's gesture.

And out comes Saraph. The real Saraph.

It's him, Saraph from my dream. A seven-headed snake with brilliant emerald-green horns and glistening diadems. The giant snake has the bali, the poor sheep, in its mouth.

Nausea hits me, and bile rises to my mouth. The sight makes my head go around and around in circles. I press my temples with my palms. Saraph's seven heads swirl around me as Aana continues to scream. And scream. I stumble and twirl on my wobbly feet. The whole forest canopy seems to rotate at full speed above. My brain is barely able to catch up. I collapse. My consciousness prances with the sub-conscious. Reality merges with dreams.

My eyes flutter, and the last thing I see is the thread-like legs of the sheep, dangling from the snake's mouth as if floating in the air. The legs have stopped moving.

Chapter 9

Michelle! Michelle!

He was in a whirlpool.

He kicked his legs. He thrashed his arms. All in vain. The water current was too strong for his feeble limbs. It carried him – where? - he didn't have a clue. Only one thing was certain – he was drowning.

What do I do? The thought pricked his brain.

It was curious how the mind sometimes forgets to think, especially in dire situations. You put it under pressure, and – puff! – the fuse goes off. Lucky for him, his lungs answered the brain. Air! You need air, you fool!

So, he kicked his legs and gyrated his way up the whirlpool. He swiveled like a ballerina. It helped. He kicked again. And up he went, till his head crashed through the gossamer-like surface of the river. He gulped and quaffed the essence of life – air!

Bright sun rays hit his eyes like poisoned arrows. He blinked.

Where am I?

He flapped around in a moment of frenzy. Frothy water currents nudged him forward. He went along with the turbulent flow. But then, suddenly, he remembered.

"Michelle!" He shouted.

No answer.

"Mich– " Water gurgled in his mouth.

He pushed with his hands. His head bobbed above the surface again.

"Michelle! Michelle!"

He turned haphazardly in a circle but couldn't see his girlfriend anywhere. He looked on either side of the river. Serrated stones lined the riverbank, and thick, towering forests stood guard beyond. But no sign of Michelle.

He pirouetted and turned around to examine the way he had come. A magnificent view of the waterfall greeted him – soft, fluffy cotton streaming down a mountain, bisecting the arc of a glistening rainbow.

The waterfall. And it all came back to him.

The cave.

The spiders.

The jump.

"Michelle!" He shouted again, but his voice fell flat against the fury of the enraged river that kept pushing him forward.

But then, the river turned a sharp corner and lost its temper. The water calmed. The flow slowed.

"MICHELLE!" This time the shrillness of his own voice pricked his ears.

He floated in his position, waiting for the river to bring Michelle to him. It was then that he noticed it – a giant ripple moving toward him. Like an alligator making a silent move for its prey.

What the hell!

The ripples became wider and kept coming toward him. His limbs quivered, his brain flickered. In a moment of panic, he dove for the nearest river bank. He propelled himself through the water toward the bank. Even as his feet flapped rapidly, he sensed something behind him. Something fast. Something dangerous.

And barely yards from the riverbank, something grabbed one of his legs. Sharp, pointed teeth dug into his flesh.

He froze.

He was dragged into the river. Inch by inch. He jerked his leg. No success. Water buzzed in his ears. He gurgled as water made its way into his lungs. There was no getting away from the creature in the river.

In a last-ditch effort, he gathered his strength and pushed the creature away with his foot. It worked. He was suddenly free.

He swam with all his might till he felt the sharp pangs of jagged stones on his palms. He was on the river bank. He jumped to his feet and lurched away, as if being jostled by an unseen force. He kept moving from the river; from the creature, without looking back.

"Hehehe!" Loud, unsuppressed giggling erupted behind him.

He stopped. Turned around.

And there she was. Michelle! Her shoulders bounced, her chest heaved as she giggled with abandon. Water dripped from her chin and her fingers. Tiny droplets glistened in the sunshine as they ran down her sleek arms. Her pink overalls were drenched. They had turned into a darker hue of plum. The overalls were also ripped all over. It was a gruesome reminder of their perilous journey through the cave.

Split between relief and rage, he just stood there, half admiring and half detesting her.

Michelle saw the annoyance radiating from his face. She pressed a hand over her mouth to suppress the giggles. It only made it worse.

He couldn't take it any longer. He stormed toward the forest, leaving Michelle behind.

"I am sorry," said Michelle, still recovering from the fit of giggles.

He kept walking.

"Come on, darling. I said I am sorry. I was just having some fun."

No reply.

She ran to him and grabbed his arm. He stopped and looked at her.

"I am sorry," she said again.

One look at her and he felt his heart melting already – her head slightly bent, eyes wide, eyebrows raised, and bottom lip stuck out into a pout. She was a little puppy waiting to cry.

He sighed.

"Sorry?" She repeated, her pout more pronounced. "Really sorry."

"It's okay," he said, finally.

"No, it's not okay. I am really sorry."

"I said it is okay. Really." He breathed deeply. "But you better not do something like this again."

"I won't. God promise!" She pinched the front of her throat.

"Oka–"

She suddenly jumped and hugged him. He was startled for a moment. But then he pulled her into a tight embrace.

"I thought I lost you." He whispered the words into her ear.

"Oh, it's not so easy to get rid of me. I am the witch who'll latch onto you even in the afterlife." She beamed.

"Would you? Oh no!" He smiled playfully.

"Yep, you are stuck with me for life."

He chuckled, pushed aside flecks of wet hair sticking to her lips and kissed her.

"I love you," he said.

"Hmm..." She looked skyward, pretending to think. "I am not sure I love a meano who gets angry at me." She smiled.

He kissed her again, his mouth hungry and full of desire.

Suddenly, he stopped. "Meano? Is that even a word?"

"I don't know if it's a word," she said with a twinkle of mischief in her eye. "But it's definitely a person, and he has me locked in his arms."

"You!" He went in to kiss her for the third time.

She stopped him with her hands. "Okay, okay. Enough kisses. Time to go."

Reluctantly, he let her out of the embrace.

"So, which way?" she asked.

He unzipped a side pocket in his water-proof pants and took out his compass. He unlatched the tiny lid, shifted in his place and aligned himself in the direction of the true north.

"This way," he pointed. "Guess we need to follow the river."

"Come on then!" She clapped her hands once. "Let's go!" She grabbed his hand.

He screamed.

He extracted his hand from her grasp. Stroked it with his other hand, like it was a fragile baby.

She was confused for a moment. Suddenly, she realized as she noticed a scarlet stump of dried blood where his thumb should have been.

"I am sorry. I am sorry!" she blurted out.

"It's fine," he said through gritted teeth.

She rummaged in her satchel and came out with a plastic tube of antiseptic ointment and a scarf, wet from falling into the river. She dabbed the antiseptic on his wound. He winced at each dab. Then, she wrung the water out of the scarf and started to swaddle his hand in it.

"Shouldn't we use a dry cloth on the wound?" he asked.

"Yes, if we had one. We don't. So, better covered than dry."

His forehead creased with pain every time Michelle wound the cloth around his missing thumb.

"All good?" she asked once she was done.

"What do you think?" He grimaced.

She patted his shoulder. "You are a big boy. You'll get used to the pain."

He stared at her with wide, unblinking eyes. She smiled and gingerly took hold of his arm.

Arm-in-arm they started to walk along the river. Neither spoke a word. They were tired and famished. The journey thus far had been demanding, and both knew, it was far from over.

Within minutes they reached the end of the river. An earthen dam had cordoned off the flow of water. The wall of the dam was a fond remembrance of a bygone era. Made of clay, stone, and soil, it had weathered over the years. Large chunks had fallen away, leaving behind a delicate structure that might give way to the charging river any moment. But despite all odds, it still stood tall – about five feet tall. It was equally thick. One could simply scale the wall and walk over to the other side of the river.

The forest, which ran on either side of the river, merged beyond the wall. It was as if the wall had been built to unite the trees that were perennially separated by the river. And unite they did. The forest beyond the wall was thick like concrete. No going through the forest.

Where to now? he wondered.

He turned his gaze to the river. "That's strange," he said after a moment.

"What?" she asked.

He walked to the edge of the river bank and dipped his hand in the water.

She walked to him. "What's strange?"

"This." He nodded toward his immersed hand. "The river flow is quite strong. And there is a perpetual flow of water from the waterfall. I wonder why is it not flowing over the wall into the forest? Or, filling up the banks on the side? All this water must go somewhere. Where is it going?"

He stared hard at the flowing river. And then at the patchy wall. The water flowed, hit the wall and vanished. No change in water level.

"Let's check out the wall," he said finally.

He walked over and bent to examine the flat end of the wall.

Suddenly, he exclaimed, "Saraph!"

Michelle jumped in alarm as if she'd spotted a cockroach. "What! Where?"

"Not real Saraph, stupid." He smiled and shook his head. "A seven-headed snake is carved at the head of the wall."

She let out a deep sigh and bent beside him to take a closer look.

Michelle dusted away grains of dirt with her hand and said, "There is something written below the carving." She leaned in. Her face was barely inches from the wall.

"It doesn't make any sense," she said.

"Let me look." He squinted at the markings. And then smiled, immediately grateful for the language lessons Dr. Costello had given him. "It's Sentinelese. It's supposed to be read from right to left."

"Thank you for the history lesson, professor. Tell me what it says," she retorted.

He wiped his smile off and trailed his finger along the text, right to left. He read the text again, translating it in his mind from Sentinelese to Somali, his mother tongue. Like a beginner does when learning a new language.

He read the text a third time, this time aloud, translating it further in English so Michelle could understand, "The path… to paradise… goes… through the Temple… of God Saraph."

"Well, that's super helpful…" she said, her tone filled with sarcasm. "…considering we started our journey from the Temple of God Saraph."

They pondered over the text for a moment. Finally, Michelle said, "Let's see if there are more markings on the other end of the wall."

She levered herself up on the wall and started crawling toward the other end. She moved slowly, her eyes scanning every inch of the parapet for markings.

He followed. His eyes, though, kept roving at Michelle's butt as she crawled ahead of him.

"I can't see any more markings," she said.

He didn't answer. He was busy chasing her curves from behind.

"Do you see anything?" she asked.

He didn't hear her. His gaze had single-minded focus.

Michelle stopped. Turned around. "All this while you have been checking out my butt, haven't you?"

"Huh! What?" he fumbled as words tumbled out of his mouth.

She rolled her eyes. "Nothing!" She turned and went to work.

"Sorry," he mumbled.

She didn't hear him, or, pretended not to. They crawled to the other end of the wall in silence. There was no text, no carvings anywhere else on the walkway.

They jumped off the wall. Scanned the other side of the river bank. An old banyan tree stood at the edge of the forest. Its numerous aerial prop roots had reached the ground and grown into thick, woody trunks. An oddity jumped out at them. They hadn't noticed it from afar. But, now it was clear like freshwater. A hollow, as large as a grown elephant, had been carved into the central trunk of the banyan tree. A human could practically live inside the hollow in the tree.

They looked at each other. The Temple of God Saraph?

They walked closer to the temple. It was an odd sight. Human skulls formed a circle around the tree. A large rock, like a tombstone, had been planted right outside the circle of skulls. Sentinelese was scribbled on the tombstone in red paint. Or was it human blood?

They came to a halt.

Seven jet black king cobras, like seven heads of the God Saraph, sat in attention at the foot of the temple. Each hissed and jerked its head in unceasing warnings.

He looked at the tombstone and turned ashen.

"What's the matter? What does it say?" asked Michelle.

"It says…" he gulped and read the text aloud, one character at a time. "Death… to the man who… steps inside …the Temple… of God Saraph."

Michelle shuddered. "Well, the way those cobras are hissing at us, I believe every word."

"So, what do we do now? We have to get inside a temple where no man is welcome."

"Yep…but what about a woman?" muttered Michelle.

"What do you mean?" he asked.

And then, his eyes widened, and his lips broke into a smile as the sudden realization of Michelle's words hit him.

He nodded his head. "Yes! Maybe, you are right." And then, just as suddenly, he stopped smiling. "But what if the solution isn't as simple as it seems?"

"Simple?" Michelle poked him in the ribs. "Did you even think about the solution before I said it?"

"No," he said sheepishly.

"Think about it now. Someone must have created the wall, the inscription on the wall, and the temple. Right?"

He nodded.

"Has to be Sentinels as they are the only humans who ever roamed this island. Now tell me –who wields power among the Sentinels? Enough power to order the construction of a dam and a temple, inside a frickin' banyan tree, in the middle of the jungle."

He remained stumped for a moment. And then his eyes lit up. "The queen!" he exclaimed.

She smiled and nodded. "Yes, my dear. Men are considered vile in Sentinel culture. Only a woman can enter and unlock the door to a temple per religious protocol. That's what Dr. Costello told us. So, no offence my love…" Michelle pumped her chest and held her head high. "…but please step aside and let the woman pass!"

He grinned.

She brushed past him and marched to the edge of the circle of skulls.

"Michelle!" he called her.

She stopped.

"What if you are wrong? What if those king cobras rip you apart like a rag doll?" He jogged to her. "I can't let you go alone. I am coming with you."

"No, you are not." She took a step toward him and held his forearm. "This is the only way. I can feel it. Trust me."

She held his gaze for a long time. Finally, he relented.

"Okay, but if those snakes come within a yard of you, promise me, you are getting out of there. Okay?"

She grinned. "Okay."

She faced the temple and straightened. And without waiting another moment, she stepped inside the circle.

He swallowed hard.

She moved slowly, a step at a time. Her arms locked by her side, her hands bunched into fists.

On seeing her approach, the snakes reared up their bodies in unison, like a dance, and stood tall in an aggressive stance. They hissed vehemently. The collective hissing sounded like a low growl.

She stopped three yards from them.

The snakes didn't move. They remained at the temple entrance, spread in a semi-circle.

She took another step.

The snakes remained still. Their forked, blood-red tongues moved in and out.

She stood there, not knowing what her next move should be.

But then he saw her figure out her next steps. She thumped her forehead. "How could I have forgotten it?" She said aloud. She bent and in one fluid motion sprung out the dagger strapped to her boot. She brandished the dagger in front of her like a sword.

That was the missing link – the dagger of God Saraph. The king cobras slithered aside, revealing a clear path to the temple entrance.

She smiled at him. He stood cross-armed, literally hugging himself. He didn't smile back. He was too worried for a smile. Worried for her, for her life.

"Be careful!" He finally replied to her smile.

Michelle nodded. This was it. She knew she had to walk in. The path to Eden would reveal itself inside the temple. That's what the clue had said. But she couldn't bring herself to move forward. Her feet remained rooted. She couldn't pin-point what was stopping her. Fear of cobras? Fear of the unknown? Or – and this troubled her most – the gut instinct of a woman?

"It's okay, sweetheart. You can do it!" He encouraged her.

Her fear melted away, but the gut feeling remained. Don't go in, it said. She brushed aside the nagging feeling and stepped forward. *There was no turning back now*, she said to herself.

The cobras lay on either side of the path to the temple door, three on each side. All Michelle had to do was walk straight into the temple. And that's what she did. She walked like a woman on a mission with short, brisk steps. No fear, no hesitations. The cobras hissed loudly, but this time it sounded more like a song of respect than trepidation.

"Yes, show some respect," Michelle hissed as she walked past the cobras. "All six of you, show some respect."

She walked on. But, two steps later, she suddenly stopped at the temple threshold. Something didn't add up. Something she had just said. She wheeled around on her heels. She pointed her forefinger at the snakes and counted. One, two, three… six in total.

One missing!

There were seven cobras, like the seven heads of God Saraph, when they first came about the temple in the banyan tree. Where was the seventh?

She looked around, suddenly frantic. Fear gripped her nerves. *I told you so*, hissed her gut.

"Shut up." She spoke aloud.

It hissed in her ears again. And she realized. It wasn't her gut feeling. It was an actual hiss.

Very carefully she rotated her neck, as if her neck was the second hand of a clock, taking its own sweet time to rotate half a circle. Bright yellow eyes greeted her. They were five inches from her face. She froze. A slimy forked tongue poked at the tip of her nose. She was face to face with a king cobra. The seventh. It dangled from a tree branch, blocking her entry into the temple.

Even before she could react, two razor-sharp fangs, white as pearl, dug into her forehead. In and out, like it never happened. Except it did. She collapsed in a heap, as though a puppets strings had been dropped.

I told you so, hissed her gut as she closed her eyes one last time.

Chapter 10
The Riddle

Michelle had fallen. The cobra had bitten her, and her feet had buckled like a tent without poles.

He replayed the fall like a video in his mind, again and again. His ears whizzed with Michelle's shriek, again and again. It was as if his mind was copying and pasting that memory into every conceivable mental space available. Copy and paste, copy and paste. And on it went in an unending loop. But his body was a sea of calmness. On edge, but calm. Some would have shouted, even shrieked, on seeing their beloved fall. Some would have blasted howls through the jungle. Some would have collapsed with shock beyond belief. But he was calm. At least, his body did not betray the horrors that were terrifying the innocent lover inside him.

He was calm because it was a time to act, not grieve.

He looked around. Saw a tree branch that had fallen a few paces away. He rushed to pick it up. It was a tiny stick, with fleshy green leaves on its ends. It felt wet and crusty in his hand. Without wasting a moment, he jumped over and entered the circle of skulls, ready to take on the seven king cobras with a tree branch.

He stopped dead in his tracks. The cobras had suddenly vanished. Not one was visible from where he stood. What the hell? He shook his head, making sure it wasn't his imagination playing tricks with him. But, reality remained unchanged – Michelle lay unconscious at the temple entrance and the cobras were nowhere in sight.

With measured steps, he made his way toward Michelle. His eyes kept dithering, his ears extremely attentive. He brandished the tree branch in front of him, like a sword, in case the cobras lay in ambush.

Nothing happened. No sound. No movement. No cobras.

He reached Michelle. Bent and felt her wrist for pulse. It was there, barely pulsing, but there. He let out a breath he didn't realize he was holding. Michelle was alive, barely.

What should I do? What should I do?

The question hammered his brain. He knew the venom had to be removed from Michelle's blood. He recalled a movie he had once watched where the hero had sucked venom out of the heroine's hand. Would it work? He shook his head, answering his own question.

He looked around, hoping to find the antidote sitting on the ground, waiting for him to take and revive Michelle. There was nothing, least of all medicine.

He got up. With long strides, he went this way and that. He wanted to do something, anything. Beads of desperation arose on his forehead. He ran haphazardly – to the edge of the forest for any medicinal plant, but he was no medicine man; to the river bank for water, but what use was water in this case; to the tombstone for any clue, but all it said was go through the Temple of God Saraph to find paradise. Oh, the folly of it all! What use was paradise, when your goddess lay half-dead in front of you? What use was home with no one to share it with?

It was now that his body betrayed his internal turmoil. He ran about – this time to the temple. Tears rolled down his cheeks as he ran. He screamed, "*help*", and choked on his own tears. He cursed the cobras, the banyan tree housing the temple, the island, but words babbled out of his mouth, one toppling over another, as he shuddered between long sobs and deep sighs. He collapsed next to Michelle's body.

Suddenly, the fog in his head cleared. The answer was right there. He had to go inside the temple, finish what Michelle had started.

He stood, jumped over Michelle's body and thrust himself inside. He was transported to another place immediately. It was chilly inside, down-to-the-spine chilly. His body immediately contracted as he wrapped himself into an embrace. He heard the constant hiss of a barely audible chant. It sounded like "Sarp-Sarp-Sarp" in a deep, guttural voice. The temple was filled with the luxurious smell of musk. Like a sweet-smelling nymph, it tempted and pulled his heart deep into the bowels of the temple. He walked further in, entranced.

In the middle of the temple was a stone idol of God Saraph, as tall as Michelle. Saraph's stone idol clasped a footed goblet in the two hands protruding from its belly. He narrowed his eyes to look closely at the goblet. It was made of gold and shone in the dim light. Seven snake-heads were engraved on its crown. There was an inscription in Sentinelese below it.

I hold the Elixir of Life.
I reveal Paradise.
Six drips from acre-foot I prescribe,
Use the nine and four drips pails, be precise,
One hour, else I take the sacrifice!

He read the inscription again, not understanding it the first time. He read it the third time. And the fourth. Suddenly, jubilation filled his heart. All I need are six drips to revive Michelle! …Smart, old Sentinelese had planned it all along.

The inscription was straightforward, only if one knew the metric system used by the Sentinels in ancient times. And he knew.

Acre-foot referred to a million liters of water, usually a reference to a large water body. Like a lake, or a river. It wasn't exact science, just a reference. But six drips were exact, rather "precise", as was inscribed on the goblet. It referred to six ounces. He needed six ounces of water, precisely, to concoct the elixir of life, or Michelle would become a sacrifice to God Saraph.

Suddenly, he was brimming with gratitude – to himself for knowing Sentinelese and to Saraph for holding a goblet of the antidote. Now all he had to do was precisely measure six ounces, fill the goblet, and revive Michelle.

But how do I measure six ounces of water, exactly? He read the inscription again.

Use the nine and four drips pails, be precise

"Pails? Where do I find two pails in the jungle?" he said aloud.

His gaze flickered in the hollow. He looked left. He looked right. He looked at the foot of the idol. No pails. Nothing. The place was devoid of any material objects.

Tentacles of worry sprung up in his heart again. Time was running out. The inscription was clear. He had one hour. And he had wasted much of it running about, crying and cursing. He had to prepare the antidote. Fast.

Maybe the pails are in some corner and I had missed them in the faint light? he thought. He bustled about, checking the four corners of the compact hollow. No pails.

He got more and more agitated. "No! No! Nooo! How can you write a stupid inscription and not provide the stupid props for this stupid planned drama?" He was seething, his head rocked left and right in distress.

Anxiety was starting to overwhelm him, when suddenly - Clang! Clang! Clang! - a continual metallic sound rumbled through the temple. A steel tumbler crashed, rebounded, and crashed again on the stony floor. He stood transfixed. In his rush, he had accidentally kicked a tiny metallic pail. The pail had rolled away, hit the wall, and came to a stop. Its metallic rim beamed resplendently as it rolled. He looked around. Right next to his foot was another pail. It was a miniature version of the one that he had just kicked across the room. The four and the nine pails!

He grasped the rim of the pail next to him. The ice-cold metal stung his hand. Six ounces. I need exactly six ounces. He reminded himself. He rushed to pick the other pail and darted out of the temple. He jumped over Michelle, over the circle of human skulls, and ran across the patchy grass to the river. He was huffing furiously by the time he reached the river bank.

There was no time to catch his breath. He set the nine ounces pail on the ground. It landed with a soft thump on the stones wallowing in mud. He squatted. With the four ounces pail he scooped water out of the river into the larger bucket. He did it twice. Eight ounces in the big pail. *Now I just need to take out two ounces of water.* And, suddenly, it struck him. There was no way he could precisely take out two ounces of water.

The riddle was tougher than he initially thought.

He unburdened himself of the pail, thinking. But he couldn't concentrate. His brain was both agitated and impatient, and his thoughts kept returning to Michelle.

Is she still alive? "Okay, six ounces can only fit in the nine-ounce pail, not in the four- ounce pail. So, I need to get rid of three out of nine ounces in the big bucket to get to six." *What if Michelle is already dead?* "And I'll need the smaller pail to get rid of those three ounces. But how do you measure three ounces with a four-ounce bucket?"

Suddenly, he flung his arm and slapped himself hard across his face. The crack echoed through the forest. The burn spread across his face like lava through vein-like fields.

"Concentrate! Concentrate, you fool!" he chided himself.

He shook his head, cracked his neck like he was a boxer getting ready for a fight, and closed his eyes. The fight was on!

"Okay, let's work backward," he said to himself. "Need to get rid of three ounces from the big pail to get six ounces, right?" He nodded in reply to his own question. "To accurately measure those three ounces, I can use the small pail. Three plus one equals four. So, the small pail should already have one ounce in it when I transfer three ounces from the big pail into it. That way I'll know I have transferred the correct amount. So, the key question is - how do I get one ounce in the small pail?" He rubbed his chin, deep in thought.

His eyes shot open. "That's it! One!" he exclaimed.

"Oh, God! This was easy. How did I not get this earlier?" He slammed his forehead with his palm, just as his lips parted into a smile.

He picked up the big pail and strode a few paces into the river, till water was in-between his ankles and knees.

"One is what connects the four and the nine," he mumbled. "Four plus four plus one equals nine. And three plus one equals four. One is the connector!"

He filled the nine ounces pail up to its brim. Awkwardly—he had never thought how much he depended on two working thumbs—he took measured steps and walked to the bank.

"Now, to get one in the small pail…"

He lifted the big pail and poured water into the four ounces pail, up to its brim. His hands quivered in silent anticipation the whole time. With a soft shove, he toppled the small pail. Water gushed out and crawled across the muddy river bank.

He repeated the action – filled the small pail and emptied it on the bank. By doing so, he was left with one ounce in the big pail. He transferred the one ounce of water, with utmost alertness, to the small pail.

"…and ladies and gentlemen, we have one drip in the small pail!"

Now, the finishing touch!

He filled the nine ounces pail to its brim and emptied three ounces into the small pail which already had one ounce of water.

He now had six ounces of water in the big pail.

Relief flowed through his veins. He lifted the pail and admired it with pride. He had done it!

He left the small pail sitting on the river bank and ran to the temple, as fast as his legs could carry him without spilling water from the pail. He was out of breath when he reached the tombstone. Hunger, exhaustion, and blood-loss were equally culpable.

He read the inscription on the tombstone again – Death to the man who steps inside the circle of God Saraph – and was suddenly filled with dread. Would the cobras be there?

How would he pass through them? But there were no cobras, no movement. No birds, no noise.

He reached the spot where Michelle lay sprawled. Her face was ashen. Time was running out according to the white froth effusing from her mouth.

He wanted to sit beside Michelle, put her head on his lap, and whisper words of encouragement. But he had to hurry. He looked away from the only woman he had ever loved. With stoic determination he entered the temple. The sweet smell of musk greeted him. His ears hummed with the melodious mantra. Sarp-Sarp-Sarp! It had a calming effect on him. His nerves relaxed, his breathing slowed. He was stripped off 'fear' before he entered the temple. It was as if "fear" was not welcome into the hallowed portal.

He ambled to the stone idol of God Saraph. Delicately, using both his hands, he lifted the pail that held six ounces of water. Six ounces of redemption for Michelle and for him. He tilted the pail. A steady stream flowed into the footed goblet. The goblet illuminated with golden light. Water turned into a bright golden, life-giving elixir. The light from the potion lit up the entire temple. Like the sun had burst through the night, pouring light into every dark nook and crevice.

He stood there transfixed. His eyes glowed, partly from the golden light, but mostly from the wow that it elicited. He watched in silent amazement, like a kid watching a magic trick for the first time. Beyond logic, but real. Indescribable, but true.

Once he had emptied the contents of the pail, he put it on the floor. His heart overflowed with anxiety. He stepped forward. With trembling fingers, he held the cup in-between his hands. Warmth from the cup permeated every cell in his body. It pacified him.

And then, something extraordinary happened. Saraph let go of the cup. The stony hands of Saraph, which had held the cup thus far, simply moved apart, dropping the cup. He stumbled slightly as he grappled with the sudden weight in his hands. The cup was like a compact bar of lead. Dense and heavy. Intense pain, like fire, surged through the stump that once held his thumb. He groaned and cursed loudly, but tightened his grip on the cup. There was no way he was letting it fall.

With long strides, he made his way to Michelle. He held the cup like a newborn child. He reached Michelle and went on one knee, and then the other. His hands remained firm on the neck of the cup, disregarding the searing pain and stream of blood that oozed from the stump of his missing thumb. He shifted the cup into his right hand. With his left hand, he grasped Michelle's head and pushed her forward into a reclining position. He held her there. Her head weighed like the cup, like lead. He brought the cup to her mouth, still covered in poisonous white froth, and tilted it against her lips. The golden elixir pierced the white froth, like light expelling a shadow. Drop by drop the liquid made its way into Michelle's mouth. He nudged her forward, so she could swallow the liquid.

Then, he waited.

Nothing happened.

He thrust more elixir into her mouth till there was none left.

He waited.

No movement from Michelle.

He checked her pulse. It wasn't there.

Chapter 11
In Limbo

A burst of water droplets hit my face, followed by an indistinct, muffled sound that tickles my ears. "Are you okay?" it says. It's as if I am in a deep well and someone is calling out to me from above. I concentrate, trying to decipher the face behind the voice.

"You there?"

I recognize Azura's sweet voice.

There? Where? I look everywhere. There is darkness around me. Where am I? I suddenly realize that my eyes are shut. I strain and strain, but my eyes remain glued together. Shut from the world. Shut in the gloom of blackness. I can't open my eyes. And I get caught in the rough winds of panic's hurricane. It tosses and hurls and twists me around, and flings me further into the deep, dark well.

"Is Uncle dead?" I hear Aana's voice, before I tumble into hell.

Chapter 12

Two Down, One To Go

He held Michelle's hand. But there was no mistaking it – no pulse.

He threw the cup away. Using his strong right hand he stroked her throat. Maybe, she hasn't swallowed the elixir?

No success.

Impatience grew on him like a hydra. He put aside one fear, and another grew. He shook her. He pinched her. "Why isn't it working? It was supposed to work."

He suddenly stopped. *Should I get six ounces from the river again?* he thought. Yes, maybe that will work.

With a lump in his throat and eyes glistening with tears, he scurried for the cup.

"I'll be quicker this time, sweetheart," he shouted as he ran.

Sudden coughing ripped apart the silence he was ensconced in.

He stopped in his tracks.

"Quicker? For wha-" Michelle coughed her lungs out, spilling spatters of golden liquid around her as she tried to sit up.

"Oh, my God! Oh, my God! You are alive!"

"Huh?" It was all Michelle could mumble through the grogginess.

He dashed to her. His feet were suddenly nimble. His heart lurched out of his mouth in delight. His eyes still glistened with tears. "Happy tears" is how he'd describe them later to Michelle. He let his feet slip to the ground as he neared her and slid the rest of the way on his knees. Like a celebration. Or maybe he thought a knee-slide was quicker than just running to her. Either way, he slid and bruised his knees. But at that moment, he was beyond care. He was overjoyed to the moon and back. The girl he loved had returned from the dead. Michelle was alive.

He hugged her tight. "I thought I lost you," he said, squeezing her some more.

Michelle coughed. "You are strangling me!" she protested.

He loosened his grip but didn't let go of her. "I never thought your cough would sound so melodious. I just want to keep hearing it." He chuckled.

Michelle glared at him through the swoon. Then, she cocked her head and looked at the hollow in the banyan tree and the temple inside it. It triggered a memory because she instantly looked up, directly at the branch where the king cobra had dangled from and bit her.

"I was bitten by a cobra," she said as she patted the site of the bite on her forehead. "How am I still alive?"

He smiled. "Oh, it was terrible, darling. I had to fight off the cobras with a tree branch. Imagine! a tree branch!" He shook his head and laughed, as if recalling the memory with fondness.

"Really?" Michelle sat up and gripped his arm.

"Oh, yes! It was nerve-wrecking. Seven snakes versus one me. It was a fierce battle." Suddenly, his brow contorted into disgust. "And then…" He paused.

Michelle dug her nails into the skin of his arm. "Then what happened?"

He looked at her grimly. "And then…I had to suck venom-filled blood out of your forehead to revive you. It tasted awful. Just awful!" He spat on the ground.

"Really?" Michelle asked. Her tone filled with sarcasm more than surprise.

"Yeah, baby. You don't believe me?"

"You. Big. Fat. Liar." She grinned. "I know you." She gave a short laugh. "You can't even stand the sight of blood. And you are telling me that you, you faint-hearted, scared-of-blood baby, sucked blood and venom out of my forehead?"

He eyeballed her with a straight face, chewing his lower lip, deciding if it was time to stop the charade.

"There! Now you are chewing your lip. Another thing you do when you lie." She hit him on the shoulder with a light-hearted thump. "Liar!"

His cheeks swelled into a big smile, which soon transformed into an ebullient laugh. He squeezed Michelle into a bear hug, laughing into her ear the whole time.

"So, what happened?" She pulled away from him. Looked into his eyes. "…and the truth now."

He nodded. And like a seasoned raconteur, he began to spin the yarn of what he aptly termed as the "Puzzle of Pails". He recounted the events since Michelle fell, some spiced up for added effect and some watered down. Michelle sat in stunned silence the whole time, the story too mind-boggling to respond to. She snuggled into his arms once he finished the tale.

"Thank you," she whispered in his ear.

"Uh-huh! There isn't a 'thank you' in love. Only 'I love you'." He kissed her on the cheek. "… but just so we are clear, never again am I letting you go alone into a cobra pit. From now on, you do what I say."

She snorted.

He pulled away from her. "What's funny? I am serious here."

Her eyes gleamed, reflecting the broad grin that draped her face. "Nothing. You sound cute when you put your army general hat on." She sat up and in a deep, guttural voice that sounded more comical than masculine, she mimicked him. "FROM NOW ONNNN, YOU DO WHAT I SAYYYY!" She broke into a hysterical laugh, cackling at her own imitation of him.

He raised his brow and looked at her with weary dispassion. "First of all, I don't sound like that. Second, it wasn't funny. At all."

"Yes, it was!" She swatted his arm. "It was an amazing impersonation. And it was funny." She jabbed a finger in his chest and said, "YOU DO WHAT I SAYYYY!" She guffawed, clutching her head with her hands, lest it exploded with laughter.

He got up. "You done?"

She didn't reply, or rather, she couldn't. Her body convulsed from bouts of laughter. There was no way he could get a word out of her.

He waited. Displeasure oozed from his face like lava from volcano.

Finally, the laughter died a slow death. Michelle lay on the ground, her chest heaving with deep, laborious breathing. "God," she said. "That was tiresome."

She looked at him. Raised her hand and said in her sweetest voice, "A hand, please?"

He contemplated, then sighed loudly and pulled her to her feet.

"Ouch. Ouch. Ouch!" Needles pinched her legs from inside, cartwheeling from the ankles to the upper thighs and back. She grabbed his arm with both hands. "My legs went to sleep," she explained while stretching and kicking the air, one leg at a time. It took her a whole minute before she released the pressure on his hand and stood. He let go of her, still miffed at her.

She immediately grabbed his hand. "You know I love you, right?"

He lowered his head and sighed. "Yep," he said curtly.

"And?" she said.

He sighed again, loudly. "… and I love you too."

She flashed a big smile and squeezed his hand. "Okay, now that we are okay, tell me, which way to paradise?"

"What do you mean?" he asked, bewildered.

"You said the puzzle inscribed on the cup mentioned 'I reveal paradise'. So, what was the big reveal?"

"Oh!" he smacked his forehead with his palm. "I completely forgot about it." He turned and shot a look at the temple entrance. "Let's go inside."

They hurried to the temple.

"Oh…nice!" said Michelle, as the sweet smell of musk wafted through her nostrils.

He shrugged in the dim light that percolated from the daylight outside. The temple reminded him of the frustration, the anger and the misery he felt when Michelle was dying. The place was no longer "nice".

"Oh! Do you hear that chanting?" she asked.

He nodded.

"Okay, look carefully," she said. "Is there anything different from the first time you entered the temple?"

He blinked twice, strained his eyes and scoped the area. Nothing different from the first time he had seen the place.

"Nope," he answered.

"Look closely," she said.

And he saw it. The idol of God Saraph stood in the center. Except, the idol had split into two. The hands that had held the goblet, had moved apart, revealing a cross-section on the floor that was hitherto invisible. A secret path!

He went on all fours and looked closely. He saw an unending staircase that led underground to the dark belly of earth.

The path to the Garden of Eden had been revealed.

Chapter 13

The Underground Sky

"Let's go downstairs," said Michelle.

He didn't hear her. He stood still, dumbstruck, marveling at the ingenuity of the old Sentinels. A small goblet filled with water - six ounces to be exact - held enough power to unlock a secret door.

"Hey?" Michelle touched him on the shoulder.

"Huh?"

"I said, let's go." Michelle motioned to the steps.

"Yeah."

One by one, they entered the stairwell. The soft chanting in the temple turned into a sweet-sounding, exuberant clamor. As if, after years and years of captivity, the air was dancing to the song of its newfound freedom. It was a melody for the ears, a flutter for the heart. They stood hand-in-hand for a while, soaking in the serenity, reveling in its charm.

Michelle inhaled deeply. "I wish I could listen to it all day."

He remained quiet, lost in thought.

She let out a sigh. "Anyway, let's keep moving."

The stairs were steep, the passageway constricted. It was difficult to maneuver in the dark. They clamped their hands to the rock that enclosed them. Only for peace of mind. Both knew it would not prevent a fall if they lost their footing. And a tumble might send them sprawling to their deaths, down an unending staircase.

They kept descending. The staircase seemed interminable, there was no destination in sight. It sapped their energy. A clear destination invigorates, but a limitless goal drains the mind. They trudged down the stairs.

After ten minutes and five hundred steps, finally, they saw light at the bottom - muted and unobtrusive. Relief poured over them. The stairwell had an ending. They kept moving. The light kept brightening, almost like traveling from night to day. Another ten minutes and their feet touched hard ground.

He suddenly turned and grabbed Michelle. He pulled her close. What came over him - relief, desire, or love - even he couldn't tell. Michelle looked stunned at the roughness. Before she could protest, he pounced on her and kissed her. Hard. It was long. It was passionate. Rough at the edges, but it was pure desire. He left her breathless. Her eyes glistened as he finally loosened his grip.

"Ah!" Michelle gazed into his eyes and smiled. "Where was this animal hiding all this while? I'd like to meet him more often." She winked at him.

He chuckled. "Well, that could be arranged."

He offered her his hand. "Come, the adventure awaits."

Michelle gripped his hand. "This adventure better end soon. The sleep junkie inside me is craving for the soft mattress at home."

His eyes followed the enclosed path in front of them. It was like a tunnel. The narrow path ended in bright white light. It was like gazing at an endless white galaxy from inside a telescope, watching it merge and blur with infinity.

Michelle said what he was thinking. "Where does it end?"

"Let's check it out."

"Wait. I am hungry," she announced.

"Yep, so am I."

He unzipped his cross-body satchel. Rummaged through the contents and came out with two granola bars. Michelle laboriously extended her hand to receive one of the bars, as if it were a great effort to even accept food on a platter.

He raised his eyebrows. "Hello?" he snorted. "I am not sharing. They are both mine."

She put on her sheepish grin. "Okay, give me one bite."

The Apple

He looked at her as if she had asked for an arm and a leg. "Uh-huh!" He shook his head. "Use your own ration, sweetie."

She scrunched her nose and stuck her tongue out, like she was going to be sick. "My bran bars aren't as tasty as your granolas."

He put on his best fake smile and said, "Then who asked you to pack them? I told you not to pack those crappy bars. But, no. You had to choose the 'more healthy' bran bars over granola."

She crossed her arms.

He unwrapped both his bars, clutched the treats like a kid, one in each hand, and took a bite of each. "Mmmm… ahhh! Mmmm! AHHH!"

She burst into laughter.

He looked around and then at her, a quizzical look adorned his face. "What's so funny? I am just enjoying my bars."

"It's like…" She tried to say something, but then words got lost in the flood of laughter.

"It's like what?"

She raised her forefinger and wagged it, asking him to give her a minute. He waited.

"It's like…hehe…it's like you are making love with the granola bars!" She slapped her thigh like she had cracked a joke.

He puffed into emptiness. "Remind me, how old are you? Because I wouldn't peg you a day over fifteen!"

Michelle giggled like a teenager.

"Here, take the rest of the granola bars. I am no longer hungry."

Michelle didn't need another invitation. She jumped in delight and snatched the bars like a hungry monkey. "Thank you! You are the best!" she said.

He smiled and started walking toward the white light. Michelle followed, munching on the bars.

He suddenly stopped ten yards from the glow. He blinked and stared at the path ahead. "What is that?"

"What?" she said, following his gaze.

The white light from afar had transformed into daylight.

"Is that the sky…but…but underground?"

"How can the sky be…" She stopped speaking as the bewitching sight took hold of her. The path was coming to an end, opening into what could only be described as the sky lit up with broad daylight - a canvas of blue speckled with fluffy clouds - in every direction. The ceiling of the underground cave was the sky! The ground was the sky!

They strode to the threshold where the path met the sky. Their minds were somersaulting. From top to bottom, wherever they looked, blue sky in bright daylight pervaded their vision. Cotton clouds floated in front of them.

"Wow!" She clasped her hands in excitement. "We are going to walk on clouds!"

He wasn't the least bit excited. Skeptical, he bent to examine the blue-white ground in front of him. Was it solid ground? Or just a cliff in the garb of the sky? He ran his hand over the sky-like ground. It felt cold and wet. He looked at his palm. White sludge dripped off it. He smelled the sludge and smiled; an assured, knowing smile.

"It's insane! I wonder what arcane magic brought the sky below ground, and then, to top it, on the ground we are walking!" she said.

"Physics," he replied.

"What?" she wrinkled her brow, befuddled.

He stood and flicked white dregs off his hand. "What you see on the ground is just a reflection of the sky up in the ceiling. Like a mirage, it's bewitching us to see what it's not."

"Oh." The excitement fizzled out from her voice. "Then what is it?" she asked.

"Salt," he said, pointing to the white residue on his hand. "It's an underground salt desert covered with a thin layer of water. A perfect concoction for a perfect mirror."

"Oh," she said again, crestfallen.

He looked ahead at the expanse of sky. "I read about this phenomenon somewhere. Apparently, Bolivia has the largest of these salt deserts. Can't remember its name. What was it?" He snapped his fingers repeatedly in the hope that it would trigger the name.

"God, you are such a geek!" she admonished him. "I don't want to know the name of a similar desert in Bolivia. It might be a scientific phenomenon to you. But, to me, it's magical. So, if you don't mind, let me pretend that I am walking on clouds, okay?"

With that, she stepped onto the reflection of a fluffy cloud. She spread her arms, like wings, and soaked in the idyllic beauty that enthralled her eyes. She looked down and saw her reflection.

"My hair is such a mess!" She adjusted her hair with her hands. "I should have packed a hairbrush."

He laughed. "Yeah, maybe we should have packed your whole dressing table."

She rolled her eyes and went about fixing her hair.

He took out his compass. It pointed their destination in a north-east direction from their current location. He pointed his hand. "This way," he said.

He crossed the threshold and stepped on the mushy salt. The sludge squished beneath his boots. The moment he entered the desert, the compass needle swung ninety degrees. It now pointed in a north-west direction.

"That's odd."

Michelle stopped adjusting her hair. "What is?"

He stepped onto the narrow path. The compass needle swung, pointing again to the right.

"The magnetic fields are laterally inverted," he answered.

"What do you mean?"

"A compass aligns itself to Earth's magnetic field, right? But the magnetic field of the salt desert is laterally inverted to the rest of Earth, like a mirror image."

"How does it matter?" she said. "The physical location doesn't change, even if the magnetic field changes. It's not like China is now in United States. China remains in China."

"True. But the question is which way to go now, north-east or north-west? We were meant to follow the true north. Does 'true north' mean the physical north, or the magnetic north?"

She stayed mum.

He continued. "I think it's a trap. One way leads us to our destination, the other to our deaths, possibly."

Michelle rolled her eyes. "Oh, you are such a skeptic." She huffed in exasperation. "We can't be sure of anything. You need to stop over-thinking and get going."

She adjusted the strap of her satchel and walked away. "I am going right."

He gnawed his lower lip, like the conundrum gnawed at him. Left, or right? He didn't move.

Michelle looked at him. "Are you coming?"

He sighed and dragged his feet after her, despite a gut-wrenching feeling that she had chosen wrong.

Chapter 14
The Witch Test

Walking on clouds was bizarre, yet amazing. He looked at his own reflection in the underground salt desert as he walked; each step up created a surreal dream of floating on clouds, each step down smashed that dream with reality.

They had been walking for an hour. The staircase had long been left behind. Infinite sky had engulfed them completely. It was like walking inside a crystal ball of sky. There was nothing else in sight for miles, except spatter of white clouds on a sky-blue palette.

"I am starting to doubt my decision," said Michelle. "Maybe you were right. Maybe we should have gone the other way."

A smirk wrinkled the edge of his lips. "Maybe."

He paused, and then said, "But let's not worry about it till we are sure we chose wrong."

They walked on.

A mile later, Michelle stopped. She bent, put her hands on her knees, hung her head, and took deep breaths. He came closer and patted her back.

"Are you okay?"

She huffed loudly, once, and straightened up. "Yes, just tired. Can we rest for a while?"

He circled the area. There was nothing to be seen in any direction. No shelter, no trees. "Yes, of course," he said. "This place is as good as any to rest for a while."

Michelle slumped to the ground. Her chest heaved, her breathing grew irregular. He came and stood next to her. He opened his satchel, rummaged through his essentials, and came out with an energy bar and a bottle of Gatorade. He nudged her. "Here, you need energy."

Michelle stood straight. She took the Gatorade and gulped it in a single swig.

"Slow down, girl! I don't want you to throw up in my face later."

She snickered. Gatorade spewed out of her mouth and nose. "Shush! Don't make me laugh." She giggled. "Let me drink in peace. Else, I'll be more than happy to throw up in your face."

He raised his arms in surrender and watched her. This was his favorite activity in the whole wide world: watching Michelle from a distance and finding joy in her every movement, no matter how silly. He watched her gobble an energy bar. Her mouth distended into a balloon, the lines on her forehead strained, while she munched away. Her face reddened as she chewed harder. And slowly, as she swallowed the bar, the balloon burst into a smile. He saw the faintest hue of a dimple. There one moment, and then, gone. He smiled with her. This was the reason he loved watching her: she always made him smile.

"Hello!" Michelle snapped her fingers. "Where are you lost?"

He shook his head. "Nowhere."

"I have been thinking," said Michelle. "This place is bewitched," she blurted out.

"What?" he said. "There is a scientific explanation for everything that we have encountered on this island so far. We don't know why there is broad daylight a mile below earth's surface, but I am sure we'll figure it out in due course."

"Ever the man with the logic! What scientific explanation do you have for a seven-headed snake or a spider-scorpion? You don't even see an enchantment when it's staring you in the face."

Michelle's hand instinctively grabbed the silver cross hanging from the chain across her neck. She was a firm

Christian who had never missed a Sunday Mass, so much so that they had started the mission on Sunday night, after the weekly mass. She'd thought it would bring them luck. He thought better than to start a religion versus science war and attended the mass. As for luck, he carried an extra bottle of water in his bag and a Swiss Army Knife in his pocket; definite, pragmatic essentials in case of bad luck.

"Doesn't matter if the place is enchanted," he said. "The path to Eden goes through here."

"But, we are going in circles. Not getting anywhere."

"Have patience, sweets. The salt desert has to end somewhere."

"Not if the place is bewitched," she returned to her original point.

He shook his head in frustration. "Okay, the way I see it, we have two options. We either stay the course or we start all over again in the other direction. Either way, we are not sure which path leads to Eden. Having come this far, let's keep going. It's our best-"

"Are you kids lost?" A meek voice interrupted him.

Michelle shrieked. He spun around in the direction of the voice, groping his boot for the Swiss knife.

Standing a few feet away, cloaked in scruffy black overalls, was an old woman. White streaks of hair covered half of her severely wrinkled face. The skin on her cheeks and jaw was flabby and sagging, as if the ground was pulling it down. The neck was the worst, leathery and crumpled. She stood there, frail and wilting, supporting her weight on two walking sticks, one in each hand. The sticks were as feeble as she was.

Unruffled, the old woman asked again. "You kids lost?"

He stood, the Swiss knife hidden in his palm. "Who are you?"

The old woman narrowed her deep-set eyes into slits. "I live here. Might I inquire who are you? I have never seen you in the White Sea."

"White Sea?" Michelle repeated loudly.

The woman shifted her gaze to Michelle, and it remained there for a long time. It was as if she had seen another woman, a young woman, for the first time. Or she was plainly awestruck by Michelle's beauty. Whatever the reason, she kept staring.

Michelle became uneasy. She kept darting looks at him, her eyes beseeching him for help.

"Ahem." He tried to divert the crone's attention. "Is this desert the White Sea?"

"Deserts are dead." The woman said flatly, her eyes still fixed at Michelle. "The White Sea is living. A reflection of our lives. A mirror that shows you the naked, ugly truth - you."

Her penetrating gaze slowly shifted to him.

Michelle leaned closer and hissed in his ear through clenched teeth, "Mental, this one".

The woman spun her head and glowered at Michelle. She had heard the whisper. "Who are you?"

"No one important. Just passing by."

"No one just passes through the White Sea. Unless they are going to…" She looked squarely at him. "…the Garden."

Michelle peered at him. He looked back. There was no point in hiding their secret. The woman knew. He inhaled deeply and sighed. "Yes, that's where we are going. But we are lost. Do you know the way?"

The woman didn't reply straightaway. She seemed deep in thought, ruminating over the question.

He took a step forward and asked again, "Do you know the way?"

Finally, she bobbed her head up and down and turned around. "Follow me," she said behind her back. She dug her walking sticks into the ground and propelled herself forward. It seemed that the sticks were her feet, and her feet were the supports.

He exchanged glances with Michelle. Both had the same question in mind. Should they follow a strange woman in a strange place where stranger things had transpired? Deep down, both knew the answer. It's the same answer that parents drill into their young ones - never follow strangers.

But, he was an explorer scientist. It was in his DNA to boldly go where no one ventured before. With a slight nod of the head, he motioned Michelle to follow the woman.

Michelle grabbed his arm. "I don't have a good feeling about this," she whispered. "The woman came out of nowhere, like a ghost. This is a trap. I am sure."

He sighed. "Maybe. Maybe not. Like you said before, we are going in circles. So, this is our best chance of finding the Garden." He grabbed her hand. "Don't worry. I won't let anything happen to you. But, we need to follow the woman if we are to find the Garden."

Michelle squeezed her lips shut, her mind running. She wasn't convinced.

"Are you kids coming?" the old woman bellowed.

"Yes. Coming," he shouted.

He looked into Michelle's eyes. "Trust me. We should go."

Michelle relented. "Okay. But if I die, you are going to hell."

He smiled, grabbed her hand, and hurried after the old woman.

"Sorry, we were just packing our things." He offered an explanation as they reached the woman. She offered no reply. She pivoted on one of the sticks and wobbled ahead, her sticks digging into the ground like she was rowing a boat. Her long, black cloak glided over the White Sea, like a sorcerer.

They followed the old woman.

Michelle whispered to him. "I am telling you again. I don't like this. She is taking us the same way we came!"

"Shh!"

He wiped away beads of sweat on his forehead with the edge of his thumb. "It's the only way to find the Garden. Keep walking."

They strode along in utter silence, saving energy for the long strides. The blue sky turned sooty. It became one of those gloomy days when the sun plays hide and seek with menacing gray clouds. Humidity hung in the air, preparing for a torrential onslaught. Suddenly, lightning flashed, and a loud thunder blasted through the quiet.

The old woman looked skyward. "We need to hurry," she said.

"What were we doing so far?" said an exhausted Michelle.

"Why? What's the sudden urgency?" He asked the woman.

Another ominous thunder cracked through the sky.

"We don't hurry, we die."

"What?" He exchanged looks with Michelle. "What do you mean we die?"

The old woman kept thrusting with her walking sticks, a fresh boost of energy propelling her forward.

"Hey! Stop!" He shouted after her. "Tell us what's happening?"

The old woman suddenly stopped. With long, decisive hops she came back. "That was a warning," she said.

"What was?"

"Lightning. Thunder."

He was perplexed. "Warning for what?"

"Death." She paused. Looked at Michelle and then to him. "No one survives when lightning strikes the White Sea."

And suddenly he understood. "Salt and water," he whispered.

"What do you mean?" Michelle asked.

He said, "The combination of salt and water is a perfect conductor of electricity. If lightning strikes anywhere in the White Sea, we are fried."

Another blast of thunder detonated in the sky. All of them lifted their chins skyward. The hide and seek game between the sun and the clouds seemed to have taken a violent turn. The sun, it seemed, was running for its life. The baleful clouds followed. Lightning flashed, thunder clashed. And the sun retreated further. The last remaining sun rays that protruded through the clouds were locked in a sword-fight with shining bolts of lightning. The sun rays were losing. Fast.

And then, it became dark. The lively White Sea became disturbingly tanned.

"There is no time. We go. Now." The old woman hopped ahead, rowing with her sticks as fast as she could. But her

The Apple

sticks could only help as much. She couldn't run. They ran and easily overtook her. Realizing that they didn't know the way, they slowed, allowing the old woman to catch up.

"Don't slow down for me," shouted the woman, her voice teeming with determination. "Just follow your nose and you'll reach the island."

"What island?" he asked, jogging shoulder to shoulder with her as she struggled to hop faster. The feeble sticks seemed to struggle like their mistress.

"Just keep going… you wouldn't miss it… it's our only hope." The old woman huffed and puffed her way through the words. She was scrambling.

Michelle grabbed his arm. "Come. Run."

"We can't leave her behind," he nodded at the old woman.

"We can!" Michelle hissed in his ear. "We stay, we all die."

"The girl is right," said the woman. "You run ahead. I'll be right behind you."

Michelle jerked him forward. "Don't think. Run. Faster."

He tightened his grip on Michelle's hand, sighed deeply and charged ahead, letting his nose guide the way. Every few paces, he kept glancing at the old woman, to ensure she was coming along. To ensure she was okay. Michelle glanced behind as well, but he knew it was to ensure the old hag wasn't playing any tricks. To ensure this wasn't a ruse where the old woman was merrily seeing them run to their happy demise.

"The island!" he shouted and brought Michelle out of her suspicion-filled reverie. She turned and was immediately besotted by what she saw. Even the gray, sinister climate couldn't dampen the lively vision unfolding before her. "Wow!" is all she said.

A tiny black island had sprung up in the White Sea. A majestic tree stood at its peak. Amid the black death of the island had sprouted a fiery green life. Even from afar, the tree bathed them in its resplendence. It gleamed all over, like a sequined dress reflecting camera flashes. The tree stood like the jeweled crown of a black emperor, brilliant and bewitching. Such was its pull that they ran mouth-agape toward the emerald nestled atop the black island. Their hearts beat faster. Had they found the Garden of Eden? The glee oozing from every pore propelled them forward. This was it! This was it! - beat their hearts.

And then, out of nowhere, something struck him on the head. He grimaced and massaged the top of his head. It was a raindrop the size of a berry. And then another hit him. And then another. The rain came down fat and hard. It felt like a barrage of pebbles had been catapulted from the sky.

How can this be happening miles underground? His logical brain gave no answer.

The pebbles stung on impact. He covered his face with his hand and saw the way forward through the gap in his fingers. His other hand tugged Michelle along. They were less than three hundred yards from the black island.

They dashed through the torrent and reached the island, just as a lightning bolt pierced through a cloud and struck the tree. They stopped. The tree illuminated. It glowed like a brilliant green diamond, its soul lit from within. Up close the tree was majestic. But, it had no fiery green leaves, as it had appeared from afar. Only fiery green... apples!

They looked at each other in utter bewilderment. It exists! They thought. The Garden of Eden exists!

Thunder cracked. A lightning bolt spread through the dark sky, like spider spooling web for its prey. The lightning bolt suddenly made him remember - the old woman! He jerked around. The old woman was nowhere in sight. He swiped the water dripping from his brow and squinted. The downpour made it difficult to see far.

"Where is she?" he said. His voice drowned in the boisterous rain.

"What?" Michelle shouted.

"The old woman!" he shouted. "Where is she?"

"Don't know, don't care." Michelle shrugged. "We found what we came here to find." She pointed to the fabled tree of Eden.

He shook his head. "You don't understand, Michelle. She'll die if lightning strikes anywhere in the salt desert, like it just struck the tree."

"But we didn't die." She protested.

"There is a reason she asked us to run for the island. It's inert. It doesn't conduct electricity."

"Irrespective, I don't want you to put your life in danger for a stranger."

He paused. Gathered his wits and said, "She helped us find the way. We owe it to her."

"We don't owe her anything!" She jammed a finger in his chest, then stepped away and crossed her arms. "You are not going. And that is final."

He looked in the direction where the old woman should have been. *Where is she?* he thought. *She was just behind us. She should have been here by now.*

He couldn't see anyone. Only the desert, no longer white, but reflecting the stormy clouds. It looked like oil in a frying pan, on the cusp of reaching boiling point. And once that point was reached, he knew, everything in the pan gets fried.

Lightning flashed in the sky. That was it. The decision was made.

"Sorry. I have to do this!" He ran, even before he finished speaking.

"NO!" Michelle screamed after him, but he was already bolting across the desert, away from the security of the island.

Rain attacked him with bullets from all fronts. He kept swatting them with his hand. A few smashed his hand. Many smashed his face. It hurt, but he didn't stop. There was not much time. Or rather, he didn't know how much time he had before lightning struck and he was charred meat. The thought propelled his feet. He ran faster.

Soon enough, he found the old woman. She lay on the ground, unmoving. Shrouded in black, she was like a dead body, waiting for burial.

He dashed to her. Bent and shook her shoulder. She moaned. Not dead yet, he thought.

"Are you okay? What happened?" he asked.

"My stick…broke…fell." Fragmented words tumbled from her mouth. The splintered head of a stick was still in her right hand. The other stick lay a few feet away. He got the gist.

The sky illuminated again as lightning flashed.

"Come on. We need to go."

He helped her sit up. She raised her head and looked at him with eyes full of despair. "I can't walk without my sticks."

"Don't worry. I can help. Use me as support. Like your sticks."

She wasn't fully convinced. She nodded half-heartedly.

He wound his arm around her waist to help her get up. It suddenly made him aware of her frail, emaciated body. The overflowing black cloak had hidden her feeble body. But now, the drenched fabric stuck to her figure, revealing the skeleton living inside.

She grabbed him. Tried to pull herself up but fell.

"My feet aren't strong enough," She huffed.

"Forget it. I'll carry you."

He scooped her up. For a human being, she was weightless - exactly the word that crossed his mind as the bony figure nestled into his sinewy arms.

"Hold tight!" he announced and scurried across the White Sea.

"Why did you return?" The old woman asked as he rushed to the island.

"I couldn't just leave you here to die," he replied.

"No, you could have left me behind. Isn't it what the girl asked you to do?"

He focused on the task at hand, as he always did in such dire situations. The old woman was messing with his concentration, as was the rain that pelted him unrestrained. "Can we not talk? Let's get to the island first and talk later."

The old woman pursed her lips. But, the storm opened its mouth. And out came bolts of lightning that streaked the dark sky white, followed by booms of thunder that left his ears whizzing for many seconds.

He sped. In the distance, through the barrage of raindrops, he saw the silhouette of the island. Perched atop it was the resplendent tree. Its aura oozed with soft radiance.

Fifty yards to go, he thought.

"You came for me because you felt it your responsibility, didn't you?"

He didn't look at the old woman. He didn't answer.

She said, "You cared for a stranger."

Forty yards.

He saw Michelle. Her arms crossed, her hair in disarray. She saw him and ran toward him, leaving the safety of the inert island.

He shouted, "Stay on the island!"

Michelle disregarded what he said and ran even faster.

He huffed a sigh.

Thirty yards.

"You have a good heart young man. You pass."

He was taken aback with the mutterings of the old woman. "What do you mean I pass?" he said.

Twenty yards.

She smiled. "You may enter the Garden."

With that, the old woman gazed at the sky above and exclaimed loudly, "Sarp-Sarp-Sarp!" It was as if she were invoking heaven itself.

Ten yards.

He looked up as he ran. The entire sky was on fire, it seemed. The clouds were bursting into flames. And suddenly, the sky opened its belly and spewed a golden bolt of lightning. It was marvelous, a sight to behold. The golden bolt fell into the White Sea, creating a ripple of electric current that traveled toward them. Fast and furious.

Suddenly, the old woman slipped out of his hands. He toppled over her and fell. Quickly regaining composure, he looked back. The old woman was gone. The black cloak lay abandoned, drenched, and crumpled. There was sudden movement underneath the cloak. And rising from ashes, like a phoenix, rose the towering Gatekeeper of Eden - God Saraph!

He gasped. Saraph was the old woman! A shape-shifting, form-changing God!

"You pass the three divine tests. You are worthy. Welcome to Eden!" said God Saraph, just as a surge of electricity powered through his veins, zapping him unconscious.

Chapter 15

The Arthur Connection

"It's working. He is waking up." I hear a faraway voice. I shake my head in desperation, struggling for air. I gasp and open my mouth. Water rushes in. It's salty. It tingles my tongue and stings my throat before gushing into my lungs. The pain hits me like an anvil dropped on my chest. It's excruciating. My whole body convulses, trying to cough out salty water from the lungs. But all it creates is a gurgling sound and a tiny ripple in the belly that is swallowing me whole. Is it the belly of Saraph? Am I being swallowed alive by a snake? Like the sheep?

My eyes flutter. My mind tosses. And then a thought knocks me over. I am going to drown and die. I am going to die without knowing who I am. A spur kicks deep inside my heart and incites every cell in my body. Fight! You can't give up!

My eyes shoot open. I jump to my feet, chest heaving and nostrils flaring. Water trickles down my brow and drips from my chin. I look down. My legs are half-submerged in water. A frothy white wave rushes in and pushes at my knees. White sand shifts beneath my feet. I am on a beach. Relief pours over me. I am not going to die!

I wipe my brow with my palms and gaze at the vast ocean in front of me. It's arctic blue and glows with an irresistible radiance on a bright, sunlit day. Seagulls squawk from far away. I arch my back, breathe deeply, and let the ocean breeze caress my face. As I crane my neck, my eyes spot something huge in the ocean. I look closely. It's an abandoned ship, anchored a few hundred yards away. Old and tarnished, its rusty red hull has come off at places. A ghost-ship. No way it can ride the ocean waves again. It sits motionless. Frost colored seagulls sit atop its worn-out mast.

"Are you okay?"

I jump.

Standing a few feet away on the beach is Azura. Her feet are dug in the sand. White grains fleck her ankles and lower shin, it's as if she is wearing grainy white socks. Clinging to her thigh is Aana. Scared and stiff. She holds a tiny spear in her hand. Skinny stands guard behind them.

"Yes…what happened?" I say.

"You fainted," Azura replies.

Someone snorts at the answer. I wheel around. Standing next to me, maybe two yards away, is Mammoth, the huge guard. How did I not see him before? His smirk vanishes the moment he sees me staring at him.

An irritating drop of water trickles down my forehead to the end of my nose. Just as I rub the bead away, an enormous wave comes hovering in and shoves at my legs. I stumble and fall in the shallow water. Mammoth snorts again. The same wave had hit him. But he stood tall, like the unmoving ghost-ship stranded in the ocean.

"Don't just stand there. Pick him up." Azura's authoritative voice fills my ears as I scramble in the knee-deep water.

Mammoth grabs my shoulders and picks me up like a rag doll. He quickly releases me, as though I am plague-ridden. An untouchable.

I plant my feet firmly and plow through the beach toward Azura. Beyond Azura, the white sand disappears into the dense forest. The towering trees stand shoulder to shoulder. It seems there is no path into the deeper reaches of the island. No visibility to the deep, dark secrets within.

"You!" I point a finger at Azura. "Were you trying to drown me?"

Skinny steps forward. Trident drawn. Ready to pierce my heart if I dare touch Azura.

I lower my finger and stop a few feet away from her.

This time it's Azura who snorts. "We were trying to revive you, not drown you. We splashed some water at first, but it didn't work. So, I decided to go full throttle and let the survival instinct in your brain wake you up."

"By drowning me?"

"Yes," she says with complete confidence. "It's a proven Sentinel method."

"Proven for what? To kill someone?" I hiss.

She laughs out loud as if I cracked a joke. I stay quiet, unsure of how to respond.

"You wouldn't have died," she says, finally, in all seriousness. "Sentinels protect each other, like a family. The Sentinel code forbids us from harming another Sentinel."

"But…" My brow contorts in confusion. "…I am not a Sentinel."

Azura smiles, "Yes, you are." She comes closer and holds my shoulders. "You are one of us now. A Sentinel."

"But I passed out. I didn't finish the initiation?"

She lets go of my shoulders. "So, what? You can't keep God Saraph waiting. You finish what you start." She looks at her daughter and tousles her hair. "Even Aana slept through her initiation ceremony."

I don't know what to say. I hadn't really given much thought to the initiation. According to me, it was the only option available. The only option that kept me alive. The only option that kept me in the good graces of the Sentinels. So, I had to do it. But, now that I am a Sentinel, it feels good. Maybe, it feels good to belong. I had felt like an orphan stripped of his past. Now, at least, there is a future I can build and belong to.

Azura snaps her fingers. I look up.

"Stop daydreaming," she says.

I gaze into her sweet, beautiful face and say, "Thank you."

"For what?"

"For accepting me. For making me one of your own. You could have had me executed. I was a prisoner, after all. But, you didn't. You offered me life instead." I give a short laugh. "Guess what I am trying to say is…thanks for not chopping off my feet and leaving me on the beach to die."

Azura chuckles. She opens her mouth to speak, but Aana cuts her. "Maa! Maa!" She waves the tiny spear in her hand. "Can I go fishing now? Pleeeease!"

Azura nods. She beckons Mammoth with a wave of the hand. "Take Aana to the fishing cove. Don't let her go deep in the water and don't let her out of your sight."

"Yes, my queen." Mammoth bows.

Aana skips ahead, brandishing her tiny spear like a warning to all fish in the ocean. Mammoth grunts and trudges behind the kid, marking a line in the sand with his trident as he drags it along.

"Laziest of my guards," Azura follows the listless trident with her eyes. "…but the deadliest of them all."

She turns her gaze on me. "Sit," she says. It sounds like a command. I obey.

She sits next to me. "I don't like people towering over me while I talk. That's why I asked you to sit."

I smile. "Well, it sounded like an order. I had no option but to obey."

She grins. "I am your queen now, you know. You have no option, but to obey." Her voice is filled with childish charm.

I laugh out loud. "Oh, no! I should have thought of that before agreeing to become a Sentinel." I put on my best fake voice.

"Oh, you did! I remember someone thanking me for the 'opportunity'."

"Did I now? Sorry, I don't remember the details. You see, I was woozy from this drug called Truth Essence. Amazing stuff, by the way. You should try it sometime. I can hook you up with my dealer, the queen."

She eyes me, one eyebrow raised, head tilted sideways. Her whole face blossoms into a smile, like a newborn flower. "You are weird, in a good way," she says.

"I am not sure if that's a compliment, but I will wear it as a badge of honor from my queen." I put my hand on my heart as if taking a pledge.

She doesn't respond. Just smiles and looks away to the ocean. I follow her gaze. The frothy ocean waves sway rhythmically, landing with soft thuds on the beach. We remain quiet for a few minutes, absorbing the enormity and serenity of the ocean.

"Can I ask you a question?" I break the silence.

"That's a first," she smiles. "Since when did you ask for permission before speaking?"

It seems like a rhetorical question. Without answering, I ask, "So, who is Azura?"

She looks puzzled. "What do you mean? I am Azura, the Queen of the Sentinels."

"No, no." I shake my head. "I mean, who is 'Azura, the girl' behind 'Azura, the queen'?"

She looks away, at the ocean again. "There is no different girl behind the queen. I was born to lead my people and protect my land. And I will live and die doing it."

I nod, fully aware of the wall she'd erected to hide Azura, the girl. I decide not to press.

"So, when is your husband coming home?" I change the topic, rather abruptly.

Azura curls her lips. "Who told you?"

"Sorry, didn't mean any disrespect." I look away and scratch my head. Tiny, freshly cut hair prick the end of my fingers. I wince as my missing stump scrapes against my head. I keep forgetting and then feeling the pain. "Aana mentioned about her Paa going outside. Apparently, the same outside where I come from."

Azura shakes her head. "Talks too much. Just like her father," she mutters, more to herself than me.

She looks up. "Yes, every five years we send an emissary to the outside world. To spy, to learn, to survive. My grandmother started the tradition some fifty years ago after the Indian government sent spies under the garb of well-meaning anthropologists. Of course, at the time we didn't know who they were or who sent them. Heck, we didn't even know of India or the English language. It bothered my grandmother. Not knowing. She thought it'll lead to the end of us. Very soon. So, we decided to educate ourselves in world affairs. And here we are, talking in a language that connects us."

I nod. "What happened to the Indian spies?"

Azura shrugs her shoulders. "The same. We killed the ones who got too close to the island."

We grow quiet, both unsure where to begin again. Moments turn to minutes. Minutes to more minutes. Both lost in our worlds, looking absently at the ocean.

"See that old ship?" Azura points to the tattered ghost-ship stranded in the reef.

I nod.

"It's called *Primrose*."

I sit up, startled. I have heard that name before. Where?

Azura says, "*Primrose* landed here some twenty years after the Indian spies. Before I was born. My mother was a teenager then, a princess, while my grandmother ruled the island."

And suddenly, I remember. Primrose was the rally point. In the dream. Michelle had promised to meet me at the Primrose if we ever got separated. The Sentinels never found Michelle. Should I tell Azura? Maybe Michelle is still on the ship?

Azura continues, "My mother told me that the Sentinels marveled at the ship's enormity but dreaded the enemy within it. Outsiders. Sentinel elders were convinced it was a ploy. Outsiders lay in wait to attack and steal what we had protected for centuries. They patrolled the ship deck during the day. At night, tiny fires lit up every corner of the ship. It was as if they were celebrating, even before they had attacked. Their drunken guffaws could be heard right till the village center, sending chills of fear into the hearts of every Sentinel. Something had to be done. And fast."

Azura hesitates. "But to my mother, it was a fairy tale. Like a sea monster had emerged from the ocean and she, Lianna the princess, had to tame the monster. One night, while my grandmother, the queen, convened another meeting of the elders, my mother crept out of the hut. She thought meetings were a waste of time. You kill the enemy first and talk later about how to dispose of the dead. At least that was what she'd been taught. She took matters into her own hands. She was the princess after all, trained to become the Sentinel Queen one day."

Azura smiles to herself, looking intently at the ghost-ship.

"You have to remember that she was a teenager brimming with youthful exuberance then. And you may be able to understand how that hampered her judgment. My mother carried a tiny spear, her weapon of choice against the sea monster. She reached the beach. The night was young. The tide was high. Nothing deterred her. She was a good swimmer, even better when she was young. She holstered the spear behind her, in the vines that held the skirt at the waist. And she was off, gliding in the water, guided by the tiny fires on the ship. She swam with determination, with courage. You need courage, she told me, when you go hunting a sea monster."

Azura quietens all of a sudden. Her face contorts in pain. Pain that simmers on the surface all your life, never boiling over, never dying out.

"Halfway to the ship, her spear got caught in the reef. She pulled at it, again and again. It made matters worse. She was out of breath. She tried coming up for air, but, of course, the spear didn't budge. It never entered her stupid brain to untangle the spear from the vines or simply remove the skirt. She told me it was her favorite spear. She didn't want to lose it."

Azura sighs deeply.

"She thrashed her arms. Shouted for help. No sound came out, only more salty water gulped into her lungs. She tugged at the spear again in desperation, hoping and praying for it to come loose. It didn't."

She looks at me with shiny eyes. She felt her mother's pain. Imagining the horror of that experience brought tears to her eyes.

"Then what happened?" I ask.

"Well, I am here, so my mother didn't die, of course." Azura forces a smile. "The next thing she remembered, she was coughing out water. Her chest was on fire. She coughed and coughed. When the coughing stopped, crying started. She said she had never cried so much and so hard. It was a cry of relief, a cry of prayer to God Saraph. She was not dead."

Azura looks at the ghost-ship, her face devoid of emotion.

"A young man took her in his arms and embraced her. Water dripped from his smooth, beard-less chin. My mother panicked in the arms of a stranger. She jumped away. She looked around and, in the darkness, lit by small fires, she realized that she was on the very ship she had come to take down! Some twenty men stood in a circle around her. Like she was a monkey, and they stood watching her antics for entertainment. She was terrified. This was the enemy she had come to fight. And now, they had surrounded her. No way to escape. She was trapped."

Azura looks at me. "I think the young man realized she was afraid. He didn't come near her. Just kneeled where he stood and said, 'Don't be afraid, dear. You are safe now.' His deep baritone only terrified her more, but she was relieved she could understand his words, though the accent was odd. She cringed and wrapped her arms around her legs. He barked an order to a bald man who stood next to him. The bald man, suddenly anxious, rummaged in the pockets of his half-sleeved shirt and pants. He searched and searched, getting more nervous before he heard a crackling sound in his shirt pocket and stopped. He produced a bar that glistened gold. Even in terror, my mother said she was awestruck. The young man took the golden bar and offered it to her. She was confused. She thought he was bribing her with gold. The man seemed to understand. He held the bar between the thumb and index finger and tore through the golden wrapper. Inside was a bar as dark as mud. He removed the bar from the golden wrapper and offered it to her again."

Azura chuckles, "My mother thought it was poison. She said she had never shaken her head with such vigor."

Azura shakes her head, as one does when fondly remembering a time of pure foolishness. "The man broke a piece and ate it. He ooh-ed and aah-ed as if it was the most delicious thing he had ever eaten. My mother hesitated, but she wanted to know what was so delicious that made a grown man go crazy." Azura laughs, her eyes beam. "And that was the first and last time my mother had chocolate!"

I nod and smile along.

"My mother finished the bar like she was a poor kid who had not eaten for days. The man smiled and asked her name. He had given her a delicious bar of chocolate, so she figured the man was trustworthy. She gave him her name. 'Who are you?' she asked. The man said his name was Arthur. He was a sailor transporting chocolates. 'Why are you here?' she asked. She remembered his shoulders flagged, and he sighed deeply. He said they had hit a storm and veered too close to Sentinel Island. It was night time. They didn't see the coral reef surrounding the island. The ship rammed into the reef and got stuck. It was his fault, he said. He was the captain of the ship after all. They had tried everything for days, but the ship didn't budge. He said they were waiting for help. Another ship was coming to get them."

Azura pauses. Seagulls flock the stranded ghost-ship, squawking merrily. She peers at the birds, before resuming the story.

"'Help the needy' was a motto we are raised with. She told him that she was the princess. It was her island, her people. And her people would help the sailors. They had smiled and nodded at each other. They were relieved, I guess."

Azura pauses, gathers her thoughts. "The relief was short-lived. Suddenly, a loud, shrill horn echoed from Sentinel Island. It was deafening and tore through the stillness of the night. It was the Sentinel battle cry. My mother recognized it at once. The sailors stood transfixed, not knowing what was happening. A second horn sounded. And then a third.

"Soon, figures emerged from the forest, marching in battle formation. The Sentinel army. There was sudden chaos on the ship. The sailors scattered, like rats from a raging fire. Only Arthur, the captain, stood his ground. He barked orders to his scampering rats. 'Get the weapons. Take positions,' he shouted. A few took out knives from their pockets, others went below deck and returned with swords or pikes, and Arthur himself took out a revolver. It was the first time my mother had seen a gun. 'Don't let the bloody Sentinels on the ship,' he shouted, brandishing the tiny revolver above his head. Then his eyes lit up, as if an idea had suddenly entered his mind.

"He rushed forward and grabbed my mother, driving the pointed end of the revolver into her temple. 'Sorry, sweetheart. This is the only way we'll come out of this alive,' he yelled into her ear. She thought she'd die. She didn't know how a gun worked. She thought he would drill this new weapon into her head. She screamed. She cried. But, of course, he didn't drill the gun into her head. He picked her up with one hand and ran to the front of the ship. Suddenly, he stopped. He strained his ears as if he heard a mosquito buzzing above the hubbub on the ship. My mother stopped crying because she heard something too. It didn't sound like the buzz of one mosquito but of a hundred mosquitoes. The man swiveled on his feet, in the direction of the noise. He looked up. A hundred arrows, like dark mosquitoes, fizzed through the air, charging menacingly at the ship."

Azura chuckles, "My mother thought it was beautiful. Against the shimmering light of the full moon, the synchrony of the arrows diving toward the ship was spellbinding. She was mesmerized. And had it not been for Arthur, she would have met the arrows head-on in that trance.

"Arthur shouted to his men - 'Take cover!' He shoved my mother with immense force, and she went flying into the recess underneath the staircase that led to the top deck. He dived after her, seconds before the arrows banged into the hardwood deck, like tiny darts inflicting a hundred wounds."

Azura goes quiet. She sighs. And sighs again.

"My mother crouched in that recess. Scared. Holding onto herself for dear life." She looks at me. "Do you know what she remembered most vividly of that moment?" she asks.

I shake my head.

"The head-splitting scream of a grown man who had fallen in front of her. A crimson puddle of blood swaddled his body. He died right there. Struggling, fighting, frothing blood from the mouth like venom, before giving up on life. Sometimes, in her worst nightmares, my mother said she could hear the dying man's wails for help." Azura forces a smile. "She used to cover her ears while narrating this part of the story. I guess it didn't help."

"Then what happened?" I urge her on.

"Arthur waited. I think he was afraid of another string of arrows wheezing toward the ship. He didn't look afraid, though. He was composed, thinking of his next move. When nothing happened for a minute, he crept out of the recess. He grasped my mother's hand and pulled her out. Grabbing her by the waist, he took the staircase to the top deck. My mother looked behind her. And oh, the horrors she saw on the ship! An arrow had gone right through the eye of one sailor. He lay on the deck unmoving. Another was shrieking in pain. His foot was stuck to the ship as an arrow had pierced through his foot into the hardwood floor of the deck.

"The captain halted as they reached the top deck. My mother craned her neck and looked ahead. There were no Sentinels on the beach anymore! No army, no one! She swiveled in her position, looking in every direction. She squinted in the moonlight, trying to focus. There was no one on the beach and the ocean seemed tranquil as ever. It was queer. It was as if the Sentinels attacked once, and then, realizing it was past their bedtime, went home to sleep. Arthur heaved a sigh of relief. 'They are gone!' he shouted to the few men who remained standing. 'Help the wounded!' he cried. He looked at my mother and asked if she was hurt. She shook her head. She wasn't physically hurt. But, mentally, it was a different matter. She had never seen so much bloodshed. She had seen animal sacrifices to God Saraph, but the brutal killing of so many people was all new and gross and heart-wrenching.

"Suddenly, they heard a shrill croak, like a frog's. It came from the rear end of the ship. Then another croak from the starboard side. And another from the port side. Very soon, there was incessant croaking all around the ship. No one knew what was happening. Was the ship being attacked by an army of frogs? 'What is it?' Arthur asked his men. Sailors looked at each other, their eyes dilated, filled with fear. She saw a bead of sweat run down Arthur's neck. Fear was palpable, and it spared no one. The croaks sounded like a death knell.

"Just as suddenly as it had started, the croaking stopped. They waited. The silence was eerie. She heard a sailor's stomach growl on the deck below. They waited another minute. Nothing happened. Arthur instructed two of his men to check overboard, one on the starboard side and one on the port side. The men didn't move. Fear had frozen their spines. Arthur reprimanded them, called them cowards, and questioned their masculinity."

Azura snorts. "It's funny how men get competitive if you question their masculinity. It's like questioning their very existence. The men complied. Torn between terror in their hearts, and with a pretense of bravery across their faces, the two men crept closer to the edge. They looked for support from other sailors. None responded. With hesitant fingers, the two sailors held the edge. With measured movements, they looked over. All seemed to be happening in slow motion. The sailors stretched their necks and looked overboard, rotating their gaze from right to left.

"And slash!" Azura makes a chopping motion with her hand. "There was a sudden slashing sound. And another. The two sailors fell on the deck. Their chopped heads splashed in the water below. Their bodies writhed in shock, spluttering and spraying blood from the neck, no longer able to reach the butchered head. Within seconds, blood had pooled everywhere around their decapitated bodies. Within seconds about fifty Sentinels jumped onto the ship from all sides. Carrying spears and tridents, they howled and roared, slashed and chopped. Within a minute every sailor on the ship had been sliced to pieces. Except Arthur. He jammed the revolver to my mother's head, shouting warnings to the Sentinel warriors who had surrounded us. 'Drop your weapons or I will kill her!' he shouted in her ears. 'Drop them, drop them now!' he circled in his position and roared again and again, strangling her with his hard grip.

"The Sentinels were suddenly alarmed. They had not expected to find their princess on the ship. They dropped their spears and tridents and fell to their knees. All of them. All fifty of them kneeled. That was the moment my mother realized she had let her people down."

Azura drops her head as if haunted by the shamefulness of her mother. "Her heart ached, remembering them on their knees. Helpless, despite the means and the numbers to fight. She made them helpless. She made them weak."

Azura straightens her spine and raises her head. "Bani, the Commander of the Sentinel army stood. She kept her head bowed in deference to my mother. 'Release the princess and we will let you go!' she said to Arthur."

"Arthur shook his head vigorously. 'No!' he shouted. 'How do I know you are not lying, you filthy Indian?'"

Azura snorts. "Bani got confused when referred to as an 'Indian'. I am sure she didn't know if it was a compliment or a slur. But, 'filthy' she understood. And she went hysterical. No one on Sentinel Island dared to talk her down, except my grandmother, the queen. She reminded Arthur that they were fifty of them, and he was only one of his people left alive. Arthur reminded Bani that he just needed one shot to kill the princess. And killing the princess would be on the Bani's conscience. Bani gritted her teeth in frustration. Her opponent had the upper hand in the negotiation. All Sentinel warriors, including the commander, take the unbreakable vow to protect the queen and her kin. There was no way Bani would let my mother die. Finally, she asked Arthur, 'What do you want?'

"Arthur said, 'If there is a princess, there is a king or a queen. I will only speak with the highest authority, not you.' Bani was furious. Fumes of anger bubbled from her bald head I was told. She composed herself. She told Arthur that she would escort him to the Queen of Sentinel Island. Arthur shook his head. He demanded that the queen come aboard the ship. They debated, but of course, Bani had to relent. She called the warrior closest to her and instructed him to bring my grandmother. The warrior nodded, bowed, jumped overboard, and swam to the island.

"Bani asked my mother if she was okay. However, Arthur cut her off. 'No talking, or I'll kill the princess,' he threatened. No one spoke a word for a long time. The waves lashed against the hull of the ship. Insects buzzed and made their presence felt. My mother said she also saw a rat scamper across the deck, unnerving a few warriors who jumped in surprise. Sights and sounds one wouldn't notice above the hubbub of the battle. But there was no battle, just troops waiting, watching, and yawning.

"Soon, they saw light. Some eight to ten torches burst onto the beach. The flames burned bright and rushed back and forth, left and right. Loud, incoherent voices spoke with urgency. There was utter panic. My mother saw the silhouette of my grandmother; her tall, bulky headdress clearly visible in the gossamer gleams visible from the ship. My grandmother sat on a dinghy. Two torches accompanied her. Unseen hands pushed the dinghy into the ocean. Slowly, the boat made its way to the ship. The tension, which had subsided in the long wait, was again palpable among the Sentinel warriors. Nobody yawned. Everybody fidgeted. The stalemate was about to end. It was only a matter of time.

"My grandmother, as nimble as the rest of the warriors, climbed onto the ship. Her torch-bearing guards escorted her. All Sentinels dropped to their knees and bowed as she stepped onto the deck. She saw my mother and stopped. She adjusted her headdress and strode to where Arthur stood. Her face gave away nothing. No panic. No edginess. She proclaimed, 'Let go of my daughter, and I promise no harm will come to you. You are a free man. Take my boat and go wherever you desire.'

"Arthur laughed. 'A boat? A boat in exchange for your daughter? Is that how much you value your daughter, queen?' he said.

"My grandmother told him to take whatever he wanted - silver, gold, platinum - whatever precious metal he desired. The Sentinels had plenty. Arthur's eyes glistened with greed. He nodded and said he wanted the queen's boat loaded with all those metals. And food, he wanted food for the voyage. He said he would exchange my mother, the princess, for the bounty. Within an hour, his boat was ready, filled with precious metals and fruits and nuts.

"The exchange happened on the boat. Arthur boarded with my mother and only allowed one other person aboard. Bani volunteered. Arthur said he would let my mother and Bani jump off the boat and swim to safety once he had a head-start of five hundred meters. He needed the head-start as he didn't want Sentinel guards swimming after the heavy-laden boat and catch him. He kept his promise. He let my mother and Bani go.

"But my grandmother didn't keep her promise. You see, she had gotten the fruit and nuts adulterated with Sentinel's special blend of the sleep serum. She sent swimmers who found Arthur fast sleep on the boat not even a mile from the island. He was captured and incarcerated. There was no trial. He was to be roasted over the fire, like an animal. 'Death by Roast' it was called. A common form of execution for unpardonable crimes."

"He was executed?" I ask.

"No, he wasn't. My mother saved him. She told my grandmother how Arthur had saved her from drowning, and he had held her at ransom because he saw no other way to save himself. He was a good man, a kind man. My grandmother didn't relent. My mother pleaded. She had seen too many deaths on the ship to let another human being die. Finally, my grandmother relented, but on one condition: that Arthur became one of us, one of the Sentinels. Arthur was only too happy to agree. Anything was better than a roast, he reasoned.

"He was initiated into the tribe in front of God Saraph. He learned our ways, our culture, our language. And soon, he became one of us."

"Happy ending, I guess?" I say.

"Not really. There is more."

Azura takes a deep breath.

"Arthur learned that deep inside Sentinel Island existed the Garden that bears the fruit of immortality. He was immediately besotted with the notion of immortality. He learned the key to the door was the dagger of God Saraph. But the path to the Garden was ridden with old spells and sorcery. Old Sentinels had ensured that only the worthy found the treasure of immortality. The issue was: as a Sentinel he was forbidden to eat the fruit of immortality. Plus, getting past God Saraph was no easy task. So, he played the long game."

"The long game?" I ask.

"One night, while my grandmother slept, he crept into her hut. He tried to steal the dagger of God Saraph. Unfortunately for him, my grandmother was a light sleeper. She woke up and caught him red-handed. His hand was still inside her skirt, clutching the dagger strapped to her thigh. Fortunately for him, she neither raised the alarm nor killed him. She made a deal with him, only God knows why. She wanted him gone from the island, never to return. Ever. In exchange, seeing his black, greedy heart, she gave him a boat and sack full of diamonds. Arthur was gone by the next morning. No one heard from him again. Till-"

Azura fidgets in her position and removes not one, but two snake-head daggers strapped to her thigh. She tosses and catches the daggers, one in each hand, like playing a game of catch. "Till you found your way to Sentinel Island."

She plays with the daggers, slashing the innocent air in front of her.

Azura forces a smile. "Do you know these daggers are two of a kind? Both were forged the same day, with the same hands. God Saraph's hands. Both daggers are identical, down to the last serration on the blades. Two keys to unlock the Garden. One for the queen, one for the king. One for me, one for my husband."

She looks me straight in the eyes, her forced smile gone. "My husband is an honorable man. A true Sentinel, sworn to protect what is forbidden. He went into your world seeking knowledge. I don't know how Arthur found him, but he did. This dagger is proof that he was forcibly apprehended, and maybe…" She bites her lower lip and sighs. "…and maybe killed for the dagger!"

Azura shudders. Grabs the coin-like silver locket around her neck, rubs it, massages it, as if comforting her thumping heart. She wobbles her head, like shaking away any thoughts of her husband's possible death.

She looks at me, calm and composed again. "Which brings me back to you. You are somehow related to Arthur. This dagger is proof of that relationship. You could be his son, his nephew, or simply hired help."

Her gaze accuses me of crimes I cannot fathom. "That day, years ago, Arthur saved my mother from drowning. We owed him. That is why I saved you. A favor for a favor. And then, Arthur had held her at ransom. One could say I am returning the favor … by holding you for ransom in exchange for my husband."

Chapter 16

Did I Tell You about My Dreams?

I stare at Azura. "So, I am a prisoner held for ransom? Then what was all that initiation charade? The opening ceremony with God Saraph. This access to 'Queen' Azura. Why not just keep me in a cell and let me rot in there, till Arthur, my supposed uncle, comes and exchanges me for your husband?"

Azura smiles. "Like I was saying, one *could* say you are being held at ransom. But you are not. You are one of us now. A Sentinel. I told you my story because I want you to understand the past. Because some day in the future, you may regain your memory. That day you will question your identity and choose - the Sentinels or Arthur."

Azura leans forward and touches my hand as if offering a truce. "I want you to choose us. This is your future. This is where you belong. Memory or not, I don't want you to forget who you are NOW."

I am stumped. "Oh…" I barely manage to utter a word.

We both sit in silence for a while, absorbed in our thoughts.

I ask, "At the waterfall, before the initiation, you had said I came here and stole something precious. You hadn't mentioned what. Did I steal the fruit of immortality from the Garden of Eden?"

Azura looks at me, her face expressionless. With a slow, forced movement, she nods.

"Is that why I survived the gunshot? Because I am immortal?"

Azura's face explodes into laughter. I look around embarrassingly, waiting for her to stop.

The Apple

"I am just checking." I try to explain myself.

"I am sorry to have to break it to you, but you are not immortal." She manages to say. "You really should thank Ayurvaid Yoni for her gift of medicine, not the fruit of immortality that you stole."

I sheepishly rub my head. "Clear. Not immortal."

Azura regains her composure. "If you must know, you stole an apple from the Garden of Eden. I want you to tell me where you hid the apple, when you remember."

"A real apple?" I ask.

"Yes."

"How does it matter then? It was plucked from the tree. It would have gone bad by now anyway."

Azura's eyes light up. "No, it will not go bad even if plucked from the tree. It is enchanted. Like the gift of immortality that the apple contains, the fire of life keeps burning in it. It dies and rots after it transfers immortal life to whomsoever, man or animal, eats the fruit."

"Are you immortal, Azura?"

She grins. "No. The Sentinels are the protectors. We are forbidden to even touch the fruit. You don't devour what you protect."

"You are telling me no one in your history was ever seduced by the power of the fruit. No one has slipped up, ever?"

"Only once. Millennia ago. The tale of that treachery haunts every Sentinel even today. Our kids grow up listening to that story, keeping the fear alive and palpable in our community."

"What happened?"

"Six thousand years ago, the *first* Commander of the Sentinel army was enamored with the apple. Deep in her heart, she was convinced that she was worthy to enter the Garden of Eden. The issue was not a question of being worthy for the Sentinels. Unlike you, she did not have to pass any tests. As guardians, we cannot proclaim what we protect. Period."

Azura leans back, crosses her arms, and breathes deeply. "One night, the commander stole the dagger of God Saraph while the queen was sleeping. She entered the Garden, unnoticed by the guards. God Saraph woke up the moment she gained entry. You see, no one can go in and out of the Garden without God Saraph knowing, as he is bound to the Garden. But the commander was quick. She got to the apple tree before God Saraph caught her. She plucked the apple. And took a bite."

"Oh! Wow! She became immortal. Where is she now?" I ask.

"Dead."

"What? How can she be dead? She became immortal, no?"

"Yes, the commander ate the apple. And then God Saraph ate her."

My mouth drops.

Azura explains, "The apple keeps you forever young. You cannot die of natural causes. Doesn't mean you cannot die."

I nod, my mouth still open in surprise.

"That is exactly the reason why we tell our young ones this story in the same breath as we tell them the existence of the Garden. Knowing you will be eaten alive keeps the greed at bay in Sentinel hearts. And we haven't had a breach since that incident."

"No breach, till we came along," I mutter.

"What?" Azura looks startled.

"I said there was no breach for so many years till we came along."

Azura narrows her eyes. "What do you mean 'we'? I thought you came to Sentinel Island alone?"

I bite my tongue, suddenly realizing I never told Azura about my dreams or Michelle.

I sigh. "Okay, don't freak out. I am not sure, but I think there was another person who came with me. A girl."

"Oh, God. This is bad." Azura abruptly stands, her mind doing cartwheels in all directions. She looks at me squarely. "What do you mean you are not sure? You remember or not?"

I stand up too. "The thing is, I don't remember. But I have been having dreams which seem to be so real. I dreamed of

The Apple

the dagger of God Saraph before I saw it for real. I dreamed of my thumb getting snipped off…" I raise my hand as proof, a stump jutting out where the thumb had once been. "…before I realized my thumb had been mutilated. The dreams feel so real, almost like memories showing up in a dream instead of reality."

"Since when have you been having these dreams?"

"Since the first time I woke up after you found me. Remember I had fallen from the bed when you first came and visited me in the hut? That was a dream too. A nightmare. But I didn't know at the time if it was real. It was just a dream, after all."

"It clearly wasn't a dream." Azura becomes more agitated, her tone accusatory. "There is more to these dreams than figments of your imagination." She steps closer, chest out, hands on her waist. The wind rustling her hair makes her look more menacing.

"What else did you dream?"

I pause, my eyes darting up and down, trying to jumpstart my brain.

"Don't think! Just tell me!"

"Okay, okay." I raise my hands in defense. "In all the dreams I was with a girl. Michelle. We came here with the single purpose of finding the Garden. God Saraph put us on the path to the Garden. It was clearly a test to prove ourselves worthy. We journeyed across the Sentinel Island, fighting monstrous animals, solving riddles, trying to stay alive while we uncovered the fabled Garden of Eden. And we finally did."

"Then what happened?"

"I don't know. Last thing I remember, God Saraph welcomed me to the Garden, just before I got electrocuted."

Azura nods, as if she knew one had to get electrocuted to enter the Garden. "God Saraph welcomed you only? What about the girl?"

"I don't know. She was there. I left her by the apple tree, while I went to bring this old woman to safety. I fought the torrential rain, got to the old woman, picked her up, and was running to the tree. A few yards from the tree, the old woman turned into God Saraph…I think it was some kind of test and I passed. But then I got electrocuted. I thought I was going to die. Nobody shot me in the head though. Makes me think it wasn't the end of it. There is more to remember."

"Of course, there is more. You took an apple from the tree. Do you remember it?"

"No. I don't."

"Did you see the girl pluck an apple."

"No, I don't think so."

"Are you sure?"

"Of course not. It was a blur. Everything happened so fast. But no, I don't remember the girl plucking an apple."

Azura takes a deep breath, as if relieved. She clasps her hands behind her and paces. Measured, mindless steps while her mind raced to find answers.

She stops, looks at me. "You clearly passed the three divine tests of the body, mind, and soul, and proved yourself worthy of the Garden. That is the only reason God Saraph welcomed you. Else he would have eaten you alive. But we never found this girl you speak of…Michelle…on the island. Makes me think that maybe she didn't pass the test and died. Or maybe she did, stole the apple, and found her way out before we even realized she was here with you. The question remains: who took the apple? If you did, then it is on the island. If she did and escaped, then we are in trouble. Big trouble."

"It is one apple only. How much trouble can it be?"

"You underestimate the greed a single apple can inspire in people. One bite is all it takes. We have protected its existence for millennia. There was a time mankind knew about it, fought over it, and died over it. That's how the Sentinels were born. To protect it. And the best way to protect it was to hide it. It took years, centuries, and then, no one remembered it anymore. The balance of life and death was restored as God intended it."

"It may sound counter-intuitive, but isn't the best way to protect the Garden to destroy it?"

Azura shakes her head. "Why would you destroy a gift of God? A gift out of which human life was born. A gift for the worthy, to pass on the goodness to generations to come."

She inhales deeply. "History does not matter anymore. Tell me more about this girl, and where can we find her, dead or alive?"

"Like I said, I last saw her on the island."

"There was no one else apart from you on the island. Maybe Michelle escaped from the tree. But she couldn't have left the island. The Sentinel guards would have found her. I think she is still on the island. But where?"

Azura turns toward the ocean, gazing blankly at the horizon. "Where are you hiding, Michelle?" Azura whispers to herself.

I turn toward the ocean as well, matching shoulders with the Sentinel Queen, gazing directly at the *Primrose*.

"I think I know where you might find Michelle."

Chapter 17

The Primrose Search

There was complete mayhem on the beach. Azura barks orders to Skinny the guard, the moment I tell her about the possibility of finding Michelle on the *Primrose*. Skinny takes out a big shell, a war horn, and blows long and hard into it. A battle cry, deep and shrill, shrouds the entire island.

Mammoth, who was watching over Aana while she fished, picks up the little girl and runs toward us, as if running away from a tiger that was chasing him. It is almost a funny sight as his mushy belly fat wobbles this way and that while he runs with the little girl stowed like a small treasure chest in his armpit. His puffy legs, like that of a baby elephant, strain every invisible vein to reach safety fast.

Another war horn blows from somewhere deep within the island. A response to Skinny.

"Commander Bani is on her way, my queen," says Skinny.

"I heard it!" Azura brushes aside Skinny's remark. "You go get the boat. Now. Be quick," Azura says, her eyes fixed on the ghost-ship, *Primrose*.

Skinny scampers away.

Azura clenches and opens her fists. She fidgets, preparing for action like a boxer before a fight.

"She better be on that ship." Azura proclaims. "Otherwise we have a bigger battle coming our way."

"My…my…queen." Mammoth halts before Azura, completely out of breath, completely confused about the chaos that has unfolded in the past few minutes. "Wha… what are my orders?"

The Apple

"Take Aana to the village. Go now."

Mammoth nods. Aana cries. "But I want to fish, Maa."

"Stop behaving like a child, Aana. You are a big girl now. If I say you go, you go."

Aana pouts, tears waiting to burst through the gates.

Azura sighs. "I will let you fish tomorrow, okay? For now, you have to go home." She looks at Mammoth. Raises her hand, points in the direction of the village, and says, "Go!"

Mammoth doesn't waste a moment. He darts into the forest, stamping and stomping through the shrubbery. I think I hear Aana sob softly just before they disappear.

"Were you on *Primrose* anytime during your dreams?" Azura asks me.

"No."

"I hate that ship. It brought the enemy upon us all those years ago. And now it's harboring the enemy again."

I try to protest. "Michelle is not the enemy. I am sure she will give you the apple if she has it. Let me do the talking, okay? She will listen to me."

"And why would she listen to you?"

"Because I think she loves me. And I think I loved her."

"Is that why she left you to die when you were shot in the head? Or worse, did she shoot you?"

I am aghast. Completely blank.

Azura notices my quandary. "Did you ever wonder who shot you in the Garden? Let me lay it out for you. There are only three possibilities. First, my guards shot you with your own gun, which they didn't. They found you left for dead. So, we can rule it out. Second, Michelle tried to kill you, shooting you in the head. Or third, you shot yourself. Maybe it was an accident or maybe suicide or maybe you were stupid enough to test if you were truly immortal."

I had not thought about it. It was all logical, all in front of me in white and black. There were only three possibilities. Only three outcomes. Unless I am missing something? But the real question is, whom should I trust - Azura or Michelle? Azura is only concerned about the long-kept Sentinel secret.

Is she playing games with me, not telling me honestly what happened to suit her needs? Or Michelle. She was, or is, my lover. It was so clear in the dreams. Why would she try to kill me? But truth be told, the third possibility scares me most - did I try to kill myself? But why?

As if reading my mind, Azura says, "So there you have it. We cannot trust Michelle. You cannot trust Michelle. We are Sentinels. We can only trust each other."

I nod, controlling every muscle on my face to not show the predicament I am wrestling with. Truth be told, I don't trust anyone at this point. Not even myself.

"Let's get on the *Primrose* first and see if Michelle is even there," I say without emotion.

A sudden rustle in the bushes behind us grabs our attention. It grows louder and louder, like a juggernaut making its way through the jungle by trampling everything in its path. We turn around together.

An army of twenty-odd Sentinel guards rushes onto the beach. They file into a military-style formation, standing at attention together with their spears. Bani, the commander of the army, bolts out from behind once her warriors are in formation. Following Bani is Skinny and another guard, the two of them carrying a dinghy on their heads. It looks like a toy boat as they set it against the backdrop of the mighty *Primrose*.

Bani rushes toward us.

"My queen." She bows and pays her respects.

"I believe we have an intruder on the *Primrose*, commander. A girl. The accomplice of our friend here."

Bani looks at me for a moment and shakes her head, her eyes oozing a mix of surprise and hatred.

"I want Sentinel warriors on that ship now. And I want that girl captured if she is alive."

"As you wish, my queen."

"One last thing, commander. I have reason to believe that the girl has the stolen apple. Secure it."

Bani affirms her orders with a nod. She turns to her warriors and barks quick orders. All twenty warriors shout in unison, a battle cry I presume. They bolt toward the ocean without breaking formation. They dive into the water and a wave of twenty warriors swim hurriedly toward the *Primrose*.

Bani shouts to Skinny, "Get the boat in the water."

Skinny and the other guard struggle with the dinghy and set it at the edge of the ocean. The boat is thin and long with wooden demarcations that separate the seats into four quadrants, a two-by-two matrix.

"I want to go with them," I say to Azura.

Azura eyes me. "No, you will slow my warriors."

"Only I have seen Michelle. I can identify her if she is there."

"You can identify her for me when Bani drags her here."

"Look, we don't need a fight or a struggle. I can convince her to come with us peacefully."

Azura twirls her tongue around the lips, mulling over my words.

"Okay. Go."

I am caught by surprise. Didn't expect her to agree.

"Bani!" she calls out. "Take him with you. He says he can convince the girl to come with you in peace."

The commander grimaces as if someone lashed at her face and left a scar. But she knows better than to protest the queen's orders. She simply bows. No word is spoken.

I walk to the boat. I flash a friendly smile to Bani, trying to break the thick, cold ice between us. She looks away and gets on the boat. I follow and sit next to her. Her body stiffens as I sit.

"Go!" she orders.

Skinny and the other guard push the boat from behind, struggling initially at the edge of the beach before the boat floats on its own in few feet of water. Both guards jump into the boat and sit on the two vacant seats opposite Bani and me. They pick up small oars latched underneath their seats and start rowing.

"Fast!" Bani bellows.

They row faster.

"I am a Sentinel now, like you," I say to Bani. "You can trust me."

She looks away to the *Primrose*. "Doesn't mean I need to like you."

The boat moves into the coral reef surrounding the island. Beautiful and colorful; ominous and full of traps. The two guards maneuver the boat with skill, knowing the areas to avoid lest the boat gets trapped in the reef.

Bani looks at me. "You see this coral reef?"

I nod.

"More than anything, this coral reef has protected North Sentinel Island from invasions for centuries. The British, the Spanish, the French… they all tried to conquer our island once they mastered the craft of ship-building. But their big ships could never breach the deadly reef that encircles the entire island. They tried many times. The ships rammed into the reef and sank. Then they tried sending small boats to the shore." She chuckles. "Men in small boats were like target practice for our archers. In the end, they gave up. I guess they found bigger, more bountiful islands nearby. We were forgotten."

I don't know what to say. Not sure why she is giving me a history lesson.

"You see, I would rather trust this reef that has proven itself than an outsider who is no different than the British or the Spanish or the French." She glares at me. Doesn't blink. "You are an outsider with no pedigree, no honor, no valor. And that is why I can't trust you."

I suck in my lips, not knowing how to respond. Azura thought me a Sentinel, but Bani wasn't convinced.

"How do you know about the British or the French?" I mumble, abruptly switching gears.

"We are isolated, not uneducated," Bani retorts angrily.

A hush falls on the boat. The two guards keep their eyes ahead, unbothered by the tension that now fills the void in the conversation.

Bani sighs. "Maybe Queen Azura already told you? Every five years, we send an emissary to the outside world to learn and stay abreast with the affairs of other civilizations. I was a Sentinel emissary. From knowing nothing, I learned five of your languages in five years. Studied world history in Britain and political science in USSR. Meditated with Buddhist monks in Tibet and Hindu priests in India. It was new, it was exciting. In fact-" She puffs her chest. "I was the *first* Sentinel emissary."

I raise my eyes, surprised at how old she must be, but doesn't look her age.

"What?" And you survived?" I ask.

"Ha! How else am I here? But I'd also be surprised if I were you. How did I survive a perilous world with more pathogens than are found on North Sentinel Island? A cold should have killed me! Or measles. Or chicken-pox. My body didn't have the immunity to fight against any of these common ailments of your world. But I did. I survived."

"Did you…" I hesitate, unsure if I should ask. "Did you eat the Apple of Immortality?"

She is taken aback. "It is forbidden!"

And that is the end of the conversation. We ride in silence, the only noise coming from the repetitive splash of wooden oars cutting through water and the deep grunts of the two guards.

Bani inhales deeply and sighs, as if letting go of the affront I caused by questioning her integrity about eating the apple.

"Ayurvaid Yoni foresaw it. Somehow she knew about the onslaught of bacteria and viruses that cripples your world. My travel sack had more medications than food. I was the first one to step outside the island. Didn't know what to expect. I over-prepared."

I nod. Mull over what she has told me. "Help me understand. You have been sending out emissaries for years now. And yet, I don't see signs for progress on the island. Why?"

"What do you mean?"

"I mean, and don't take it the wrong way, the Sentinels are still stuck in a hunter-gatherer age. You have seen the infrastructure, the amenities, and the possibilities in the outside world. And yet, I don't see any signs of it on the island."

She smiles. I realize it's the first time I have seen her smile.

"And that is how you define progress? By how tall the buildings are?"

I shrug my shoulders. "Yeah, maybe."

"You may have been initiated into the Sentinel tribe, but you still have a lot to learn about us. We are proud of our culture, our traditions, our way of life. What we seek is the progress of the mind, not the progress of the material world as you define it."

Bani looks to the *Primrose*. We are almost there. Within minutes we reach the hull of the abandoned ghost-ship. The guards stop the boat next to rectangular metal bars that double as a makeshift ladder. Up close the ship looks even more ghastly, like a monster turned to stone years ago, waiting to pounce the moment the spell of aging lifts away.

Skinny puts his oar in its place and drops an anchor in the water. For extra measure, he picks up the rope fastened at the end of the boat and ties the other end around the first bar of the makeshift ladder. Once the boat is secured, he climbs up the ladder, like a monkey bouncing from one step to the next. Within ten seconds, he is on the deck of the ship. He looks overboard, gestures us to follow suit.

"You go first." Bani says to me. "If you fall, there better be someone here to save your butt."

I nod, ignoring the patronizing comment.

I gingerly put my foot on the first step of the ladder and move to the second step. It is flimsy and rusted. I realize why Skinny spent so little time putting pressure on the protruding metal bars - you never knew when one would give way.

I climb a step and then another. The step beneath my foot creaks and bends a little. I stop.

"Can you hurry?" says Bani.

"I am trying," I respond.

I push down on the step to climb and the step bends completely. I pull up with my hands just in time. I stop to breathe, adrenaline building in my veins.

"Hurry, we don't have all day!" Bani orders, her tone agitated. The friendliness I felt before is gone.

I become infuriated. "Can you shut up for one second? I am trying to concentrate."

I think Bani has had enough of me. With one yank she pulls me into the water. The sudden fall takes me by surprise. Water gushes into my mouth and nose. All four of my limbs dance out of tune, scrambling for air. A heavy hand grabs me by the hair and, suddenly, I can breathe again. The hand pulls me up into the boat. It's Bani.

"Listen, you scum!" She shouts in my ear. "You may be a Sentinel. But you are an ill-mannered animal. You need to learn to respect. Next time I hear you disrespect me, I will kill you with my bare hands."

I cough the water out. And I keep coughing. It leaves me breathless.

Bani turns to the guard. "Let's go. I don't have time to wait for him."

Even before I recover, Bani and the guard climb to the top of the ship.

I am livid. At Bani, yes, but mostly at myself. I brush away water from my brow and stand up. I get back on the ladder. I turn anger into determination. Slowly, I move up. Three minutes in and halfway through, I stop to catch my breath. I look down and immediately tense. I hold the bar tighter. I close my eyes, gather strength, and move up again. Another four minutes and I reach the deck of the ship. I climb over the railing and squat, hands on my knees, trying to catch my breath.

I look up. There is commotion on the ship. The Sentinel guards run helter-skelter searching every nook and cranny. Like ants running amok in a fire, going everywhere and yet nowhere. I walk across the top deck. There are faint, almost faded patches of dried blood, blood spilled all those years ago when the Sentinels stormed the ship and killed off the entire crew, except Arthur. The wooden boards of the floor have given away at most places, leaving behind large gaping holes. I can see guards searching beneath the deck through the holes. Some holes run across decks such that the inside of the hull can be seen from the top deck. I watch my step and take the stairs to the deck below.

I hear Bani's voice before I spot her. "Look who is here," she proclaims to the guards within earshot. "It only took you ten minutes. Record time, I must say."

"If you must know it took me no more than seven minutes."

She guffaws. "And that is much better than ten minutes?"

She dismisses me with a wave of the hand and returns to ordering her men around.

"Don't take it personally."

I turn around in the direction of the voice. It's Skinny.

"Has she always been like this?" I ask Skinny.

"Always." He smiles and returns to searching the many drawers and cupboards in what used to be the living quarters of the ship.

I smile, touched by Skinny's gesture. He didn't have to say anything. But he did, making me feel part of the team. Once again, I realize how good it feels to belong.

"Found it! Found it!"

There is a sudden uproar from the corner room. All guards in the vicinity rush the room. I follow.

I am immediately stung by the pungent smell of dried feces. It's a bedroom, the largest on the deck, but smells like an unclean toilet. There is a small cot in a corner with a mattress shredded to the core, its coiled springs clearly visible. A dressing table sits next to the cot with a tiny, smudged mirror on top. The lone accessory surviving the test of time. Dilapidated cupboards with broken doorframes cover one wall of the room. Right opposite the cot is a tiny room, its door rusted and long gone. I move closer and realize it's the source of the smell, the toilet. I gag, move back a few paces. I realize it's the only room with an attached toilet. Must have been the captain's quarter.

Bani charges into the room and immediately pinches her nose shut. She looks inside the toilet. "Someone has been here

The Apple

recently," she says. She looks at me. "It had not been used for years, until now."

Bani turns to her guards. "What did you find?"

A guard steps forward and points inside the cupboard. There are all sorts of leftovers in one corner of the top shelf - shiny brown wrappers that once held cookies or biscuits, empty mini-cups of food, soiled plastic spoons and red tubes that have been fully squeezed of the food concentrate it once contained. The stark contrast of the shiny wrappers and cups against the dusty, aged room is proof that someone inhabited it recently.

Bani inspects the leftovers. She picks up an empty cup and smells it. She recoils at the smell.

"What garbage do you foreigners eat!" she says without looking at me.

She examines a wrapper next. And then a spoon. Like a dog sniffing through the trash.

"All recent, no more than few days old," she says with the seriousness of a detective.

I stifle a giggle. The sight was proof enough. She didn't need to snuffle to make the deduction. But then, as the leader of her army, she has a reputation to maintain and a face to save.

She turns to the guard who had made the discovery. "Collect it all. The queen would want to see proof."

The guard bows and gets to work.

She says to the other guards, "Search every crevice of the ship. The girl might still be here, hiding. I want her found."

The guards scatter away like rats.

Bani turns to me next. "I am convinced that the girl was here, though she is not here now. But I know the queen. She always wants to be hundred percent sure. She may say a stranded fisherman took refuge in this ship before help came and rescued him. It's probable, yes. But is it true? I don't think so." She takes a step closer. "I want you to search this room. Find me something, anything that is a hundred percent proof. You have five minutes, and then we leave."

Even before I nod or say anything, she storms out. I am left alone with the guard busy collecting leftovers from the cupboard in a jute sack.

I decide to start with the worst location - the toilet. I squeeze into the dark recess. It's a toilet with a hole in the floor to collect the excrement. There is nothing of interest except the dried feces. I am about to walk out when I notice a tiny, white paper roll on the inside corner, barely visible in the scant light forcing itself into the recess. I can't hold my breath any longer. I quickly grab the paper roll and rush out. The guard looks at me as I dash out of the toilet and take deep gulps of air. I toss the paper roll to him.

"An addition for your sack."

He turns the roll in his hand, inspecting every inch of it.

"What does it do?" he asks.

I point to my butt. "You wipe it after you are done."

He looks confused. "But…there is a leaf for that. Why not use it?"

I snort. "You guys have a leaf for everything, don't you?"

I leave him wondering and go to the bed next. I look inside every spring of the mattress. Nothing. I bend and look underneath the bed. Nothing.

I check out the cupboard next. The guard has cleaned out the leftovers. Nothing else is there. I find it surprising.

"Where are the rest of the items?" I ask the guard.

"What do you mean?"

"The queen told me that there were many foreigners on the ship when it first landed and got stranded here. The crew of the ship was taken by surprise at night and killed. There must be belongings left behind by the crew, even if old and dusty."

The guard looks at me as if I am stupid and can't figure it out. "We took everything, of course. We wiped the place clean after we won."

I want to tell him that they only won if we count the number of kills. But they lost the secret that they had sworn to protect. To me, they lost everything. I hold my mouth shut and move to the dressing table.

The Apple

I pick up the smudged mirror and wipe away the grime with my hand. The mirror reflects the faint image of a gaunt man with cropped hair and deep dark circles underneath the eyes.

"Charming," I say to my haggard, disheveled self.

I put the mirror on the top of the dresser and open its two drawers. They are empty.

I sigh. "There is nothing else in the room. Let's go." I say to the guard.

He nods and walks out of the room, holding the jute sack. I follow.

I am about to step out when I notice an oddity. I stop.

Light reflects off the wall opposite the mirror on the dresser. The reflection is circular, the size of a walnut. It wasn't there before, until I cleaned the mirror.

What is the mirror reflecting? Itself or another reflecting surface?

I go to the mirror and move it to identify the path of light. The light reflection on the wall doesn't move in tandem with the mirror. The source is not the mirror itself. It's something else.

I follow the reflection to the source and find something stuck in one of the mattress springs. I had missed it earlier. I squeeze my fingers inside the spring and take out the object.

It's a pink digital watch. Elsa, the Snow Queen from the movie *Frozen*, winks and shows me the time. There is now no doubt that Michelle was here.

Chapter 18

Dream, Dream, Dream

I clutch the pink watch and walk out of the room. A part of me is excited to hold and touch something that belonged to Michelle. It's the part that misses Michelle from the dreams. There is no denying it - we were in love. And for that reason, I am thrilled that she escaped unharmed from Sentinel Island. The question is - where did she go? Maybe to get help to rescue me?

"What did you find?" Bani is waiting for me on the deck.

I handover the watch. "It belongs to Michelle."

Bani studies the watch closely. "What is it?" she asks.

"It's a watch. It tells time. Doesn't matter. What matters is that Michelle was here. Thankfully alive. Did you find her on the ship?"

She pouches the watch and shakes her head. "This is bad news. The queen will not be happy."

She turns to Skinny. "We are done here. Tell the warriors to head home."

Skinny nods once. He squeezes his lips and whistles, a shrill cry like the buzz of a cricket. All warriors stop what they are doing and, within minutes, jump overboard. There are loud splashes of water all around the ship. And soon, the army is swimming to the island.

I follow Bani to the ladder. She descends first with a guard, leaving me with Skinny. I go next. It takes me five minutes to reach the boat. Surprisingly, Bani makes no fuss, no sarcastic remarks. She sits quietly, studying the watch in her hand. I realize that she is in no hurry to deliver bad news to the queen.

The Apple

The guards take us to the beach. Azura is waiting, her hands crossed, prowling in anticipation. The army of guards, dripping wet from the swim, stands to attention.

Azura strides over. "Did you find her?" she fires at Bani.

She bows. "No, my queen."

Azura inhales loudly, trying to calm herself.

"But, we found this."

Bani hands over the flashy pink watch to Azura. She points to me. "He says it belonged to the girl."

Azura immediately looks at me. "How do you know?"

"I saw it in the dream. She was wearing it when we arrived on the island."

Azura closes her eyes, controlling the fire building inside. Her body stiffens, her hands clench into fists.

"She escaped. The girl escaped," Azura says in a deep, guttural voice.

She starts prowling the beach again, her mind at work. After a minute, she stops. She looks at her army chief.

"War is coming, Bani. We need to prepare. You have one day. Take your women and men, and do what is necessary. If there is an invasion, I want us ready to fight at a minute's notice."

Bani stands to attention. "We will be ready, my queen."

She bows and walks away. There is newfound excitement in her stride, the queen's instructions giving her purpose.

Azura turns to me next. "And I have work for you. I need to know if the girl entered the Garden with you or not? Did she take the apple or not?"

"I have already told you what I know, Azura."

"I know. But I need more information. And I need it urgently."

"Well, sorry, but I don't remember. And I am not sure what can be done to recover my memories."

"I am not talking about your memories. I am talking about your dreams. And for that, there is a solution."

"What?"

"Come with me."

Azura strides off toward the forest. I follow. Like the rest of the island, the forest is replete with tall, bushy trees and thick undergrowth. The trees are crammed together, forming a giant canopy, leaving virtually no room for daylight to invade. I blink as my eyes adjust from complete daylight on the beach to sheer darkness of the jungle. Azura moves quickly through the undergrowth, knowing her way through what can only be described as nature's chaos. I keep up.

Soon, she finds the beaten path that takes us to the Sentinel settlement. There is mayhem in the settlement. I see Bani standing in the square. Trident-carrying guards run from hut to hut, calling out residents to gather in the square. The residents trickle out of their homes and move with urgency. It's like someone pushed the emergency button. Come to think of it, that's exactly what Azura did by giving Bani one day to prepare for a war she foresees.

Azura disregards greetings and respectful bows from Sentinels we bump into. She moves with purpose, her mind focused. She stops in front of a hut.

"Dai Ma!" Azura calls out. "Dai Ma, you there?"

"Come in, come in." The hoarse voice of Yoni invites us to enter.

I follow Azura into the hut. Yoni is sitting on the floor, twisting and beating a concoction of herbs in a stone grinder. She tries to rise.

"Keep sitting, Dai Ma." Azura sits next to Yoni. "There is an emergency."

Yoni studies Azura. "How can I help, my child?"

"I need the sleep serum. Now." Azura looks at me. "We need to put him to sleep."

Chapter 19
The Garden Of Eden

He had been electrocuted. Tremors ran through his body. He twitched and convulsed uncontrollably, his body contorting with each tremor and relaxing as it passed through. Before long, the tremors subsided. He lay there. Still. Silent.

He opened his eyes, only to be blinded by sun rays streaming through cotton-like clouds. His eyes flickered, adjusting to the brightness. It was a gorgeous day, a warm day.

His mind took him two weeks back. After nonstop preparation for three months, he and Michelle yearned for a timeout to relax their minds and bodies before the mission. They had trekked to the Valley of Flowers, a UNESCO World Heritage Site nestled at the cusp of the Great Himalayan and Zanskar range in India. An endless meadow of lush green flora, swathes of alpine flowers, and weather that was the right degree of perfect, the Valley of Flowers was how he had always pictured paradise. Not Lauterbrunnen in Switzerland, not Milford Sound in New Zealand, not Isle of Skye in Scotland; the Valley of Flowers, for him, was paradise on Earth. Period.

He thought of the endless walks he had taken hand-in-hand with Michelle, cocooned in the sweet and enchanting fragrance of fresh grass, daffodils, alpine asters, and rock jasmines. They had spent hours reclined on cushy rolling hills, talking, thinking, and napping. They had vowed to settle for good in the Valley of Flowers after the mission. The apple of Eden held no charm for him. It was only a job. He smiled, picturing himself as a farmer rearing his cattle on the Himalayan slopes.

He stopped his racing mind. Why am I thinking about the Valley of Flowers?

And suddenly, he realized that he was enveloped in the sweet aroma of flowers. He breathed in. The fragrance kindled the loving memory. He chuckled, marveling at the way memories were stored in the mind. A whiff had the power to kindle a flood of memories.

He pushed himself and sat up.

The treat that met his eyes was truly magical. The exuberance of Nature the Magician. It transfixed him. A carpet of fresh, bright-green grass was spread as far as he could see. He brushed his hand over the velvety grass. Interspersed on the canvas of green was a riot of colorful flowers blooming at the same time. Pink tulips embraced yellow daffodils. Red roses sat shy of the violet orchids. Orange marigolds were intertwined with white lilies, as if making love. Purple lilacs called out to its lover, the blue iris, across a tiny stream of water that glinted in the mid-day sun. It seemed like a playground of companionship, a garden of love. He instantly fell in love with the place.

He craned his neck to the right. A single tree stood tall atop a petite hill.

The apple tree!

The tiny hill on which the tree stood was no longer of black soot. The fresh grass had veiled it in dazzling green. Brilliant red apples had replaced the green, unripe apples from before. The apples shimmered in the morning light. He smacked his lips as his mouth watered for a bite. He was suddenly hungry.

He stood. Looked at the grass-covered meadow again. And then at the apple tree, single and dignified, standing tall on the hill. It was at this moment that he realized the scenery was the same, only the colors had changed. The black and white painting from before had been infused with refreshing colors after the lightning struck; as if electricity were all that was needed to bring the Garden alive.

The Apple

A sudden movement in his peripheral vision caught his attention. He wheeled. Some ten yards away, close to the hill, was Michelle. She sat on the grass, groggy and disheveled in the aftermath of electrocution. Her thread-like hair had toppled over her face. Blades of grass were entangled in the mess that was her hair.

Relief swept over him. Mirth embraced his heart. He ran to her.

"Michelle!" Joy rang in his voice.

She squinted and peered at him through the gaps in her tousled hair. He dropped to his knees and embraced her. No words escaped his mouth. Her touch was enough.

"Where are we?" she said.

He spread his hands. "Take a guess." He smiled.

She flicked strands of hair from her face. Sweeping the area from left to right, she said, "Don't know where we are, but it's definitely beautiful."

"Look behind you," he goaded.

She heaved a huge sigh, as if he had asked her to move a mountain. She rotated in her position.

"The tree!" she gasped on seeing the glorious apple tree.

He nodded, his face flushed with an immense smile.

"The Garden of Eden! We found it!"

He nodded, this time more vigorously. "Come!"

He sauntered up the petite hill with newfound zeal. Michelle followed. He reached the top of the hill. The horizon gleamed a glamorous gold as the sun stood shy behind a thread-like veil of silver clouds. Just below the horizon, wherever he looked, his eyes met the grass – green, vibrant, and endless. The crease on his forehead ebbed away.

He heard Michelle come and stand behind him. He placed his hand on the sturdy trunk of the apple tree. It was smooth, yet firm. He looked at a low hanging apple. Bright red radiance throbbed within it, like life itself was pounding from inside.

Slowly, his hand moved away from the trunk. He couldn't stop himself. He had to touch the apple, so overpowered were his mind and heart. He gently cupped the apple, feeling it was almost a live animal. He felt invincible. He felt spectacular. Every cell in his body oozed energy. Every hair on his body stood to attention.

He was but a mortal. With one quick jerk, he plucked the apple.

Nothing happened. No thunder, no rumble, no trap.

He marveled at the fruit in his hand. A gorgeous piece of creation. Does it make one immortal as is rumored? he wondered. Instinctively he brought the hand clutching the apple close to his mouth. He wanted a bite. A big fleshy juice-dripping bite.

"Stop!" Michelle barked, just as he was about to bite into the flesh of the apple.

He stopped.

"Give me the apple!" Michelle ordered.

The sharpness in her voice alarmed him. She had never spoken to him with such harshness. He turned around. What he saw left him mouth-agape. He stood there, stunned.

Michelle stood tall. Feet apart. Hands outstretched. Pointing the flare gun directly at his head.

Chapter 20
Goodbye Love

"Michelle?" he murmured.

"Give me the apple," said Michelle. Her hand remained stable. The barrel of the flare gun pointed at his forehead.

His expressionless face didn't betray the agony of his heart. Why is she doing this? His mind was running through plausible reasons. Why the betrayal? I love her. She loves me… no, apparently not.

"I said, give me the apple. Now!"

The usual glint in Michelle's eyes had been replaced with a cold, lifeless stare. The warmth and enthusiasm he had come to associate with her were gone. She seemed as cold as the dead corpse of love between them.

Why did I not see it coming? he thought. We have been going out for over a year now. Since the firm contracted me for this assignment. His mind suddenly stopped. He smiled. Ah, the firm!

"Let me guess," he said finally. "You are the firm's lackey."

Michelle shifted in her position. Her grip on the gun hardened.

"The firm uses you for their bidding. And you manipulate people they are interested in. It's like a brothel. The firm is the Madam and you are the-."

"Shut up!" Michelle shouted.

He smiled. He wanted her agitated. He wanted her roused. In all his experience, the more distressed a person was in pressure situations, the easier it was to push them off a cliff, figuratively. But, he didn't want to just push her. He wanted to shove her off the hill and take the gun, literally.

"Well, the truth can be bitter, sweetheart," he said. His voice was calm and polite.

The politeness only enraged Michelle. This was not the reaction she was expecting.

"I am not your sweetheart. Never was!" she flared. So did her nostrils. Tiny tremors fluttered through the muscles of her arms.

"Well, thanks for clarifying, darling."

Michelle winced at "darling", oozing with anger.

He continued, "But why the charade? I was happy to help the firm. Happy to search for the long-lost Garden. Happy to endanger my life and come here, knowing well that if discovered by Sentinels, death was the only way out."

"Stop humoring yourself. I studied you for months before the firm hired you. You are a junkie. A treasure-hunting junkie. But, the best treasure-hunting junkie out there. You were happy to do this for yourself and for the money, nothing else."

He smirked. "Then, why the charade?"

"Because we didn't trust you. We feared that if you discovered the Garden, you'd take all the apples for yourself and screw us over. We needed someone to watch over you. And don't lie now, but you didn't trust us either. Remember the first meeting?"

He nodded, slowly, remembering the time when he was invited by Dr. Costello, the chairman of Immunos Pharmaceuticals, to their London office. He was in Egypt then, cooling his heels after his last adventure. The private jet of the chairman had flown him from Cairo to London. A chauffeur-driven limousine, courtesy of the chairman, had picked him up from a private runway at Heathrow Airport and driven him straight to the business headquarters of Immunos Pharmaceuticals at Canary Wharf. Housed in a fifty story skyscraper, Immunos Pharmaceutical overlooked the Thames River and its bustling wharf.

Michelle had greeted him in the office lobby, smartly dressed in a hot pink chiffon dress. She wore matching lipstick and pumps. He remembered admiring her toned arms, clearly noticeable through the sleeveless dress. She had welcomed him with a broad smile and a firm handshake. He was immediately infatuated with her. She had led him to the private office of the chairman on the 50th floor.

In sharp contrast to the rest of the office building, which was sleek, modern, and well-lit, the chairman's office looked like an ancient church. "Biblical" was how he had described it to a friend later. A dome hung over a niche in the far back wall which drew attention to a massive statue of Jesus on a cross. The office was lit only with the dancing flames of tall, white candles. A beautiful fresco, depicting the Virgin Mary as the Queen of Heaven, adorned the dome. Christian art permeated the room - Renaissance paintings on the walls and stained-glass windows featuring vivid scenes from the Old Testament. The floor was sleek and smelled of fresh linoleum.

The chairman, a heavyset, bull-necked Italian named Dr. Arthur Costello, stood behind a mahogany desk in the center of the room. Even at seventy, he had a head full of long, shoulder-length white hair. He wore a classic three-piece suit, well fitted and crisp, not a wrinkle in sight. The same could not be said about his sagging face with deep wrinkles gracing the eye area. Costello had welcomed him with a grim face and a throaty cough. A smoker's cough.

"I am Dr. Costello. You have already met Michelle. And that…" Dr. Costello twisted and pointed to a corner of the room. "…is my associate, Rana."

He hadn't noticed the man standing in the shadows wearing a black baseball cap. He strained his eyes to see the man's face, and just as suddenly, he looked away. The man suffered from vitiligo, half his facial skin dark, half discolored in patches around the eyes, nose, and mouth. On the color spectrum, if he was milk chocolate, Rana was dark chocolate randomly sprayed with patches of whipped cream. He wore an all-black suit that covered every inch of his skin except the face. Standing still in a dark corner of a dimly-lit room gave him the aura of a spy. Or a bodyguard. Or, maybe, the secret boss.

"Coffee?" he was asked.

"Black, no milk."

Costello snapped his fingers, like beckoning a servant. Michelle walked to the state-of-the-art Nespresso machine placed on an antique teak-wood table. No words were exchanged while the coffee brewed. Michelle distilled the steaming liquid into a cup and handed it to him.

"Don't be fooled by appearances," said Costello, his baritone voice booming in the enclosed room. "I am as much a man of science as I am a believer of Gospel. I believe the Bible is a treasure map, replete with mentions of holy herbs and elixirs." The chairman had paused then, expecting the usual incredulity he received on this statement. But, he had just nodded, as if what he had heard was normal, routine.

Costello gave a wry smile and continued, "My life's mission has been to find these elixirs and transform them into medicine for the common man."

He had chuckled.

Costello looked at him with contempt. "What's funny?"

"The mission isn't about relieving the suffering of the 'common man'. It's about minting billions of dollars in drug sales. Isn't it?"

The chairman's face had contorted into disdain. He opened his mouth to say something on impulse, but a bout of coughing overtook him. He started again.

"Every great company is built on the foundation of a meaningful purpose. A purpose that is far beyond profit and revenues. Don't get me wrong, profit ensures the maintenance of a business, but it's the purpose that ensures its sustenance in the long run."

He had laughed. "You don't need to convince me with corporate speak, Dr. Costello. That's one reason why I don't work a nine-to-six corporate job. Tell me why I am here?"

He swigged a mouthful of the coffee.

The chairman came to the point, his creased brow barely hiding the disdain for this treasure hunter. "I need you to find the lost Garden of Eden."

He spat out the coffee in surprise. Jets of black liquid stained the carpet on which he stood. His face went blank, his eyes focused, his mind attentive. "The Garden of Eden is a myth," he had said.

Costello took out his handkerchief and coughed into it. From the deep, guttural sound, it appeared he'd cough his lungs out. Costello peered at his stained handkerchief and shriveled his nose in disgust.

Costello continued, "You don't need to know how, but we now, finally, have the key that unlocks the gateway to the lost Garden." Costello had looked at Rana for the briefest moments.

"Okay. We find the Garden. Then what?"

"Not we. You. I want you to come on-board. Find me the lost Garden. And bring me the Apple of Immortality."

He had smiled broadly. "Let me guess. You want to extract immortality from the apple, suffuse it in your drugs and sell to the 'common man'?"

"Not immortality. If I sell immortality, very soon I will run out of people to sell to on Earth. That's bad for business. A sustainable business model would be to sell a drug that increased life expectancy for a few years. And people will keep coming back for more. Forever profitable."

Costello had smiled, satisfaction shining bright in his eyes.

"So, you are going to sell an addiction?" he had asked.

The chairman stopped smiling. "What I do with the prize is none of your business."

He had walked up to the chairman, looked him in the eye, and had said, "I am the hunter. I find the prize. I don't care if you take the prize for yourself, old man. I don't care if you last forever. But I care if my find makes billions of people addicted to a drug. I care if I give absolute power to a self-serving, self-righteous old man!"

"Since when did a kidnapper grow a heart?"

There was uneasy silence for a minute. Costello knew about his past, a past he had buried together with his baby sister. Never to be revealed, except in the nightmares that plagued his sleep.

"That life is behind me." He had seethed.

"Doesn't mean it no longer defines who you are," Costello retorted. "Just quote your price, young man. You will be paid handsomely for the hunt."

He had needed the money to set up his next private quest. That was all he cared about anyway. But Costello had pricked a nerve: deep-seated, always throbbing, never forgiving.

He had placed the cup of coffee on the chairman's desk and said, "It was nice meeting you, Dr. Costello. But I am not interested." And he had left the office.

"Hello? Hello?" Michelle snapped her fingers, bringing him out from his reverie. Her other hand held the flare gun, still pointed at his head.

She said, "Thinking about the first meeting? Or thinking about how I 'accidentally' bumped into you the second time?"

He narrowed his eyes. "What do you mean?"

"We knew you weren't coming back after the first meeting. Dr. Costello didn't like you or your attitude, but he wanted only the best for this job. He'd tried others over the years, but no one else had come close. So, it had to be you. The question was how to convince you?"

A devious smile passed over her face. "It was my idea. To make you fall for me. And then, coax you to do my bidding. Of course, the blank cheque from Dr. Costello also helped."

She chuckled. "Men have fallen head over heels around me all my life. I knew you could be easily manipulated. After all, you are nothing but a man."

Hatred filled his heart and raced through his veins. His head throbbed with indignation. There was only one thing on his mind - vengeance!

"Now," Michelle said. "Give me the apple." She straightened her outstretched arm holding the gun.

He lost all patience. "Heck! Why don't you take another apple? The tree is full of apples! What difference is this apple going to make?"

Michelle stood silent as if mulling to answer him or not. Finally, she sighed and said, "Each apple is precious. Very little bio-extract can be squeezed out of each fruit and made stable for drug synthesis. We want to be certain the apple is what the legend says it is. If it proves its worth, we are going to return for more."

He wanted to ask "How much more?" but he stopped as he realized that greed and power knew no bounds.

"I ask one last time. Give me the apple or, by God, I am going to shoot you."

He snorted. "Stop kidding yourself, Michelle. You don't want to kill me. If you wanted to, you would have already done it, and taken the apple."

"I don't want to, but I will shoot you if you don't comply." She fidgeted, her arm was tiring out. "I am making it easy for you. Give me the apple, and I will spare…"

Suddenly, a loud, shrill horn blared somewhere on the island. Somewhere above ground, but somewhere close.

"What was that?" Michelle said. Her voice was tense and worrisome.

A second horn boomed. Same pitch, same tone. But longer and louder.

"What's happening?" said Michelle.

He stood still, listening intently, as if waiting to hear more.

"Answer me! What's happening?" Michelle shouted at him.

A third horn tore through the air, deafening everything in its path. The entire island heard its ear-shattering boom.

Michelle made a half-hearted attempt to shield her ears. She wanted to keep the gun aimed at him.

As suddenly as it had started, the blaring horn stopped after three blasts.

"We need to go. Now!" He hurried toward Michelle.

"Stop right there! Or I'll shoot!"

He stopped mid-step.

"You stupid girl!" Harshness echoed in his voice. "That was a battle cry. They know we are here. And they are coming."

Michelle pursed her lips and swallowed hard. It took her another second to regain her composure. "Then stop wasting time. Give me the apple!"

Certain death was behind him. Possible death in front of him. Possible trumped trumps certain death. He took his chance.

With a quickness that caught Michelle off-guard, he swung his arm and threw the apple. The apple hit Michelle's wavering hand. The gun fell. Michelle wobbled for a moment, lost and uncertain.

But she was young and nimble. Her reflexes were fast.

She dove for the gun. He dove for the gun. He latched onto the gun barrel. She caught the stock frame. She pulled. He pulled. But he was stronger. Michelle knew it was a losing battle. In despair, she pulled back her knee and smashed it in his groin!

He collapsed into himself, wailing in pain. But rather than letting the gun go, he tightened his grip on the gun barrel. As if channeling the pain into a harder grip.

Michelle pulled and pulled. But she couldn't yank the gun away from him.

He stared at Michelle with eyes ablaze, teeth gritted. He screamed, his own little battle cry, and pulled at the gun with unbelievable strength.

Michelle was no match. She knew it would be seconds before he took away the gun. A decision had to be made.

She stopped pulling the stock frame. She wriggled her finger into the trigger guard and pulled the trigger with all her might.

Part Two
Saving Eden

Chapter 21

God's Power Is Mine

Michelle was in the Canary Wharf headquarters of Immunos Pharmaceuticals in London. It was half-past midnight. The weather was gloomy and wet, in typical London style.

Michelle sat on a plush five-seat sofa in Dr. Costello's private office. Her satchel, ripped and worn out from the mission, lay at her feet. Costello sat next to her, his shoulders tense and hands clasped together. He coughed uncontrollably, his condition much worse than the last time he'd met Michelle. He moved forward. The golden cross hanging from his neck beamed as a stray ray of light from a votive candle reflected off the frescoed dome and struck the cross.

Michelle hadn't spoken a single word since her arrival. She sat there, staring at the linoleum floor beneath her feet, lost in thought.

Costello had been briefed about the situation. At 2200 hours local time, the rescue team, which had been on standby on an anchored ship near North Sentinel Island, had received the pick-me-up signal from Michelle. Her pink Disney watch had been fitted with a satellite transmitter before the mission. All she had to do was press a button for pick up. Like calling a cab by pressing one button. A team of three was immediately dispatched via speedboat. The speedboat anchored one mile from the rendezvous point - an old ship called *Primrose*, stranded in the reef surrounding North Sentinel Island. While one manned the speedboat, two rescuers swam the last mile to the i. They searched the old ship for half an hour before, finally, finding Michelle. She was in shock, acting "mental" according to the rescue team leader. He thought she had lost it and needed urgent psychiatric attention. She was brought back to the rescue ship, sedated, and put on a glucose drip. A doctor on-board monitored her as she was flown to London on Costello's order. It had been another forty-eight hours before she was aware enough to respond. Before she made sense. And he'd had to be patient—something he wasn't used to being.

Costello appraised Michelle from head to toe. She looked jaded. And pale. A bony skeleton had replaced her usual alluring figure. He almost felt sorry for her.

He put a hand on her shoulder. "Michelle, how are you doing?"

Michelle jerked on contact, suddenly coming back to reality. She looked at him with tired, bloodshot eyes. "Sorry, what did you say, sir?"

Costello narrowed his eyes. Concern washed over his face. "I asked, how are you doing, Michelle?"

Michelle shook her head once. No words left her mouth.

"Michelle?" The chairman persisted.

"I killed him, okay! I killed him!" she shouted all of a sudden.

Costello sighed. He was not one to be disrespected. He did not get to where he was by letting lackeys like Michelle ride over him.

Michelle immediately realized her mistake. "I am sorry, sir! I am so sorry!" Tears welled in her eyes. "I did not mean to shout."

Costello sighed again. He decided to let the indiscretion pass. For now.

He said, "Why is it troubling you, Michelle? We planned to kill him all along. What changed?"

"I don't know." Michelle hung her head, as if abashed, and shook it vigorously. "I don't know," she said again.

Costello was getting impatient now. All he wanted to know was if they'd found the Garden of Eden. And the forbidden apple. Was it just a myth, or did the treasure hunter actually discover it? He was glad the treasure hunter was dead. Moron! He cursed in his head.

He controlled his impatience and remained silent. He gave Michelle a minute to recover, trying to physically control the restlessness that was smothering him.

"I only meant to take the apple from him," she said finally, patting the satchel at her feet unknowingly.

The chairman's heart jumped with excitement. He peered at the satchel. He'd told his men to bring Michelle and her belongings intact. He hadn't wanted anyone else to be tempted. The crease of a faint smile appeared on his face. The apple is real! And it's here!

Michelle rotated her head to look at him. His smile vanished as soon as it had appeared.

He nodded grimly, "But?"

"But I didn't mean to kill him. If he had given me the apple and not fought over it, I would have…" She hung her head again, just as she left the sentence hanging.

The chairman was suddenly alarmed. In his business, you never left loose ends. There was no knowing when a loose end would bite you. That's how nemeses were born. He had let the earlier indiscretion pass. But this! No way! Michelle had clear orders to kill the treasure hunter. Crystal clear! He reminded himself.

"But you did kill him, right?" he inquired.

"Yes," she said, her voice a bare murmur.

Doesn't matter, you stupid girl! Costello thought. You were given clear orders. He made a mental note. Michelle cannot be trusted again. Ever.

But he still had a use for her.

He stood. Bent and gripped Michelle's shoulders.

"You did well, child," he said. "Like you said, he made you do it. It wasn't your fault."

"But I pulled the trigger." Tears rolled down her cheeks. Her whole body shook.

"You had no choice. He gave you no choice."

He gripped her shoulders firmly and nudged her to stand up. Michelle stood grudgingly. Her head hung in shame.

"Look at me, Michelle," the chairman urged.

Trembling, biting her lower lip, Michelle raised her head.

He said, "We will pray for forgiveness. God is benevolent. He understands. Pray, and He will forgive."

Michelle nodded.

"Good!" he said. "Come with me."

He took her to the rear of the room, his personal praying area, and stopped at the feet of Christ on a wooden cross. He picked up a white votive candle and lit it. Fumes from the burned wick tickled his nostrils. He whispered a short prayer.

Placing the candle at the altar, he said, "Pray, Michelle."

Michelle stepped forward. Then, unsure, she looked at him.

"Go ahead, pray of forgiveness. You have all the time you need."

She nodded. With shaky hands, she lit a candle. Bowing her head in prayer, she closed her eyes. Almost immediately, she started to cry uncontrollably. Her feet gave way. She dropped to her knees. Her loud sobs filled the room.

Costello grimaced. Weak! He thought. He stepped away, leaving Michelle to pick herself up once she was done. He traced his steps to the sofa. His heart cartwheeled as he moved closer to the prize - the satchel! He stopped at the edge of the sofa. The excitement was palpable. His fingers went numb as the thought of holding the apple took over his mind.

He had waited a long time. And the stupid girl was making the wait unending with her sob story. He looked behind him. Michelle was crouched on the floor, crying, looking away from him.

He wasted no time. Grabbed the satchel. Maneuvered the zipper. He didn't have to rummage through the bag. In the dimly-lit office, the apple sparkled like a freshly cut ruby - crimson, translucent, and luminous. It had been days since it was plucked, but the apple showed no sign of decay.

On the contrary, it teemed with ripeness, waiting to impart everlasting life to its bearer.

Carefully, Costello picked up the apple. He dropped the satchel, which hit the floor with a weak thud. He held the apple in both hands, completely besotted. He saw life beyond the lung cancer that gripped him.

Costello whispered to himself, "God's ultimate power is now mine!"

Chapter 22
Thank You, Michelle

Costello walked over to his ornate, mahogany desk. He put the apple down with both hands, as if it were a fragile vase that needed careful attention. He felt invigorated. His chest calm, his breathing normal. He had not felt this strong in years. He cleared his throat, an act which would have invited incessant coughing just two minutes ago. Now, he didn't cough. Just holding it had given him renewed life.

He opened the top desk drawer. A 9mm Glock 26 revolver lay there snugly. Designed for concealed carry, its small frame and short barrel looked like a cute toy in the large drawer. He took the revolver out. It had been years since he last used the revolver. But it was a Glock. If someone told him to put his trust in a weapon not fired for fifty years, he would pick a Glock. Trust the Americans to know their guns, he smiled.

He walked over to Michelle. She sat with her head bent, hair falling over the face. The sobs had stopped. He could not tell if she was watching him through the hair covering her face. But he didn't care. He came and stood next to Michelle, pointing the revolver at Michelle's head.

"Are you going to kill me, sir?" Michelle spoke first.

Sly woman, he thought. Has been watching me the whole time while pretending to sob.

"We had a deal, Michelle."

Michelle pulled her hair back and stood. The barrel of the tiny revolver followed her movement.

"Yes, and I delivered," she said.

The Apple

"You did. Unfortunately, by accident. I cannot have dissenters in my team. You are now a dissenter who knows too much. Goodbye, Michelle!"

With that, he unlatched the gun safety and aimed at Michelle's head.

"Wait! I have another apple!"

He was halfway through pulling the trigger. He stopped. His mind racing.

"Where?" he asked, lowering the gun.

"Let me go. And I will bring the apple."

"I asked, where?"

"I can't tell you. I tell you, and you will kill me."

"I will kill you even if you *don't* tell me."

"You don't have to do this, sir. We can reach a compromise."

"The thing, though, is that I don't trust you anymore, Michelle. And you knowing that makes you an even bigger threat. I can't trust you, and you can't trust me. Moreover, I don't need your apples, which I am pretty sure you are lying about to save your skin. I can walk through the front door now to get apples from the tree directly. I only needed you and that treasure hunter to confirm the existence of the Garden. And I am mighty grateful for your effort."

With that, he raised his revolver again.

"Well, then go right ahead. Try killing an immortal woman."

A sudden hush fell upon the room. It took Costello a moment to realize the gravity of what he had heard.

"You ate an apple!"

A sly smile escaped her lips. The charade fell and out stepped Michelle in her naked, cunning self. "The truth is, I have never trusted you, old man. I have done your bidding for twenty years, ever since you bought me from my pimp. In hindsight, selling my pubescence to Slavic arseholes was probably more rewarding than bending over backward for you. But, I am done with you. This was my exit ticket to freedom. So, I plucked an extra apple. I ate it. Now, I am immortal. You can shoot me, but you can't kill me."

Costello burst into laughter. "Dumb! Dumb! Dumb woman!"

Michelle looked perplexed. She clearly didn't expect such a reaction.

Costello pulled himself together. "Well, you are right about that, Michelle. I *can* shoot you."

A single shot reverberated through the room. The tiny bullet hit Michelle in the middle of the forehead and ricocheted inside her skull, damaging nerves and gray matter alike. Michelle was dead even before she hit the floor. She lay there, her eyes wide with shock. Blood streamed down her forehead and formed a tiny puddle on the floor.

Costello bent over the dead body. "What a waste of beauty. What a waste of an apple." He spat on Michelle's face.

Costello walked to his majestic chair and sat. He was exhausted by the release and relief. He gathered his strength and thoughts. He picked up the apple. It sparkled despite the muted light and the late hour. He wanted a bite so bad. He wanted to pierce the crisp skin of the fruit with his incisors and pull out a chunky, juicy bite. His cancer-ridden lungs begged him to take a bite.

Not yet, he told himself. It'd have to wait. Just a few more days. Till every remaining apple is mine.

He got up. Walked to the safe behind his desk. It was a small granite safe, as big as a shoebox, built directly into the concrete wall. He pressed his thumb on the fingerprint scanner and placed his face in front of the facial recognition sensor. A green LED light switched on, a cursor started blinking, and a thirty-second countdown began. His pulse raced. He punched the ten-digit password into the keypad, as fast as his trembling, wrinkled finger allowed.

The safe opened with a sharp click. He sighed. He placed the apple inside, gently, like it was a newborn baby. He kept gazing at the apple, brimming with vitality inside the dark, lifeless safe. He inhaled deeply. Gulped the saliva building in his mouth. Not yet, he told himself again and closed the safe.

He rummaged in his trouser pocket and pulled out his mobile phone. He tapped twice to speed-dial a number.

"Hi, Shawn. It's me," he spoke into the phone. "We are going to North Sentinel Island. I want your men ready for action in forty-eight hours. It's going to get ugly."

Chapter 23
Call for Arms

I jolt up in bed, distressed, anxious, and sore. I clutch my head where the bullet had pierced through the skull. I feel a crusty indentation, the size of my thumb.

The room is partially lit by incense candles burning in one corner. The sweet aroma of fresh lilacs engulfs and lifts me. Calmness sweeps away the anxiety. I let out a big yawn.

Yoni is sitting on the floor next to me, her legs crossed, her hands on the knees, open palms facing the ceiling. She seems to be meditating. Her eyes closed. Her body still.

"Woken up, have we?" she says without opening her eyes.

She brings up her hands, rubs the palms together as if generating heat, and presses the palms against her eyeballs. She breathes in deeply as she lets her hands fall. Opens her eyes and looks at me.

"How are you feeling?" she asks.

"Like I just got shot," I say, pressing the bullet-wound on my head.

She nods with a smile. She pushes herself up with a grunt, the effort betraying her age.

She turns toward the door. "I will call the queen," she says on her way out.

"Wait!" I exclaim.

She turns, as slowly as the aged gears in her machinery allow her.

"I never thanked you for what you did. Azura told me. You saved my life when I got shot in the head. I am here only because of you, Yoni. And for that, I will be forever indebted."

She dismisses it with a wave of the hand. "It's what I do. Nothing I wouldn't have done for anyone. The human soul is sacred, you know. It does not deserve to go in tatters from a gunshot."

I nod my appreciation. She turns again and leaves.

I take a deep breath, reflecting on the last dream in the Garden.

"Michelle, Michelle, Michelle," I murmur, calling out the name of my killer like a mantra, committing her crime to memory. She was my lover, bait to get me to Sentinel Island. She was my killer, a plan hatched deep within the confines of her dark heart. I do not know why she turned. But she did. I do not know if she ever loved me. Doesn't matter. All that matters now is revenge.

I hear hurried footsteps outside the hut. The next moment Azura strides in, followed by Yoni.

"Where is the apple?" she comes straight to the point.

Through clenched jaw, I say a single word. "Michelle."

Azura straightens. She nods continuously, as one does on receiving confirmation for what is already known.

"I still don't believe it," I say. "I loved her. She loved me. Why did she do it? All for an apple?"

I am sure Azura can see the fire of vengeance burning in my eyes, the struggle going through my mind. She disregards the trivial matter of lost love and says, "Forget about her. Where did she take the apple?"

I sigh deeply and shake my head. "I don't know. She could have gone anywhere."

"Not anywhere. Back to where both of you came from. Do you remember where? Or who sent you?"

I start to shake my head. But then a faint memory from the dream hits me. "Dr. Costello."

Azura narrows her eyes. "Who? I thought Arthur sent you."

"Yes, Dr. Arthur Costello. The name doesn't matter. What matters is that he is the chairman of the biggest pharmaceutical company in the world."

Azura looks completely confused. "Pharmaceutical?"

"Medicines. He makes medicines. He wants to extract the essence from the apple and sell 'longer life' to whoever can afford it."

"And who doesn't want a longer life?" Azura responds. "It's the very greed that brought the Sentinels to existence. For six thousand years we have protected the Garden from being ravaged by human voracity. And we will not fail now. *I* will not fail now."

Without warning, Azura walks away. She stops at the door and addresses Yoni.

"Go to the village hall, Dai Ma. Gather with all children and their mothers. You will be safe there." She pauses and points to me. "Take him with you."

Azura scurries from the hut, leaving Yoni and me staring at each other.

"Wait!" I get up from the bed and hurry after Azura. Warm evening breezes caress my face when I step outside the hut. Dusk peeks through the horizon while the sun prepares to set. The calm and beauty of the evening is in sharp contrast to the commotion that greets me. Every Sentinel I see seems to be in a rush. Every Sentinel I see has a weapon in hand - a spear or a club or a set of bow and arrows.

I catch up with Azura. "Wait! Azura, wait."

She slows but keeps walking. "I do not have time. Be quick."

"Take me with you. I don't want to be safe with children. I am a Sentinel now. I can fight. I want to fight, if there will be a fight."

She stops.

"First, there *will* be a fight. War is coming. I know it. Second, I cannot let you fight shoulder to shoulder with Sentinel warriors. You have not been instructed in any of the fighting disciplines. You can't shoot an arrow. You don't know the art of operating a trident. You will be a liability in my ranks. It's in your and our best interest that you stay away from the fight. Yoni will guide you to the

The Apple

village hall. You can help the children and mothers stay warm, fed, and safe."

"But I know the enemy best. Even with my limited memory I know more about their capability than any of you. I can help, Azura. I want to help. I brought this upon you. The least I can do is stand with you and your people, my people now, and fight back."

Azura chews her lower lip, her mind racing.

"Okay. Only on one condition. You join as an adviser to the queen. Me. You will not join the ranks of my warriors. You are too taken by vengeance. It will cloud your judgment in combat. The best place for you is next to me, advising me. Understand?"

I nod quickly and vigorously.

"Come with me," she says.

She darts off again. I stay close to her heels. She marches to the village center. A Sentinel guard stands in the middle of the street, shouting orders at the top of his lungs, diverting weapon-carrying men and women one way and unarmed children and mothers the other way. Bani, the Commander of the Sentinel army, stands a few feet away, overseeing the operation. She jumps to attention when she sees Azura.

"You had one day, Bani," she says. "I hope the preparations are done."

It is only now I realize that I had been knocked out for close to twenty-four hours. All thanks to the sleep-aid Yoni had given me.

"Yes, my queen," says Bani, her voice overflowing with confidence. "All under control. Every able-bodied Sentinel has been provided a weapon of choice and will be at the front before sunset. I am sending half the warriors north and half the warriors south, the two possible fronts from where we can expect an invasion."

She sees the quizzical look on my face and sighs. "The village is in the middle of the island. It's impossible to invade the island from the eastern or western fronts. The forest is impenetrable. If they survive the forest, they would not survive the ferocious lions or the venomous cobras that rule those parts of the island."

She turns to Azura. "The southern beach is where I expect the enemy to attack."

Bani glances at me briefly when she utters "enemy".

"But…" I interrupt. "Michelle and I sneaked in from the western beach. Our surveillance report showed that it was the only area not patrolled by Sentinel guards."

Bani's face reddens. A nobody not only interrupted her but was now challenging her.

Sensing the animosity, Azura answers, "And you would have reached a dead end at the giant redwood tree, am I right?"

I nod.

"The only way is through the enchanted door in the tree, for which you had the dagger of God Saraph. They don't have the dagger anymore. And it is impossible to break through the door, even if you know it exists."

She turns to Bani. "How many warriors?"

"We have about a hundred and twenty. Like I was saying before I was interrupted…" Bani gives me a stern glance. "…the warriors will be equally divided between northern and southern fronts. I will personally be going to the southern front as it is most susceptible to invasion."

"And how many warriors will be guarding the children here?"

Bani looks sheepishly at Azura. "Two," she mutters.

"Two? That's it? Why, commander? We need to make sure our children are safe if the enemy sneaks through our defenses. I want ten warriors posted at the village hall, guarding the children and the mothers."

Bani nods. She immediately turns to the Sentinel guard closest to her and relays the order.

Azura says, "A few other important matters. First, if you are headed to the southern front, I will lead the army on the northern front. Second, I want a two-warrior patrol manning the western and eastern fronts at all time. I agree they are likely impenetrable, but if the enemy tries to invade from those fronts, the patrol can give us an early warning of the enemy's arrival. Third, if you are heavily outnumbered, fall back to the village center. Don't be a hero and become a martyr. We can re-group here."

Bani gives a confident nod and turns to the hundred-odd women and men now assembled in the square. She instructs half of the army to turn around and follow her to the southern front, and the other half to follow the queen straight to the northern front. Then, she puts her hand on the chest and shouts, "Victory to Sentinels!"

A hundred warriors shout the battle cry in unison.

"Victory to Sentinels!" Azura returns the cry of strength.

The two armies march out, seeking war.

Chapter 24
The Siege

We are on the forest path, underneath the cushion and protection of tall, canopied foliage. I walk alongside Azura as the newly appointed adviser to the queen. We are in the middle of the pack, shielded by the Sentinel army in case of an ambush. Through the thick canopy, I barely make out the last rays of sunlight being swallowed by darkness, only to be replaced by the resplendent white light of the full moon.

"Do you think we will be attacked today?" I ask Azura.

"We may already be late," she says, looking straight ahead, disinterested in conversation.

We walk in silence, navigating the zig-zag path trampled and opened by the guards in front of us.

I hear the release of a deeply held sigh from Azura. "The attack may not happen for months, or even years. Or it may happen tonight. I do not know. But we need to be prepared for all eventualities. We need to protect Eden with our lives."

"You need more than just lives," I retort.

Azura finally looks at me. "What do you mean?"

"Granted you have a hundred warriors. But they carry spears and bows. They will stand no chance against the modern weapons of today. I think we will lose faster than we think."

Azura laughs. "Have some confidence, young man." Azura jabs at me, knowing full well she is years younger than me.

She says, "We may be backward. Our weapons may be traditional. But we have heart, a strong purpose shared by every Sentinel in the army. The purpose connects us like beads on a necklace. The enemy does not come with a shared purpose beyond riches. That will be their downfall, you mark my words."

"It's good to have confidence, young lady," I jab back. "But over-confidence has seen the demise of many a king and queen. And your strategy is wayward. You divided your army in half. No focus. You are taking half to the open beach. If the enemy starts firing bullets from their ships, they would have won the battle even before they land."

Azura smiles. "You know you talk too much and assume much more. I hope the enemy is like you, presumptuous and self-absorbed. Exactly what we need to win."

I chew the inside of my cheeks as blood bubbles through my veins. "I am not the enemy here, Azura. I just want to make sure we don't die at the hands of a foolish leader who does not know what she is up against."

Azura stops. Raises her hand. The whole caravan comes to a stop. She turns, faces me. I feel the heat of the fire bursting in her eyes.

"I was five when I got my first lesson in warfare. Six when I could hit my mark with an arrow from a thousand feet. And seven when I killed a lion with my trident." Her words, even whispered, echo in the deep forest. "Every Sentinel goes through that training. Every Sentinel either kills a lion or gets killed. No other way to become part of the Sentinel army. Even for a foolish queen."

She takes a step toward me. "When bullets fly from enemy guns, I do not want my army of a handful hundred focused together in one spot. It's the easiest way to disintegrate within seconds. We need to be spread thin, camouflaged by the jungle, playing to our strengths of close combat. We remain invisible, force the enemy to play with our rules, not with theirs."

She pauses to see if I react. I don't.

"There you have it. That is the simple strategy. We are not going to the beach to have a holiday, my smart adviser. We are going close, yes, but not so close to be in the direct line of fire."

She takes a step forward and jabs a finger in my chest. "Don't take me for a fool. Ever. And worst, don't call me that. Next time, I will put you in the line of fire myself."

She doesn't wait for an answer, turns, and shouts to her men. "Keep moving!"

Azura strides to the front of the line, determined to lead from the front, I presume. I walk alone, in the middle of the pack, trying to keep up with the sharp turns and climbs in the dim light. After walking for the better part of an hour, squeezing through tight spaces and fleshy branches, the forest suddenly opens up. The sound of waves lashing against the rocky beach becomes pronounced. Each lash seeming more menacing than the last. A hundred yards from the beach, still within the confines of the forest, we come to a halt.

Azura orders her men to separate into five companies of ten each and spread out across the northern front. "I want five men on watch duty in each company, and five men resting in the pits at all times. Rotate every six hours. I want complete vigilance from men on watch duty. You are accountable for watching every speck of the northern front. You see any movement, raise the alarm. Am I clear?"

"Yes, my queen!" the men shout in unison.

"Victory to Sentinels!" Azura cries.

"Victory to Sentinels!" Fifty men join the chorus.

Two companies of ten men march out to our right and two companies to our left. Azura and I are left standing with ten men of the company stationed in the middle. Five men from our company on first watch duty run out toward the beach. Just inside the rim of the forest, each man climbs a tree keeping a fair distance of two-hundred yards between each man. In this way, five men from each company, twenty-five in total, watch over the entire five-thousand-yard coastline of the northern front.

We wait. Each watchman bellows out a cuckoo bird-call, signaling they are in place, hidden and watching every speck of the coastline.

The Apple

Azura turns to the remaining five warriors and me. "Let's go rest in the pit."

I look around, confused by what she means.

One of the guards in our company bends, wriggles his fingers into the ground, and lifts a rock, revealing a secret dugout. The rock is as wide as the chest of a heavyset man, like Mammoth. It's covered with green shrubbery, camouflaging its existence. I had not noticed it was there, even when the guard bent and inserted his fingers into the ground. Now I realize why. Like an iceberg, the bulk of the rock is below ground, covering the mouth of the secret pit.

The guard puts the rock aside and jumps into the pit. He is immediately swallowed by darkness. Another guard follows and then another, till Azura tells me I am next. I gulp. Squeezing through a tiny, dark hole in the forest floor terrifies me a little. I do not know what to expect. But I saw three guards jump in ahead of me, which gives me both confidence and strength.

I do not jump in. I sit on the ground and put both my feet into the hole. My feet dangle in the air. I push in a bit more. My feet still don't find solid ground. It feels like jumping into a bottomless pit. I take a deep breath and jump in. Complete darkness shrouds me. I bounce off the sides of the earthy wall, breaking the fall. My feet land on solid ground within seconds.

It's dark. I stand tall and feel the walls around me with bare hands. There is no opening in the wall. No way to go.

Where did the other guards go? They couldn't have just vanished.

"Bend down." A muted voice beckons me from close to my feet.

And then a hand grips my foot. I twitch.

"This way. Bend down," the voice says again.

I crouch. Using my hands, I locate an opening, large enough to crawl through. I break through the tentacles of claustrophobia gripping me, and crawl inside the opening. It's pitch black. I squint, trying to see if my eyes adjust to the darkness and show me a path. Nothing. It remains as dark as a moonless cloudy night.

"Follow me," says the same voice from ahead of me.

"I can't see you."

"Don't worry. This is the only way to the central pit. You won't get lost. Just keep moving, so others can follow."

I nod to myself and crawl as instructed. A sweet, earthy scent, like quenched soil right after a rainfall, greets me as I move deeper into the tunnel. The air inside is surprisingly clean. There must be vents built by the Sentinels, I think to myself.

After about two minutes of a slow crawl, the voice in front of me says, "We are here. You will be able to stand up once you are out of the tunnel."

I dab the tunnel ceiling with my hand and locate the point where the constricted tunnel opens into the hollow pit. I crawl the last few paces and rise, slowly, making sure my head doesn't bump into the ceiling of the pit. It doesn't. I can stand straight. For the fun of it, I raise my arm. My fingertips do not touch the ceiling even when I stand on my toes. Feels good to be in an open space, even though it is ten feet beneath the ground with no visibility whatsoever.

A hand slaps my knee. "Step aside so I can enter." It's Azura.

I move further into the pit, stepping away from the mouth of the tunnel. Azura stands upright. I can't see her, but I feel her presence right in front of me as the airflow suddenly changes.

"Make yourself comfortable," she says.

I nod, staring in the darkness at the place I imagine her to be standing. "I would, once you show me to my corner. Or better, is there a bed in here somewhere?"

I hear her laugh from behind me. I immediately turn in the direction of the laughter, surprised. A moment ago, she was in front of me. And now she is behind me. She walked past me, and I didn't even notice?

"We are laying an ambush for the enemy, Mr. Adviser, not holidaying. There are no cushy beds in here. We sleep on the floor."

I follow the voice and move to the center of the pit.

"Stop!" Azura says suddenly. "Or you will bump into me."

I come a halt. "You can see me? How?"

"All Sentinels can see in the dark. It's part evolution, part training," she explains. "Throughout our history, humans have attacked Sentinel Island at night, in the cover of darkness. Our ancestors made darkness our friend. Our strength. They trained the eyes to see in the dark, and over centuries the ability became part of Sentinel DNA. We keep training. The ability keeps getting stronger in our children. A virtuous cycle. It has…"

She suddenly pauses and sighs.

"Stop making funny faces at me. I can see that tongue of yours sticking out at me," she says.

I burst out laughing. "Sorry, I was just checking how well you have trained to see in the darkness."

"No more jokes. No more funny business, okay?" She admonishes me. "We are at the cusp of battle. Be serious. If you cannot, you are welcome to hide with the kids in the village."

I sulk and mumble "Sorry."

She says, "Some ground rules for you. First, we stay at the center of the pit at all times. There are seven tunnels that lead out from this spherical pit. One is the tunnel we came through, and then there are six other equidistant tunnels completing a circle. I don't want the tunnels blocked at any time. So, no sleeping in the tunnel. No slouching at the mouth of the tunnel. Stay in the center. Second, we take turns sleeping. There are seven of us. Two of us must always be awake, guarding the pit at all times and staying vigilant of the intruder alert from men on trees outside. You…" A finger pokes at my chest in the dark. "…and I will be on guard duty first. Third, there are baskets of food placed in-between those two tunnels."

I don't know where to look in the darkness. I stay put.

Azura realizes my quandary and says, "Someone will show you later. The important point is that we may be holed up here for months. So, each of us is allowed a rice wafer three times a day. I will tell you when it is time to eat, we only eat then, ensuring our bodies get used to the routine. Any questions?"

"Is there a bathroom in here somewhere?"

"We take a bath once a day in the afternoon, the peak daylight hour when probability of attack is minimum. You may go to the beach and wallow in the ocean water. For nature calls, you will go above ground and relieve yourself wherever you want in the jungle. A guard will accompany you the first time, so you don't get lost. From the second time, you are on your own. Clear?"

"Crystal," I say.

"Guards," she addresses her men. "Get some rest."

A chorus of "My queen" rings through the pit. And then there is silence. No movement, no shifting. It's almost like the men went to sleep standing up.

A hand grabs my arm. "Come. We are on watch duty." Azura pulls me a few paces and asks me to sit. I do as instructed.

"Azura, why is…"

"Shhh!" she lightly punches me on the arm. "No talk here. We need to stay vigilant for any stray sounds," she whispers. "Can't do that if you keep talking."

I sigh and move into a sitting position. I am too overwhelmed with sheer darkness, and now I have nothing but my thoughts to entertain me. I yawn. The silence, the darkness, and the warmth inside the pit offer a perfect remedy for sleep. I soon start to feel drowsy.

I must have dozed off because the next thing I know Azura is shaking me awake.

"You are on watch duty for God's sake!" she scolds. "Stay awake."

I rub my eyes and stretch my arms, telling myself that I can get through this boredom.

Suddenly, a muted, but shrill sound breaks through the silence. It's a bird-call. A cuckoo bird-call.

My pulse quickens as I register its significance.

"Guards! Wake up!" Azura yells. "It's our lucky day. The enemy is here."

Chapter 25

Let's Fight

Drowsiness in the pit evaporated within seconds. I heard urgent movements. Joints creaked as the five guards quickly stood. Naked feet rubbed against the earthen floor as they got ready for action.

"Be quiet," Azura whispered to her men. "I want full stealth mode, not a single sound. Go to the entrance of the tunnels and wait for my orders. We will have one chance to catch the enemy by surprise. Don't blow it. In the tunnels. Now!"

The five guards shuffled away without a word into the tunnels.

Azura grabbed my hand. "Come with me."

She pulled me toward the wall. "Bend down. Feel the open passageway of the tunnel. I will go first. You follow me."

"Got it!" I say a bit too enthusiastically, despite a multitude of questions running through my head. What have I got myself into? Am I expected to fight? But how, without a weapon?

Azura crawls into the pit. "Follow me. And keep quiet."

I rush into the pit on all fours. I do not know if it's the same tunnel through which we came. But it feels and smells the same. We crawl quietly but urgently, and within minutes we reach the entrance.

"I am going to open the entrance and assess the situation outside. Wait for my command. If all is clear, we will go outside."

She does not wait for my response. I hear her groan once, and then it's silent as she climbs the ten feet up the tunnel and pushes away the rock blocking the tunnel entrance. Suddenly, there is light. I blink my eyes as sharp fragments of moonlight flood into the tunnel. It feels as harsh as sun rays after staying in pitch darkness for hours.

Azura peeks outside. Left and then right. Only the top of her head and eyes are above ground. Her feet and hands are dug into the wall, steadying her. She waits a beat, and then like a furtive cheetah on a hunt, she climbs out the hole.

She looks at me and whispers, "Come!"

I look at the wall surrounding me and brush my hand over it, trying to figure out how am I supposed to climb ten feet. My hand grazes over a depression in the wall, built like a slot. I find an exact slot one foot above, and then another a foot above it.

It's a built-in ladder, I say to myself.

I plant my hands into the slots, hoist myself up and climb to the top. I look outside. There is no one. There is no sound. Where did Azura go? I hesitate and look again in all directions.

"Here! Hurry!" A hushed voice calls out from my right. I know it's Azura, but I can't see her even in the moonlight.

I creep out the tunnel and dash to the voice, keeping my head low. I find Azura crouched behind a huge redwood tree. A guard crouches next to her, a bow in his hand and a quiver of arrows on his back. I rush to their side.

"What's happening?" I ask.

"Veera tells me…" She nods toward the guard with her head. "…that multiple enemy boats just docked on the beach. Estimated twenty men in total." She smiles. "Fewer than I was expecting."

Azura turns to the guard. "Get up the tree. Let the enemy enter the forest. Let them come close, as close as possible. Then, we attack. Wait for my signal."

The guard nods. He flings his bow around his shoulders and with the grace of a skilled monkey, climbs up the redwood tree.

We wait. The persistent buzzing of mosquitoes and the intermittent sighting of fireflies keeping us company.

The Apple

Gradually, we hear whispers coming from the beach. I peek from behind the tree. I can't see a thing on the beach as my line of sight is cut off by trees and bushes.

Azura yanks at my shoulder. "What are you doing? They will see you."

"No, they won't. I can't see them. How can they see me?"

Azura rolls her eyes. "Just stay here. Don't move if you don't want to get killed by the enemy… or by me."

I chuckle, but her unsmiling glare never leaves my face, a telling sign that she is serious.

The sharp sound of a twig breaking stops my heart for a second. The enemy enters the forest.

Azura crouches even lower and peeks. "They are spread out. Walking cautiously." She is almost whispering to herself. "Ten yards more and Sentinel archers on tree-tops will finish this even before it starts."

I see the hint of a smug smile gracing her lips.

"Stop!" An enemy soldier whispers. "Heat signatures top-front. Lock target now."

"Target locked."

"Target locked."

Urgent voices respond to the leader.

"Oh no!" I murmur.

"What?" Azura asks, unable to hide the sudden fear in her voice.

Even before I tell her what's about to happen, the leader of the enemy army shouts, "Fire!"

Successive gun shots, about ten or so, pierce the silent night. Followed by the loud grunts and groans of grown Sentinels.

Veera falls from the top of the redwood right in front of us. Dead, even before his bones shatter from the fall. His eyes are open, shocked at how easily the enemy found his hiding place. Loud thuds left and right paint the same story - the fall of the Sentinel archers, without firing a single arrow.

Azura remains frozen in her spot, unable to come to terms with what has transpired. But, she soon recovers. She peeks at the enemy soldiers, but this time she doesn't crouch low and doesn't try to hide.

"Heat signature behind that tree!" an enemy soldier scowls.

A single bullet is fired. It whizzes past Azura as she steps behind the safety of the tree trunk. Just in time.

"What are you doing? Are you mad?" I whisper as softly as possible. "You just showed them where you are hiding!"

"Shhh!" She puts a finger on her lips. "That's the plan. I want to draw them into the forest. Then they are mine."

I sigh loudly, not quite understanding her ploy. I brace myself for imminent death. Now that the enemy has locked her as the target, I would be the casualty caught in the fire of bullets aimed at her.

The enemy leader orders. "Roger, move up on the right flank. Alex, same on the left. Proceed with caution. Enemy is armed."

Azura says, "We need to get behind them."

She rolls over in her position and sweeps her hand over the ground. She locates what she is looking for and pulls open a slab of rock. The slab turns one-eighty degrees on its hinges, revealing the mouth of another tunnel.

"I will go first. Stay right behind me, okay?"

She is about to jump but stops. She bends forward and stomach-crawls a couple of yards to where Veera lies dead. She picks up his quiver of arrows and the bow. She plucks the string on the bow. It makes a slight swoosh as it springs into position. Satisfied, Azura crawls back without turning. She puts her feet into the hole and jumps.

"Come! And close the door behind you," she whispers.

I put my feet into the hole and find the ladder-slots built into the wall. I lower myself into the hole and turn over the slab of rock behind me, locking myself into complete darkness.

Azura touches my foot as it hits the landing. "This way."

I get on all fours and crawl after Azura. She moves fast, like a rat running away from water gushing into its hole. I strain every muscle in my limbs just to keep up with her. We reach the central pit within a minute. She pulls me out and leads me to another tunnel.

"This way. We will spring up behind the enemy. Faster now, we don't have much time."

I have no clue what she means by faster. The one-minute crawl to the pit was in record time in my opinion. But then, I don't have the same level as conditioning and training as her. I take a deep breath and jump after her into the second tunnel.

My limbs are on fire. Sweat streams down my face and pours over my clammy hands. I struggle to breathe in the scanty air inside the tunnel. I huff. I puff. Every muscle in my body wants to give up, but adrenaline keeps moving me forward. Within five minutes, which seems more like a thirty-minute workout, we reach the end of the tunnel. Azura climbs the ladder at lightning speed and orders me to follow suit. She reaches the top and gently turns over the rock, revealing the opening. Helped by the moonlight streaming into the hole, I find my way to the top. Azura puts up her hand suddenly, a signal to stop. I stop in my tracks. Azura peers over the hole and turns her head slowly to the left and then to the right. She surveys again to be sure. Satisfied, she crawls out the hole. Her hand beckons me to do the same. I creep up and out the hole at tortoise pace and find myself yards from the beach. The enemy boats, which look like jet black inflatable balloons, are stranded on the beach, barely visible despite the flooding moonlight. I look behind and bask in the safety and relief of a huge tree trunk.

Azura rests her head against the tree trunk and slides into a reclining position. "Move down and stay down," she urges me.

"I confirm. No heat signatures."

"Dammit! A person can't just vanish in thin air, Alex!" the leader mutters. "Roger, what have you got?"

"Negative. Nothing on my side."

"God dammit!" the leader swears again. "Spread wider and move in. Slow and steady."

Azura steals a quick peek at the enemy soldiers. She turns and nods to herself. She cups her hands around her mouth and roars like a lion. Her deep voice sweeps the forest and ricochets off the canopy of trees, turning into a multitude of echoes.

"Stay on high alert, men!" The enemy leader's shout is on edge.

Suddenly, there are loud roars from all corners of the jungle, as if a pack of fifty angry lions is showing their displeasure on being woken up at an ungodly hour. The roars are followed by loud shouts of Sentinel men, tridents drawn and swords ready, as they come charging up above ground.

"Multiple heat signatures. Fire at will! Fire at will!"

The voice of the enemy leader is barely audible above the sudden din created by Sentinel warriors. Gunshots and grunts of grown men rise above the Sentinel cry.

Azura pulls out an arrow. She places it against her bow, pulls the string, turns to face the enemy, and takes aim. She waits. And waits. Bullets whiz past her. Her hand remains steady. Her eyes focused. But she does not release the arrow.

"What are you waiting for?" I shout.

And then without warning, she releases the arrow. I turn and peek around the tree. The arrow goes ramrod straight and pierces through the neck of the enemy leader. He fires wayward in every direction as he falls. I take cover. So does Azura.

"One aimed shot is better than a hundred released randomly," she says to me. "Let's see how long they last without a leader."

Azura readies another arrow in her bow. She pivots on her toes. This time she doesn't wait. She fires immediately. By the time the arrow hits the target, the unprotected neck of another soldier, Azura is ready and aiming with another arrow. She fires again. Hits again.

Within minutes the enemy succumbs. The battle comes to an end, much quicker than anybody anticipated.

"Victory to Sentinels!"

"Victory to Sentinels!"

Loud cheers go up. Sentinel warriors raise their tridents and pump the air.

Azura and I emerge from behind the tree and walk over to where the Sentinel warriors are congregating.

"Didn't expect it to be over so fast," I say to Azura as we walk, a broad grin on my face.

Azura suddenly stops. "What's that?" She strains her ears.

I smile. "What? I don't hear any…"

I stop speaking. The Sentinels stop celebrating. Dull, pulsing roars grow louder and louder. All of us cover our ears as the sound becomes unbearable. The trees sway wildly as wind picks up speed. It's like the heart-throb of a cyclone, beating the air into submission. Through the raging trees, I notice five beasts in the air, staring directly at us. Five military-grade helicopters.

Azura shouts something. But I can't hear her as the raging rotors of the helicopters numb my eardrums. Azura grabs my hand and pulls me behind the cover of a tree, right before a missile swooshes from a helicopter. The missile explodes violently, tearing apart the foliage and at least six Sentinel guards in its path. A deep crater forms where it had landed, torching every bush in its vicinity.

Another missile lands. And another, bombarding every nook, corner, and crevice of the forest, it seems. It's like the enemy wanted to smoke us out of the tunnels, before bringing in the heavy firepower.

"Run to the tunnels! Run to the tunnels!" yells Azura.

It takes me a while to understand her command in the cacophony of constant bombardment. And that's what saves me. Before I can dash to the nearest tunnel, all five helicopters release sprays of bullets. Sentinels who had heard Azura and ran for the tunnels, leaving the cover of trees, get ripped apart in the melee of bullets. Human flesh, burned and torn, gets tossed in every direction. The helicopters keep spewing bullets, wreaking the havoc of modern warfare on ancient Sentinels.

Suddenly, the firing stops.

The helicopter in the middle turns sideways, its rotor groaning loudly. It hovers for a moment before making a beeline for the heart of Sentinel Island, leaving us numb and bloody. Other helicopters dash after it, as if in pursuit.

"No!" Azura cries. She looks at me briefly. "The children... Aana!"

She bolts after the helicopters, toward the village center.

Chapter 26

Save the Children

"Azura!" I scream and dash after her.

Azura does not hear me or pretends not to. She keeps running for the village. She swerves around the deep crater formed by the missile and the raging fire that has engulfed a single tree. The fire, it is clear, is intent on spreading, threatening to wipe out the entire forest. But I doubt the green, leafy, and moisture-laden vegetation will be easy to burn down without a propellant.

I notice a Sentinel warrior standing at the edge of the crater, dazed and unmoving. His body is tattered and bloodied, shining red against the burgeoning fire in the backdrop. He looks at me. Blood streams down his cheeks.

"To the village!" I shout to him while running.

He does not respond.

I am about to shout again when he falls face-first into the crater. Dead.

A tremor runs through my body. It'd be this moment, the fall of a bloodied dead man, that would haunt me for the rest of my life.

I try to shrug it off and focus on the path ahead. It takes me a few seconds before I catch sight of Azura, right before she vanishes into the darker reaches of the jungle. I race after her, before a thought stops me.

I retreat to where I last saw the enemy leader. He lies prostate in a bush, an arrow sticking out from the neck. I pick up his machine gun. Then I reach over and unstrap his night-vision goggles, the piece of equipment that had given the enemy eyes and an upper hand at night. The headband of the goggles is dripping blood. I use the leaves of a nearby bush to clean it. Carefully, I put the goggles on. The headband still feels wet from the leftover blood. I look up, and I am immediately engulfed in a world of green and black. I rotate in my position, taking in my surroundings with a fresh pair of eyes. It's not like viewing in broad daylight, but for my untrained eyes, I can finally see in the dark. I fling the machine gun strap over my shoulder and sprint to the point where I last saw Azura.

"Wait!" says someone with a Sentinel accent.

I turn and find a figure, skirt flailing and hands waving, running toward me from the opposite direction. The figure is bright orange, as if its entire body is on fire. It boggles my mind, till I realize it's the night-vision goggles picking up human heat signature.

"Wait for me." The Sentinel warrior comes closer.

I remove the goggles to see clearly.

"Where is the queen?" The warrior asks.

It's Skinny. He looks jaded, beaten. Black soot covers his face, his chest. There is a deep gash on his right cheek, like someone slashed it with a pocket knife in a street fight. It looks raw, fresh. The blood has not crusted yet.

"What are you doing here?" I ask Skinny. "You had gone with Bani to the southern front. What happened?"

"All dead. Only I am left."

"All dead? How?"

"They came with those eyes." He points at my night-vision goggles. "They saw the watchmen on top of trees. Most watchmen were picked out one by one and killed. The few who were not jumped from the trees and ran for the tunnels. The enemy saw them flee into the tunnels. They didn't even have to search for the tunnel entrances. Once they located the entrances, they simply smoked us out."

"Smoked you out?"

"Yes. Threw in some sort of bombs that released smoke. The natural ventilation in the tunnels was not strong enough to remove smoke that gushed into every crevice. We scampered like rats. Came out coughing and heaving. The enemy was waiting outside with their guns. We were no match. It was like they were doing target practice. Within minutes, seemed like seconds, Sentinel dead bodies lay scattered. The forest reeked of Sentinel blood. The moon turned red."

"Wait, what?"

"Sentinel blood was spilled today. The moon has turned red."

"Ah!" I nod, finally understanding the expression.

I ask, "How did you survive?"

"I was one of the watchmen. There was a hollow in the tree where I sat watching the southern front. When the enemy came, I squeezed inside the hollow. My size helped."

I look at him from top to bottom. Skinny and short.

"The enemy didn't notice me. I stayed hidden on top of the tree, till I could sneak away. I came as fast as I could to warn the queen."

I shake my head. "Well, you are a little too late, my friend. Most of the Sentinels are dead here as well. The queen went to the village to save the children. I was rushing after her before I ran into you."

"Then we must go now," he says.

He curves his index finger and thumb and blows a shrill whistle.

"What was that for?" I ask. "The whistle."

A pall of sadness shrouds his face. "If there are any Sentinel survivors…" He looks around at the catastrophe that has befallen the Sentinels. "…they will know where to go."

He sighs. "Now come. We don't have much time. Those flying machines would have already reached the village."

We bolt into the thick woods. Skinny soon overtakes me. He is faster and better acquainted with the path. He uses his trident like a machete, clearing away any limp tree branches or bushes that try to slow him down. It takes us a mad run of half an hour before the edge of the village appears in sight.

Skinny stops, not wanting to run straight into a trap laid by the enemy. While he surveys the area, I collapse on the ground. My legs screech with fatigue, my heart pounds my chest from inside. I lie on the ground for the better part of a minute, before he shakes me up.

"Enough rest. We go," he says.

I push myself up. Gulp in deep tracts of air. Through the tree cover, I look at the huts in front of us. There is not a soul in sight. I adjust the night-vision goggles. No heat signatures. Slowly, we come out of the forest, staying vigilant at every step. We cross the huts on the outer rim and move in toward the village epicenter that harbors the Sentinel kids and mothers.

I suddenly stop. The flying beasts, the five helicopters, sit motionless in a single file in the clearing next to the village center. I pick up heat signatures inside the helicopters, one in each. The pilots are sitting inside, ready to fly the beasts away at a moment's notice. Or worse, fire another missile at whoever approaches from the front. There are maybe ten enemy soldiers on sentry duty outside the village center. I crouch and pull down Skinny, lest he is seen and fired at.

"We need to go around and come out from behind the helicopters," I say.

Skinny narrows his eyes, looking confused.

"Helicopter." I make a twirling motion with my finger. "The flying machine."

"Oh!"

We stay low and move along the periphery of the huts built in concentric circles. Not one candle is lighted inside the huts. There is pin-drop silence. It's like crouching through a graveyard at night, not knowing which ghost might spring up and take you by surprise. I don't encounter any heat signatures till we reach the other end of the circumference, behind the helicopter.

"What now?" I ask Skinny.

"We need to get inside and save the queen."

"I know. But how?"

"Only one way. We go through the front door."

The Apple

I slam my palm against my forehead at the redundant response. "I know that too, genius. But you can't just walk past the soldiers stationed at the front door. Easiest way to get killed."

I pause for a moment to think. "Okay, let's do this. I will go take out the pilots. Catch them by surprise and create a ruckus. The distraction will allow you to take on the soldiers at the front door. You think you can do it?"

Skinny nods. I can't help but smile at his confidence or over-confidence. A trident-bearing Sentinel having no qualms in taking on ten soldiers of a far superior enemy.

"But how will you take out the pilot?" he says. "And what noise will you create? That should be my signal to attack the soldiers."

I think for a second. I smile to myself as a simple solution presents itself. I raise the machine gun I am holding.

"This. You hear it fire, and you attack." I secure the machine gun and say, "Okay. No time to waste. Let's do it."

I leave Skinny in his place. I move sideways along the circumference of huts, such that I come out facing the side of the helicopter closest to me. I creep in further and reach the back wall of the last hut separating me and the helicopter. I peek around the corner of the hut. The pilot inside is engrossed in a handheld device. His hands twitch left and right, as if driving a car, and I realize the man is playing a video game on his mobile. I smile. Easy prey. Wouldn't even know what hit him.

My attention is suddenly diverted to the village center some twenty yards beyond the pilot. I hear loud voices from inside, the last sound waves of a heated argument dulled by thin walls. Seems like things are getting spiced up inside. The enemy soldiers outside pay no heed to the happenings inside.

I let out a sudden gasp. From afar, I had picked up the heat signatures of the soldiers at the door. What I had missed were the lifeless bodies of slain Sentinel guards strewn around them. One, two, three…I count five bodies on the ground, knowing full well that there would be more as Azura had left ten Sentinels to guard the children. My grip on the machine gun hardens as fresh rage ignites within me. I line up the machine gun straight at the pilot. The task is simple: fire indiscriminately, shatter the glass window of the helicopter, kill the pilot, and then kill a few soldiers at the door before Skinny takes over.

Click! I remove the safety switch of the machine gun. The action surprises me. It confirms that I have fired this weapon before, even though I have no memory of it. It gives me more confidence in my ability to handle the weapon.

I aim for the pilot's head.

I count in my head. One. Two…

Click! I hear the safety switch of a machine gun. But it is not mine. The cold metallic muzzle of the gun is thrust into my temple. From the corner of my eye, I see an enemy soldier snickering.

"Busted, you son of a bitch!"

Chapter 27
A Hostage Situation

"You are not going to believe who I found, Dr. Costello!" says the soldier, shoving me inside the village center, the largest hut in Sentinel dwelling.

A single oil lamp burns inside. It is cramped with people, but devoid of furniture, like a large storeroom that no one believes merits a decoration. It smells of sweat, urine, and fear. Crouching against the back wall are some twenty Sentinel children of various ages. They hang on to their mothers in desperation. Some sobbing, some shivering and some unmoving. The mothers, I notice, have formed a protective ring around the children. There is only one child outside the ring: Aana, who is clinging to her mother's leg. Azura stands firm facing Costello and his soldiers, some ten in number.

While the soldiers are in black military overalls, like the rest of their brethren, Costello is wearing a crisp three-piece suit, ready to attend his company's board meeting. It's like he has come to a charity function, doling out gifts to a destitute community. A gold pendant in the shape of a cross hangs from a thick cross-linked gold chain around his neck. It almost seems like the bulky chain and pendant are the cause of Costello's bent posture, not age.

"Well, well, well!" says Costello in unexpected exuberance. He sizes me up and then opens his arms, inviting me into an embrace. "I was led to believe that you were dead. But am I not glad to see you, my dear friend?"

"I am not your friend," I say, loud and clear.

The soldier behind me bangs the butt of his gun against my knee-cap. I immediately fall forward, searing pain pulsing from behind my knee.

"That's not how we treat our friends, Shawn," Costello says to the soldier, making no attempt to hide the sarcasm in his voice.

He comes close to me and bends over; the cross around his neck dangles. "I must thank you for finding the Garden of Eden. Michelle told me all about your little adventure. I must confess, I was not hopeful in the beginning. But I am glad you proved me wrong, boy."

I stare at him but remain silent.

He stands tall. "Now, as I was just explaining to the girl queen here…" He somehow managed to make "girl" sound like a slur. "…I do not want any more bloodshed. All I want is someone to take me to the Garden. Simple."

"Why don't you ask your lap-dog Michelle?" I say with disgust.

Costello shakes his head and smiles. "Fickle love of today's generation. One day they are in love, the next they are calling each other names."

"She tried to kill me."

"No, she didn't. She asked you, politely, to give her the apple. But you didn't."

"Levelling a gun against your head and making demands does not qualify as politeness." I fume.

"All semantics. She asked, you didn't give. You both fought, and the gun went off. An accident, if you ask me."

"It was no accident. She-"

"Quiet." Costello raises his hand and his voice, which engulfs him in a sudden bout of coughing. He recovers and says, "If it's any consolation, I have already exacted revenge on your behalf."

"What do you mean?"

Costello chews his lower lip, mulling over and deciding if he should say what's on his mind. Finally, with a slight nod and a nonchalant expression, he says, "I killed her."

The Apple

There is a sudden quiet inside the hut. No child sobbing, no mother cooing her child.

I hated Michelle until this moment. I should be glad, I guess, that I was avenged for what she did to me. But I am not glad. I am angry. Angrier than I have ever been. I am angry at Michelle for dying before I could avenge myself. I don't know how I would have avenged for what she did but killing her was not part of the plan. I am angry at myself for not being careful and getting caught by Shawn, the soldier, who I am now determined to kill with my bare hands. I am angry at Azura for running away from the battlefield and surrendering to the enemy, all for the sake of her kid. But I am mostly angry at the impostor businessman, who is playing us like puppets in a horror show at the carnival. Except, it's not a carnival, it's real life.

"You don't seem to be happy. I did your job for you."

In a split second, I am up on my feet, lunging for Costello's throat. I grab his wrinkly neck and squeeze it like a lemon. Garbled words tumble out of his mouth. He groans. His arms flail. I choke harder.

The next moment, powerful hands try to pull me away. It takes three soldiers in the room to save the old man from a chokehold that would have killed him had it lasted half a minute more.

Shawn punches me flat on the nose, while his two buddies hold my hands back. He punches me again. I hear the soft crack of a bone. Warm blood oozes out and trickles into my mouth. I spit out blood, lose my footing in the process, and drop to my knees. The soldiers let me fall. I try to breathe through the nose, but only end up making a whistling sound. My nasal airways are blocked. I take in big gulps of air through my mouth.

Costello recovers from the ordeal. He comes closer, massaging his neck. He seems to be deciding what to do. And then, without warning, he kicks me in the face. Blood and spittle splatters across the room before my head hits the floor. I grovel on the ground for some time, not knowing how to overcome the unbearable pain that has engulfed me.

Costello dusts off his suit, and says calmly, "Now, where was I?"

I cuss at Costello, but even I can't decipher the jumbled words that pour out with blood in my mouth.

"Like I was saying," Costello continues. "I don't want to go on an adventure like you and Michelle. You were sent to confirm the myth of the Garden. And now that I know it exists, I want direct entry. And only one person can give me that." He turns and glares at Azura.

"I have already told you, Arthur. I-"

"And I have told you, girl, stop calling me Arthur. Pick one: Dr. Costello or the chairman."

"But that's your name, isn't it…Arthur?"

Costello winces as if Azura had called him a bastard.

Azura continues, "The Arthur who became a Sentinel, lived among us as a brother and then deserted us. Only to return years later demanding something that was never his. Isn't that true, Arthur?"

Costello winces again at the name. "Stop. Calling. Me. Arthur." The old man's nostrils flare, as if on the verge of bursting. "I gave up that name and that pitiable life. Now, I am a beloved leader and a respected businessman. And, I demand to be treated with respect by you savages." He points his finger at the Sentinels in the room and moves it left to right and back, like his finger was a gun firing bullets at the Sentinels."

"I can't give you what you want, Arthur," Azura says flatly.

Costello takes one step forward and gives Azura a slap across her left cheek. The slap resounds in the enclosed space, dwarfing every other sound in the vicinity. Azura's feet falter, but she steadies herself. She doesn't massage the cheek, which is now burning red. She doesn't say a word, though I am sure she wants to utter plenty. All she does is snarl and glare quietly at Costello.

"Next time you call me 'Arthur', I will cut off your tongue. Am I clear?" he shouts the last bit, even though Azura is still within arm's reach.

Azura doesn't reply.

"Now, take me to the Garden, queen. Or, I will kill all Sentinel children one by one, cut their bodies into teeny-tiny pieces, and feed them to the lions."

"You dare not!" Azura's voice booms with a newfound ferocity.

"Watch me."

The old man snaps his fingers. One of the soldiers rushes forward and grabs the child closest to him - a three-year-old girl. The girl screams. Her mother squeals, intervenes, and pulls her child away from the soldier. A brief struggle ensues. But the soldier is having none of it. He backhands the mother across the face - once, twice and thrice - each slam more ferocious than the last. Realizing she is no match for the soldier, the mother grabs his feet and begs and pleads and appeals to the soldier's humanity. It enrages the soldier further. He tries to pry his foot out of the mother's grasp. Doesn't help. He shakes his leg, as one does to shake away a pesky fly. Doesn't help. The mother grasps harder, her cries of appeal growing louder. The soldier roars. Pulls back his other leg and slams the toe of his hard-leather boot into the woman's face. She immediately recoils and falls to the side, unconscious or dead, I can't tell. A hush falls over the hut before the screams and cries of the little girl come back with a deafening vengeance.

Satisfied with his deed, the soldier picks up the girl. She kicks at his chest with her tiny feet, punches with her little fists. Mute the sound and you'd find it almost comical, like an ant trying to whip an elephant. But it's the girl's heart-rending cry for help that fills each cell in my body with deep sorrow.

"Make her stop. She is killing my ears!" Costello tells the soldier.

The soldier puts his hand on the girl's mouth.

"Ouch!" he exclaims as the girl bites his index finger. He immediately pulls his hand away and massages the tip.

"The little rat bit me!" he exclaims again, only his voice is doused by the incessant cries of the little girl.

Costello tries to ignore the child and the soldier and turns to Azura. "Now, I will spare this child if…"

His facial muscles contract in frustration as he can't even hear his own voice above the din created by the squealing child. He curses under his breath, mumbling that is hard to decipher. But it's clear that he's had enough. He grabs the child by the front of the neck and dangles the little body in midair.

The little girl struggles. Her cries soften. Her face reddens.

"You are strangling her!" Azura shouts to Costello. "She will die! Let her go!"

The child flails, slamming her tiny arms against Costello's outstretched hand. Her legs flap in the air, as if paddling while swimming. Her cries have transformed into a deep-throated gurgle, an interplay of the air that wants to go in and lungs that want to inflate again. But Costello's hand doesn't twitch, his fingers wrapped tight around the girl's neck, squeezing it like a lemon.

"Stop!" says Azura.

She rushes forward to save the little girl. But the soldier, who has stopped massaging his finger, grabs Azura before she can touch Costello.

"Let me go!" orders Azura.

The soldier smiles, bemused that a queen he doesn't answer to is commanding him. He doesn't say a word, doesn't let her go.

"All I wanted was to do this peacefully. But no, you people don't listen, do you?" says Costello, his arm outstretched and unmoving. His fingers crush the fragile neck of the little girl.

"Stop. I beg you, Arthur. Please stop," Azura's voice cracks. Her eyes glisten with tears. Her resolve waning.

Costello's face reddens. "How many times do I have to tell you? Stop calling me Arthur!"

With that, Costello pulls back the hand holding the girl, like a baseball pitcher pulls back his hand to throw the ball, and slams the little girl into the ground. The girl lands with a soft thud, like a whisper announces its presence in a library. All eyes in the room dart to the girl, fearing the worst, fearing the death of innocence.

The Apple

Azura pulls away from the shackles of the soldier and rushes to the little girl. The girl is slumped face-down, her body limp. She makes no movement, no sound. Azura checks for a pulse on the hand. She checks for a pulse on the neck. She checks for air flowing in and out the nostrils. Her every movement more frantic than the last.

"NO! NO! NO!" she cries out loud. Tears flooding her eyes as she cradles the dead body of the little girl.

This is the weakest I have seen Azura, or the most humane, I am unable to judge.

Costello stands tall over Azura, his face smug, his breathing normal. He rotates his right shoulder as if pointing out the niggle in the shoulder from pitching the child hard into the ground. He moves past Azura and comes to a standstill behind Aana. He places his fingers on Aana's shoulders and grins, knowing full well that his intentions are clear enough for all to see, especially the mother, Azura.

"Maa!" Aana calls out to Azura. She tries to run to her mother, but Costello's much stronger hands hold her in place.

Azura looks up. If she was hysterical before, she goes ballistic seeing Costello towering over her kid. Her motherly instincts propel her toward Costello. But, before she can lay a hand on Costello, powerful hands grab her from behind. She twists and turns and kicks. All in vain. The soldier is stronger and has the advantage of a steady head over Azura, who is both pained and agitated.

"What will it be, queen?" Costello says calmly. "Are you taking me to heaven or shall we send your kid to hell?"

"You monster!" Azura yells.

Costello sighs. "It's all on you. You have an easy choice. I am just acting on your choice, on your behalf. Think of me as the executioner, but you are the judge, the decision-maker. So, I ask one last time, what will it be?"

Azura slumps to the ground, defeated and dejected.

"I will take you to the Garden," she whispers.

Chapter 28
The Road Back To Eden

The five helicopters zoom toward the Temple of God Saraph. Costello sits with the pilot in the lead helicopter. He holds Aana in his lap. His ransom. Azura and I sit in the back. Shawn and three of his buddies sit around us. All four soldiers have guns pointed at us, lest we instigate a fight or jump off the helicopter to escape. Some twenty-thirty soldiers follow in the other helicopters.

The cool night breeze, whooshing in from open doors on both sides of the helicopter, prickles crusts of dried blood around my nose. It hurts. Badly. Clumps of rusted blood block out vital oxygen. I take in big gulps of musty air. My mouth is dry from being permanently open against the constant bashing of cold wind. I close my mouth and swallow hard, quenching the burgeoning thirst with my own saliva. But it only ignites the deep-rooted pain in my nose. I open my mouth again, looking like a complete idiot.

"There! Turn right!" Azura points with her hand and shouts to Shawn, her voice barely reaches him above the jamming noise of the helicopter's rotary blades.

Shawn looks in the direction of Azura's extended hand. He speaks into the mouthpiece of a handheld radio, tells the pilot to turn right. Almost immediately, the helicopter swerves and jolts everyone to the side. We would all be falling out the door if not for the seat belts restraining us.

"See that tree? The tallest tree in the forest? Land around there." Azura shouts to Shawn.

The Apple

Shawn narrows his eyes, squints, and makes out the silhouette of the tree. The tree is an anomaly, at least ten feet taller than its brethren for miles. It's hard to miss, even in the barely-there moonlight.

Shawn confers with the pilot on the radio. He says to Azura, "There is no clearing to land the helicopter at the tree. Where is the closest clearing?"

Azura mulls over the question. "Go a couple of miles south of the tree. There is a river. We can land on the river bank and walk to the tree."

Shawn nods and conveys the instructions to the pilot. The helicopter zooms ahead. Within minutes the river is visible from the sky, its calm waters shimmering in the white moonlight. The pilot hovers over the river for a few seconds, searching for the right spot to land. The riverbank runs for miles, replete with stones and pebbles and rocks. The pilot notices an even patch. He nods to himself and gives a thumbs-up to Costello sitting next to him. We descend. With finesse and care, the pilot lands the helicopter.

Shawn jumps out. He beckons the rest of us. "Come, come. Let's go!"

He looks at his comrades. "I will lead. You guys follow these two. Stay vigilant and stay sharp. I don't want our hosts here to escape." He smiles for the first time, his crooked front teeth making him look more goofy than sinister.

The other four helicopters follow suit, landing haphazardly in dry, even patches on the river bank. There is barely enough room to accommodate all the flying machines.

Shawn looks at Azura. "You try to escape and your daughter…"

He motions toward Costello holding Aana in his arms. Shawn doesn't complete the sentence. He just smiles, the meaning fully conveyed and well understood.

I follow Azura out of the helicopter. The jagged stones prick the underside of my uncovered feet. I grimace and let out a groan.

"This way," says Azura, her face devoid of emotion. If the stones are hurting her, she doesn't show. If the fear of losing her daughter is crippling her, she doesn't show.

Azura leads the pack of thirty plus into the thick forest. The pilots stay behind on Costello's instructions, ready for a quick getaway if needed.

The dark grip of the canopied forest engulfs us. I have forgotten how many times I have been consumed by the jungle since arriving on Sentinel Island. Somehow, it makes me feel at peace, at home. Like getting under a snug blanket in winters. Guided by flashlights courtesy of the soldiers, and moonlight courtesy of the cosmos, we march for the tallest tree. I remember that tree more vividly than my own name. It was there that all my dreams turned to reality. It was there that I saw a creature more awe-inspiring and more fear-instilling than any on Earth. It's the tree shrouding the Temple of God Saraph. The tree out of which came the real seven-headed snake. Yellow eyes, blood-red tongues, and emerald-green horns. And two slimy hands. I shudder at the memory.

The memory also gives me hope. Saraph, the guardian of Eden, is the last line of defense for the Sentinels. It's the reason Azura gave in to Costello's demands. It's the reason she is leading us to Eden. She knows, as well as I do, that one cannot simply enter Eden without facing the challenges. Without proving yourself. Saraph won't allow it. And no human would challenge a two-story-tall snake. That is Azura's hope. Our last hope.

We reach the Temple of God Saraph. The stone idol of Saraph welcomes us with hands joined at the palms.

"Holy crap!" exclaims Shawn. He moves his flashlight up and down, left and right, taking in the idol.

"You Sentinels have quite an imagination." He smiles, his crooked incisors on full display.

Costello clears his throat. "It's not a creation of imagination, Shawn. It's a depiction of reality."

Shawn gawks at Costello, his smile gone, his mouth open.

Costello moves past Shawn toward the tree. "Yes, Shawn, there is a real seven-headed snake guarding the Garden of Eden. Sentinels call it God Saraph."

He knows about Saraph! Alarm bells ring in my head. I feel exposed and exasperated, as if someone just poured a bucket full of cold water on my sand castle. I cast a side glance at Azura. She doesn't meet my eyes, her full focus on Costello. There is no surprise on her face. No amazement. Almost like she expected Costello to know.

Costello laughs, a short, mocking laugh. "They forget that I was a Sentinel once, even if briefly. And, like all Sentinels, I was initiated to the tribe by God Saraph." Costello uses both his hands to air-quote "initiated".

"Is the snake still alive, Dr. Costello?" asks Shawn.

"My guess would be - yes."

"So, what do we do about the snake?" asks Shawn.

"Kill it, of course."

Chapter 29

Saraph, The Last Hope

Shawn looks at Costello, unsure how easy it will be to kill a monstrous snake. Costello's comfortable countenance makes him more disturbed than calm. He fidgets in his position as fear slowly spreads its tentacles, gripping him in its charm.

"What next, queen?" Costello looks squarely at Azura.

Azura doesn't look at Costello. Doesn't utter a word. She bends and pulls out the snake-head dagger strapped to her thigh. She thrusts the dagger into the tree and opens the secret door - the hole of nothingness. The hole is blacker than the shroud of night, the contrast stark and visible.

I look at Shawn and the army of soldiers behind him. Their mouths are agape, their bodies still, their eyes wide. Like kids at a magic show seeing a rabbit being pulled out of a hat for the first time. Costello, on the other hand, is smiling, marveling at the magic trick he must have seen before during his initiation ceremony. Appreciative, but not surprised anymore.

"Here you go," says Azura. "Your direct entry to the Garden of Eden."

Shawn is the first one to find his voice. "Is the…" he clears his throat. "Is the Garden inside that dark hole?"

"Yes," comes Azura's curt reply.

"The snake is definitely inside that dark hole, Shawn. The Garden, we will see when we get past the snake."

Shawn gulps loudly.

"Give me the dagger, woman," says Costello.

The Apple

Azura hesitates. Doesn't give the dagger.

"I will not say it again. The dagger…please." Costello stretches his hand, waiting to receive the dagger.

Azura steps forward and reluctantly puts the dagger in Costello's outstretched hand.

Costello sheathes it.

"I promised to give you direct entry to the Garden," says Azura. "I have kept my promise. Now, let my daughter go."

"Not so fast. You need to take me to the Garden, not just open the door for me. You and our treasure hunter here…" He points to me. "…will lead me to the Garden, pluck the apples for me, and then get me back here safely. You do that, and I will let your daughter go. That's the deal."

Azura starts to protest but stops. She mulls over the deal propositioned by Costello and sighs deeply.

Finally, she says, "Okay, let's go."

She starts to walk to the hole in the tree.

"Wait," says Costello.

Azura stops in her tracks.

"First, call the snake," Costello continues. "It's the only obstacle in our path now. We kill the snake, and then we go pluck us some apples."

"God Saraph is immortal, indestructible," says Azura. "He cannot be killed."

Costello grins. "We will see about that." He turns to his soldiers. "Guns at the ready, boys."

"I am telling you," Azura protests. "We announce our arrival to God Saraph, and we will never get to the Garden. Stealth is our best bet."

"You are telling me that the Gatekeeper of Eden will never know we stepped into the Garden. You take me for a fool? We call the snake. We kill it. And then it's a walk in the park."

Azura shrugs. I see the hint of a sly smile on her lips. Before anyone notices, the smile is gone. She wants this. She wanted to call God Saraph all along.

She faces the tree, closes her eyes and chants, "Sarp-Sarp-Sarp! Sarp-Sarp-Sarp!"

All thirty-odd soldiers aim their machine guns at the black hole in the tree.

"Sarp-Sarp-Sarp! Sarp-Sarp-Sarp!"

Costello puts Aana on the ground. He holds a pistol in one hand and the dagger in the other, ready to take on the seven-headed God.

"Sarp-Sarp-Sarp! Sarp-Sarp-Sarp!"

I stay back, not wanting to be a casualty in the massacre that is about to unfold: the massacre of Costello and his soldiers. I have no doubt that they will not come out of this alive. They may have modern guns and a tiny dagger, but Saraph is a God, a twenty-foot, thick-skinned, venomous reptile with two bulldozers for hands.

"Sarp-Sarp-Sarp! Sarp-Sarp-Sarp!"

"Aim for the eyes first," Costello shouts to his men. "And then, fire at the exposed belly when the snake opens it to take out its hands."

"Hands?" soldiers say in unison, their own hands holding the guns suddenly unsteady and limp.

"Yes, two hands," Costello says as if it's normal for snakes to have hands, like humans. "Don't be afraid boys. Remember, it's only a snake. A mortal snake."

The soldiers nod, not convinced if it'd be that easy to kill the snake God.

"Sarp-Sarp-Sarp! Sarp-Sarp-Sarp!"

A loud hiss emanates from the dark reaches of the hole. Silence follows and grips us. Azura stops chanting. The soldiers stop fidgeting. I stop breathing for a moment. God Saraph is here. Not visible yet, but here.

"On the ready, boys!" Costello tries to shore up the confidence of his men. I doubt it helps, as evident from the trembling hands of most of the soldiers. It's clear that they did not sign up for this. And now they are caught in Costello's greed and ambition, their deaths minutes away from reality.

Through the nothingness slithers out a thick, dark mass. It expands and enlarges, like the shadow of a monster rising from its ashes. The mass shrouds the door in the tree, and then the entire tree trunk and then most of the redwood tree itself, eclipsing the moonlight in its wake. A gloom befalls the forest. It's God Saraph.

God Saraph opens its eyes, two on each of the seven heads, dousing the night with yellow gleam streaming from the eyes.

"Welcome, Queen Azura."

Azura bends on one knee, her head bowed in deference.

"A talking snake?" Words tumble out of Shawn's mouth in surprise. Renewed fear entangles him. He casts a side glance at Costello, the pain of betrayal painted on his face.

"Who goes there?" Saraph's loud baritone freezes everyone in their spot, sending a chill along our spines.

Saraph slithers forward and stops on seeing Costello few paces behind Azura.

"Ah, Arthur! It's been a while."

Costello gives a mock-bow. "God Saraph! An honor to see you again."

"I see that you have brought weapons and an army of friends to honor me." Saraph's middle head acknowledges Costello, while the other heads hiss madly at the soldiers surrounding Costello, baring sharp white fangs as big as a grown elephant's tusk.

"Wouldn't be necessary if you just step aside and let us pass to the Garden of Eden."

Saraph hisses loudly, as if laughing at the request.

"You know I can't allow it. You have to go through me to get into the Garden."

Saraph slithers forward slowly but menacingly, now twenty yards from Costello.

"So be it!"

Costello fires his pistol, aiming at the shiny yellow eye on the middle head.

Saraph bows its head just in time. The bullet hits the thick skin on the head and ricochets off. No bruise, not even a scratch. The snake God hisses, mad and angry at the audacity shown by a tiny human.

Azura scrambles to the side, not wanting to get caught in the cross-fire. I jump after her, finding haven behind a large tree trunk.

Costello grabs Aana and retreats.

"Fire at will! Fire at will!" he says, as he flees behind a tree.

The soldiers bombard Saraph with heavy machine-gun fire. The blasts boom, ravaging the stillness of the night. But the bullets ricochet off the snake's skin, spraying the nearby trees haphazardly. I dig deeper into my crouching position as bullets brush past me, chipping away the edge of the tree trunk. Flying wood-splinters form a cloud of dust in no time, as if a herd of buffaloes had stampeded through sand.

Saraph's gigantic mass swoops down in one quick motion. The snake grabs the nearest soldier with its mouth. The soldier is caught off-guard. Pointed fangs pierce into the soldier's body like a sharp knife cuts through steak. The soldier shrieks.

"Help me, Shawn! Help me! Please help m-"

One second, his shrill cries boom in the forest. The next second his cries are gone, swallowed whole by the snake.

Chapter 30
God Can Fall

Saraph raises its hands in the air and hisses loudly, like a footballer does on scoring a goal. In Saraph's case, it's scoring a soldier.

Shawn rushes behind a tree. He opens fire, aiming for the snake God's eyes. Saraph lowers its head and slithers toward Shawn, flicking the bullets like lint on the shoulder.

Four or five soldiers take advantage of the tussle between Shawn and Saraph. They leap forward, throw grenades at the snake and duck. The blasts take us all by surprise, creating large plumes of smoke and dust around Saraph.

Is Saraph dead? Is the mighty snake God dead?

Dust settles and smoke dissipates away. The snake God stands tall and unscathed.

How? I look at Azura with wide-open, bewildered eyes.

She smiles, and gives a mysterious chuckle, which tells me that nothing she is seeing is out of the ordinary. But, to me, these happenings are extraordinary. Period.

Saraph changes direction. Grenades, the reason. The soldiers turn around and run. They have seen enough to know that they are no match for the snake God. Neither are their machine guns, nor their grenades. Between fight and flight, they only have one option. Flight.

Soldiers scamper away. Saraph follows. Saraph is faster and taller. It bends mid-slither, reaches out with its hands, and grabs two soldiers from behind. The soldiers look like toy dolls clutched between Saraph's fingers.

"I am sorry. I am sorry. Please let me go." One of the soldiers pleads.

Saraph hisses, but it sounds like a screech. The hands squeeze the soldiers' torsos, suffocating and crushing their frail human bodies.

"I can't…can't breathe…let…go…please."

The grip hardens, the squeeze tightens.

And, in an instant, the two soldiers explode, like a can of beer bursting under pressure, spilling and spraying its contents everywhere. Blood and fluids and gooey organs drip from Saraph's hands.

A soldier close to Azura and me, hiding behind a tree, retches and vomits. The mind-numbing graphic and nauseating stench of fresh death stir up a riot in his stomach. The retching probably reminds him of the exploding soldiers, and he vomits again, emptying his stomach of every sliver of food and every ounce of bile.

Three brave souls step forward and bombard Saraph with bullets. Saraph stands tall, hands folded inside the belly, amused at the brave ones. It's like Saraph is deciding if the soldiers are dumb or dumber. Did they not learn from the plight of their buddies, or has adrenaline rush made them dumb?

And then, without warning, Saraph pounces on them. Like a crow who pecks at grains fast and repeatedly, Saraph picks up soldiers one by one with its seven humongous mouths, swallowing them alive. It seems like the who-can-eat-the-most-soldiers contest, and Saraph is winning. Soldiers vanish by the dozen.

"You scum!" Shawn comes out of his hiding position and bombards the snake with a fresh volley of bullets. The bullets go in every direction, a perfect example of carpet bombing, of hoping one lands in the right area. None land in the right area.

"The belly, Shawn! Go for the exposed belly," Costello shouts from behind the tree, egging on the leader of his mercenaries.

Shawn stops, processes the information. He repositions himself and fires at the snake's belly. Saraph brings his hands down, shielding and parrying away all bullets from the belly.

Saraph moves forward, gains ground quickly. Shawn retreats, step-by-step, never taking his finger off the trigger. Ten feet from Shawn, Saraph lowers its impenetrable heads, protecting its belly. It frees up its hands to swoop in from the side and grab Shawn like a rag doll. Saraph picks up Shawn, clutched between both its hands.

The machine gun drops from Shawn's hands. He struggles as the grip tightens. The scene has an uncanny similarity to the fate of the soldiers whose internal organs were squeezed out of them.

"Let me go!"

Saraph stands tall and laughs, throwing its head back and guffawing as if it just heard a hilarious joke.

"You petty humans never learn," says Saraph. "Time to say goodbye."

Shawn wriggles and struggles.

Saraph opens its mouth. Venom drips from its sharp fangs. It brings up Shawn, clutched between both its hands, ready to swallow the soldier whole. At least no more human explosions, I think.

Boom! A single shot reverberates.

Saraph stops.

Boom! Another shot.

Saraph stumbles. It looks at its exposed belly, now leaking gooey, red blood. It looks in the direction of the shot. Costello stands tall, holding a revolver, a toothy grin plastered on his face.

"Time to say goodbye, God Saraph."

Boom! Another shot pierces through the snake's belly.

Saraph lowers its hands, dropping Shawn as the grip loosens. Its massive body sways and rotates unsteadily. Its eyes flicker. The next instant, it falls in a heap, its fangs biting dust, the bright yellow light gone from its eyes.

I gasp in disbelief. The snake God is dead.

Chapter 31

Welcome To Eden, Again

"A God, you said?" Costello mocks Azura, standing at the dead mass that once belonged to Saraph.

Azura looks pained and disheveled and ashen. Her eyes are unblinking. She cannot believe what has transpired.

Costello grabs little Aana by the hair and pulls her close. Aana screams "Maa!" in agony.

Azura jolts out of her trance, brought to reality by the screams of her child.

"Shall we?" Costello directs his question at Azura and nods to the hole in the tree.

"You don't need us anymore," pleads Azura. "Your path to Eden is clear now. No more obstacles, no more dangers. Let Aana go and no Sentinel will stand in your way. You have my word."

"I don't need your word. I need action. Get me to Eden, get me home safely, and you have my word that nothing will happen to your daughter."

Azura's face contorts in anger. I know she wants to destroy Costello, just like Saraph crushed soldiers with bare hands. But neither does she have the strength of Saraph or the bargaining chips. She is being blackmailed. She knows it and can't do zilch about it.

"Okay, let's go then. The sooner we get it done the better." Azura walks off to the door in the tree - the big black hole of nothingness.

Costello looks around at his men. Exactly six men have survived the ordeal. Plus Shawn.

"You coming, Shawn?" Costello snarls.

Shawn is in shock. He stands like a zombie, unmoving and silent. His clothes are dirty and dripping goo - or whatever sticky mucous dripped from Saraph's hands.

"Shawn!" Costello barks, jolting Shawn out of shock.

The soldier looks around, unsure of his surroundings. "Sorry, you said something to me, Dr. Costello?"

Costello walks over to Shawn, grabs him by the collar, and shakes the daylights out of him.

"Get a grip on yourself, boy. You are a soldier, for Christ's sake, not a sissy."

Shawn looks at his shoes. The six surviving soldiers, almost in unison, look down as well. It's like Costello is speaking to all remaining mercenaries through their leader, Shawn.

"Look up!"

Shawn instantly stands to attention, looking straight at Costello. All six soldiers look up too.

"That's better. Now, you are going to get into that tree-hole and lead the way. Understand, soldier?" Costello raises his voice, as if invoking the brave soldier inside the shell-shocked, fearful man in front of him.

"Sir, yes, sir!" Shawn barks.

"Good. Lead the way, soldier."

Shawn picks up the machine gun that had fallen and slings it on his shoulder.

"You three." He points to his men. "Stay with me in the front. The rest of you stay close at the rear."

Shawn walks to the redwood tree warily and begrudgingly. Three of his men follow him. Shawn points his gun at the hole and switches on the torch-like light retrofitted on the gun barrel. Like laser, the light pierces through the darkness inside the hole to reveal more darkness. He bends his head and enters the hole. Almost immediately he is swallowed by nothingness. Azura follows suit, followed by the three soldiers.

I look at Costello. He points his revolver at me and gestures it toward the hole. No words are exchanged.

I enter the temple. The first step falls on an even, flat surface. The air smells clean, feels warm. Almost welcoming.

The second step almost sends me packing down the steep stairs. I grab the inside of the tree trunk for support. It's surprisingly soft to touch, like smoothened wood.

"Watch your step!" says Azura from somewhere below me.

I notice the faint beams of light emanating from the soldiers' guns.

"The stairs are steep," continues Azura. "Please pass the message to Costello. I don't want Aana tumbling down the stairs because of the slow instincts of an old man."

I relay the message to Costello, who is still standing at the threshold, holding Aana by the shoulders.

He nods. "Keep going," he says.

Step-by-step, I proceed downstairs. The passageway feels like traveling inside an air vent: confined, constricted, airy. We trudge at a slow pace. Hundred, two-hundred, even after five hundred steps the staircase doesn't end. I hear Azura's even breathing in front of me. I hear Costello out of breath behind me.

"How long before we reach the Garden?" Costello squeals from behind, like a little kid snapping at his parents during a long, boring road trip.

"Halfway there!" Azura shouts.

"Halfway to go," I repeat the message.

"I heard it the first time, you moron!" Costello curses between gasps for air. "I am sweating like I am under a rain shower."

I disregard the mutterings of the old man and keep going.

The thousand-step staircase finally comes to an end, leaving my knee joints on fire, my calf muscles trembling. The air suddenly opens up, like coming out of a tunnel into an open field. Fragrance of fresh flowers and moist grass greets me. The Garden smells close, but not a light is visible in the darkness except the muted lasers from soldiers' guns.

"Welcome to the Garden of Eden!" announces Azura, much to the surprise of the rest of us.

Chapter 32

Where Is The Tree?

I am taken aback. The Garden in my dream was sunny. It was resplendent. It was like morning sunshine, radiant and blissful. Nothing close to it is visible.

"Where?" I say defiantly.

"Here," says Azura. "The Garden starts from right here."

"This can't be Eden!" says Costello, still huffing from the trek. He stands tall and points his revolver at us. "Stop messing with me, kids. This looks like a burial ground. Where is my frickin' Garden? Where is my frickin' apple tree?"

"Right there!" Azura points in the dark. "Can't you see?"

None of us can see what or where she is pointing in the dark. Of course, she forgets that only Sentinels can see in the dark.

Costello removes the safety of his revolver with a sharp click. He thrusts the tip of the barrel against Aana's temple. The little girl whimpers and cries softly. Tears roll down her cheeks that only her mother can see in near darkness.

"You take me for a fool? I am asking nicely for the last time, queen. Where is my Garden?"

"You are standing in the Garden for God's sake." Azura explodes. "You can't see because you are blind, old man. Blinded by darkness because it is night time. Wait till sunrise and you shall see."

"What are you talking about? We are five hundred feet underground. How does it matter if it is day or night outside?"

"Bend down. Touch the floor."

"What do you mean?"

"You heard me. Bend and touch the floor. Tell me what you feel?"

Costello does as instructed. I do the same because, like Costello, I am not convinced.

Moist grass.

"Grass." Costello mutters under his breath.

Azura heaves a sigh. "Right. Eden is an underground Garden. Like I said, you are standing in it."

"What did you mean we shall see it after sunrise?" I ask. "It is impossible for sunlight to reach this far below ground."

"You need to see it to believe it." Azura chuckles mysteriously.

Costello looks at his glow-in-the-dark Rolex. "Sunrise shouldn't be long now."

Azura says, "Let's walk to the middle of the Garden. It has the best view of sunrise."

Azura leads the way, followed by Shawn and his men. The rest of us follow their laser beams.

The Garden is eerily quiet. No insects, no animals. A pleasant, constant breeze glides into my hair. The soft fragrance of roses and daffodils and tulips sends a wave of calm across my body. Mind relaxed, I suddenly feel tired and sleepy. How long since I last slept?

"How big is this place?" Shawn whispers, more to himself than a question to Azura.

"Wait, you will see for yourself soon," Azura answers.

We walk the better half of thirty minutes before Azura asks us to stop.

"Let's sit here," she says.

My tired body doesn't need another invitation. I sit with a thump next to Azura.

"Soldiers," says Costello. "Stay on guard, stay standing. I don't want any mischief from these two."

Costello sits a few feet from us, his bones creaking, his revolver steady, pressed tight against Aana's temple. No one speaks for the next five minutes. It's a welcome breather. The adrenaline subsides, weariness springs up.

The Apple

"Why now?" Azura breaks the silence all of a sudden.

"Excuse me?" says Costello.

"I am asking why now after all these years? You have been gone a long time. You knew about the existence of the Garden for years. Thirty, forty years? Why come now, why not earlier?"

"Trust me, I wanted to. For more reasons than just to steal the fruits of immortality," Costello says mysteriously, his voice almost sullen as he remembers memories, good and bad. "But I needed time to gather resources. To gather more information. To take the Sentinels, you, by surprise. Most important, I-"

He pauses, thinking. It's like he is contemplating if he should reveal something that he has never told anyone. Something that betrays who he is. Or who he has become.

"What? Say it." Azura pushes him, her voice oozing a sense of urgency.

"Most importantly, I needed time to face your-"

"What's that?" Shawn suddenly interrupts Costello. "Up there!"

We look up. A single dot of light, emitting hues of red and orange, has appeared at the highest point in the enclosed space. Like a single red star adorning the night sky, celebrating its solitary existence. The dot grows larger, becoming the orange morning sun, coming closer and closer.

I stand up, no longer tired, but intrigued.

And then, without warning, a single ray of sunlight, like a bolt of lightning, falls on the ground. I jump in surprise, cover my face, blinded by the sudden burst of light. I blink fervently, my eyes adjusting to the divine light streaming from above.

Costello gasps.

Shawn gasps.

Like a spotlight, the single ray of sunlight illuminates the Apple Tree of Immortality.

Chapter 33

The Cunning Child

The tree bursts into life. It's divine. It's magical. It stands dignified and magnificent on top of a petite, velvet-green hill. Its leaves are dazzling green, the apples brilliant red. It's fresh, it's spectacular, it's enthralling.

Costello drops to his knees. He drops his head. I am not sure if in prayer or relief. The revolver remains in his hand.

"Oh my God. Oh my God." Shawn keeps running his hand through his hair, coming to terms with what he has just seen.

The single ray of sunlight expands across the entire surface area of the ceiling. Soon, the dark, night-like ceiling is transformed into the morning sky. It's dappled with furry white clouds against an azure canvas. It's like the ceiling is reflecting and mimicking the sky outside.

Azura looks up, then at me, her face beautiful, her mouth sporting a smile. "It's going to be a bright, sunny day today," she says.

"Is it reflecting the sky outside? How?" Shawn asks. His voice has an exuberance that I have not heard before.

"Well, I am sure some smart scientist will be able to answer it for you. But for now, I suggest you just enjoy the view."

The entire garden and the seemingly unending waves of fresh green grass comes into focus. The lilies, the daffodils, the iris - a riot of colors blooming with child-like abandon. And in the center of the Garden, on top of a grassy hill, the main attraction - the apple tree.

Costello finishes his prayer, bends forward and kisses the ground. When he sits up, I catch a glimpse of a shiny metal in the ankle-high grass.

The dagger of God Saraph has slipped out of its sheath. Unaware, he stands and faces Azura.

"I must thank you, Queen Azura."

Aana sits, as if tired and cranky, right next to the fallen dagger. Costello disregards the little girl and faces Azura again.

"Forced or not," Costello continues. "You did your part and showed me heaven today."

Aana discreetly picks up the dagger.

What is the kid doing?

Slowly and slyly, Aana slips the dagger inside her skirt. If I had not seen the dagger fall out of Costello's pocket, I wouldn't even have bothered to look at Aana. But now I can't take my eyes away from the little girl. I try to keep a straight face, looking directly at Costello, lest he follows my gaze and catches the kid.

"Now that I have done my part, please release my daughter," Azura begs him.

"And let go of my only leverage?" Costello chuckles. "Not happening, my queen. Not happening. And you forget, you also need to pluck these apples for me…" He points to the tree. "…and take me back safely and bid me goodbye as I fly away on a helicopter. Only then will I release your daughter."

Aana starts to bawl suddenly. "Maa!" she cries, seeking the comfort of her mother. She rubs her crotch and fidgets her legs, as kids do when nature's call is beyond control and no bathroom is in sight.

"Aana, what happened, baby?" Azura looks worried.

Aana's cry becomes louder. "Need to pee. Now! Now!" she squeals between sobs.

Azura starts to stride over to her daughter.

"Wait right there!" Costello shouts, his hand outstretched, pointing the revolver directly at Azura.

"Come on, Dr. Costello. It's nature's call. Let me attend to my daughter. Please." Azura pleads. "You can stay behind me and keep your gun pointed at my head. One wrong move and you can kill me. Just let me attend to my little girl. Two minutes is all I ask."

Aana continues to bawl while Costello contemplates.

"One minute. Behind that bush of flowers. One wrong move and I will fire. You can count on it."

Azura nods and runs over to her daughter. She picks up the crying child and rushes her to a nearby bush. She turns Aana away from prying eyes, so only Azura's back is visible to us. Costello follows them, but maintains a good distance, giving privacy to the mother and child. Aana stops crying as Azura starts to whistle, helping the kid relieve herself. Apparently.

My heart is racing. I cannot shirk off the feeling that it's a ruse. A transaction is underway. And it has nothing to do with nature, but everything to do with cunning.

"What's taking so long?" Costello grows nervous.

"Just a moment," Azura replies without turning to face Costello.

I grow nervous. Will the dagger change hands? Or will they get caught?

"Your minute is up! Come on, let's go."

"I said just a moment," Azura raises her voice.

Costello forgets about privacy and walks over.

My heart jumps into my throat.

Costello stands tall over Azura and clicks off the revolver's safety, the gun barrel a whisker from Azura's head.

This is the moment the queen dies, I tell myself.

"I gave you one minute. Now step away from the kid."

Azura adjusts Aana's pine skirt and steps back. "There. She is done."

Costello grabs the kid and asks Azura to stand to the side. Azura saunters back. Her eyes meet mine. She smiles. And then, she winks at me, letting me in on the secret.

The transaction is complete.

Chapter 34
The Rebirth

Costello tightens his grip on Aana and walks toward the apple tree. Azura and I walk after Costello. Shawn and his cronies follow, their guns pointed at us.

"Psst!" Azura whispers to catch my attention.

I keep looking straight ahead. I nudge closer to Azura, our hands brushing each other's as we walk alongside.

"Be ready to grab the gun," Azura murmurs.

"Oi!" Shawn shouts from behind. "No talking. Move apart."

I look at Shawn, my hands raised in mock surrender. I move away from Azura.

What did she mean? I ask myself. Be ready to grab the gun? Whose gun? Shawn's? Costello's?

We reach the edge of the hill on which stands the mighty apple tree. We start the short climb. After climbing a few paces, Azura, all of a sudden, slows. My heart races. My senses become more aware. Something is about to happen. Azura bends and puts her hands on her knees, as if tired.

Shawn moves forward and thrusts the gun into Azura's lower back. "Keep moving," he says.

Azura straightens up. Shawn lowers his gun.

The next moment happens in a flash. Azura swivels on her toes. In one sharp motion she rams the dagger into Shawn's wrist. The gun falls from his hand. He yelps, a loud shrill cry of pain. Even before the first drop of blood trickles down, Azura pulls out the dagger, sidesteps and hauls Shawn into a chokehold, the sharp tip of the dagger millimeters from his neck.

I jump for the gun. Grab it and point at the soldiers behind Shawn. All six soldiers have their guns aimed at me.

"Drop your weapons! On your knees. Now!" A soldier shouts.

Costello looks back. The bloodied dagger in Azura's hand, and blood dripping from Shawn's, sends shock waves to his brain. He raises his revolver and jabs it in Aana's temple. His intent clear - to threaten Aana, or worst, kill the child if it comes to that.

"Drop your weapons! Now!" The same soldier howls again.

Azura disregards the soldier.

"Let my daughter go!" Azura looks squarely at Costello.

"Or what?"

"I will kill your friend here."

She pokes Shawn's neck with the dagger tip. A single dot of blood appears. Shawn whimpers in agony, enduring the affliction to his wrist.

"Ha!" Costello guffaws. "You are kidding, right?" he says.

"I promise you, I will kill Shawn."

"Be my guest. Go ahead." The amusement is heavy in Costello's tone.

Azura shuffles in her position. She was not expecting this.

Shawn stops whimpering, stops fidgeting. He locks Costello in a cold, hard stare.

"Go right ahead. Kill him," Costello says. "There are six others ready to take his place." He points to the other soldiers with his revolver.

"Or you can stop with your antics, girl. Give me the dagger and let's get us some apples."

"So be it."

In one sharp motion Azura thrusts the dagger in Shawn's neck. His eyes balloon in surprise. Azura twists the dagger, completely butchering his jugular artery, and draws out the blade. Shawn falls face-first, his eyes still wide open, never to blink again.

Azura twists on her back and throws the dagger, like a dart, at Costello. He jumps in surprise, thinking the dagger would pierce his head. It doesn't. It falls inches from his feet.

"There, take the dagger." Azura's face is devoid of emotion.

Costello catches the lump in his throat and gulps. Without letting go of Aana, glaring at Azura, he comes forward, picks up the dagger and pockets it.

"Tch, tch! I never picked you out for a vicious girl. All this wasteful killing. Did you even think how this violence would scar your child?"

"Don't you worry about my child. We don't cocoon our kids in fake reality like you outsiders. We raise lions, not dogs." Azura burrows her glare into Costello. "Kids need to know reality from the time they are born. You cannot be scared if you embrace the world for what it is. As for my daughter, she should know the difference between saint and scum, and how to rid this world of scum like you and your friend Shawn."

Costello glares. Nobody speaks a word for few seconds.

"Good," Costello says finally. "She would be happy to embrace death when I put a bullet in her tiny little head."

Azura's face twitches, her body remains steady. No word spoken.

Costello looks beyond Azura and peers at the mercenaries. "Danny!" He picks out one of the men. "It's your lucky day. You have been promoted to take Shawn's place."

The soldier steps out and salutes. "Thank you for-"

Costello clutches Aana by the hair and walks away, leaving the soldier hanging.

Danny recovers. "Give me the gun," he orders.

I hand over the gun.

"Move. Both of you."

Azura and I start walking. We reach the top of the petite hill within minutes. Costello soaks in the glory of the apple tree. He is enchanted, almost enamored. When I had first found Eden, I had also experienced this pull, this attraction so close to the tree. It's like opposite poles of a magnet, once in vicinity you can't stop the attraction. The closer you get, the stronger the pull. I see it in Costello's eyes. The same pull, the same greed. He wants the apple. He wants to touch it, pluck it, and taste it. He can't control the urge. This is what he has waited for so long.

Costello strides to the tree. He cups the bottom-most apple in both his hands, like it's the precious face of his beloved. His hands caress the apple, his fingers stroke it. He is bewitched, it seems.

He plucks the apple with a soft tug.

Almost immediately thunder crackles. The sunny day inside the underground Garden transforms. Dark clouds gather. The light dims. It's like we are in a movie studio, and with a push of a button someone has changed the backdrop. A burst of lightning almost blinds us with its glare. We blink, in unison. When the eyes adjust, we find ourselves enveloped by gray and sinister evening.

"What black magic is this?" Costello demands of Azura. His voice betrays anxiety and trepidation.

"You are not worthy of the gift." A voice echoes in the enclosed Garden. It's not Azura's. It's not me. It's none of us. It booms from the sky above and reverberates from the ground below. It has an uncanny familiarity. I think I have heard it before. Where?

"Who said that?" The pitch in Costello's voice is high, confidence low.

Suddenly, the ground shakes. We swing back and forth. An earthquake. The sway is terribly strong. All of us are swept from our feet, unable to balance. We tumble.

The trunk of the apple tree turns fiery orange, like it has caught fire. It spits burning light in every direction, pulling our eyes to it like spotlight pulls an audience.

Crack! A deep gash appears in the tree trunk. The crack runs from the bottom to the hilt of the tree trunk, where it merges with the branches. The crack widens, slowly and menacingly, like someone is prying open the tree trunk to get outside.

With a sudden crack, the tree splits open.

"You are *not* worthy," says Saraph again, as it slithers out of the cracked open tree.

Chapter 35
The Reveal

"Kill the snake! Kill the snake!" Costello shouts to his men.

Boom! Boom! Boom! A volley of bullets is fired at Saraph.

Saraph advances. The soldiers retreat. The machine guns keep roaring. Saraph hisses, all seven mouths baring sharp fangs, dripping venom. But he doesn't even wince at the bullets, which fly waywardly after bouncing off its impenetrable skin. The snake God arches its back, like stretching its body after a deep slumber, and spits out streams of venom from its many mouths, like water sprinklers squirting all over the garden. Heaps of venom fall on the soldiers stacked together. The soldiers are fully drenched in pungent smelling, gooey fluid. Its greenish tint reminds me of phlegm from a wet cough. The goo sticks to the soldiers like glue, thwarting their every movement. The men scream and shout, struggling to break free. Slowly, one by one, they fall on their knees, grabbing their throats as if choking. Their veins distend. Purple, crisscrossed lines appear on their faces, on their arms and neck - venom flowing through the bloodstream. They writhe in pain, make gurgling sounds and spit out white foam, which froths at their mouths. The struggle to hold onto dear life is unbearable to watch. I cannot imagine how it feels. Within a minute, they lie on the ground, unmoving. Dead.

Only Costello remains.

Costello aims his revolver at Saraph's belly and fires. Tiny bullets hit Saraph's enclosed hands which protect the belly. The bullets fall away like dead mosquitoes from a zapping machine. Costello unloads bullets, till he is left with none. He still keeps pulling the trigger in the mad rush, and hope, to kill Saraph. But the revolver returns empty clicks.

Realizing he is defeated, and imminent death is moments away, Costello lets go of the revolver and falls to his knees. Doesn't flee. Where would he? Doesn't fight back. How would he?

Saraph swoops down and wraps its mighty hand around Costello. The snake squeezes its hand, slightly. Costello lets out a groan, air pushed out of his lungs, his old bones creaking.

"Arthur, the unworthy." The middle head of Saraph looms dangerously close to Costello's face, the forked tongue inches away.

"I killed you. You fell. Bit dust. How are you still alive?"

Saraph hisses, sounds like a guffaw. Its hand tightens. Costello yelps in pain, his rib cage threatening to disintegrate.

"You forget the Sentinel ways, Arthur. I am not surprised."

Saraph picks up Costello from the ground, his legs dangling in midair, and brings him closer. If Costello could reach out with his hand, he would be able to touch Saraph's tusk-like fangs. The dagger of God Saraph falls from Costello's shirt pocket. Azura rushes forward to pick it up. It's a Sentinel treasure, the key to enter the Garden. It must be kept safe. She uses the belt of vines around her waist to stow away the dagger, like sheathing a sword in a scabbard hanging from the waist.

Saraph says with a sibilant whisper, "There is a reason I have lived for six thousand years. There is a reason the Sentinels call me the God of Rebirth. I am forever charged with the protection of Eden, forever confined to the Garden. Never dying, never going out of Eden. It's my boon, my bane."

Costello's shoulders sag. He mutters, almost like a whisper to himself, "I knew you were a formidable force, God Saraph. I knew it would take an army to kill you. But I believed it could be done. With science, with modern warfare, with shrewdness. My entire plan hinged on this belief - there is no God, and if there is, it's only in our minds, mortal and vulnerable."

"Goodbye, Arthur. You will be an example for any unworthy force threatening to take Eden in the times to come. People will tell stories about you. You will be remembered as the evil that was scoured from the world."

Saraph open its middle mouth, large enough to fit a minivan. Costello cringes, his death no longer looming, but knocking on the door.

"STOP!"

Saraph stops mid-motion, surprised at the audacity.

I am stunned at the incredulity. It's not Costello who has spoken. It's Azura.

"Stop, God Saraph. Please stop."

Azura steps forward, her hands joined at the palms, praying to God Saraph.

"Queen Azura?" Saraph turns, holding Costello in midair, inches from its mouth.

"Please forgive this man." Azura lowers her head and bends on one knee.

Saraph slithers to Azura. "This man does not deserve to live. Why the kindness in your heart?"

She bites her lips.

Costello looks at Azura, a glimmer of hope in his eyes. Maybe, just maybe, he would not die today.

"What are you doing, Azura?" I raise my voice. "Remember how many Sentinels have died today because of this vile man. Remember how he smashed the skull of an innocent little girl at the village. Or what he made you do by taking your daughter hostage. Do you remember?"

"I remember! I remember everything." Azura snaps.

"Then, why are you trying to save him?"

"Because…"

Azura bites her lips again. Closes her eyes, as if she herself doesn't believe what she is going to say.

"Because he is my father."

Chapter 36

Father's Betrayal

I remain frozen in my position. Stumped.

"What?" Costello's face contracts with incredulity. "I am your father?"

"Yes," Azura nods, a single bob of the head, sure and firm. She turns and beseeches Saraph. "Please do not kill him."

Saraph hisses. "You know that all Sentinels, royalty or not, are bound by the same laws, Queen Azura. Sentinels are charged with the protection of Eden. Any defector who eats the fruit of immortality for selfish reasons is punishable by death. Arthur is a renegade Sentinel. He must be punished."

"Yes, please punish him by all means. I am not asking for forgiveness on his behalf. I am asking for leniency. He deserves to be punished, but please do not kill him."

"I can understand your pain. But the old laws are clear. A Sentinel who eats the fruit of Eden is punishable by death. I cannot grant Arthur clemency just because he is the father of the Sentinel Queen."

"No, not because he is my father. But, because he did not eat the fruit of immortality. He only plucked the apple. Didn't eat it. Yet."

Saraph hisses. Azura has picked up on technicality in the old law like a shrewd lawyer. The judge, Saraph, now sits uncomfortably, thinking.

"Interesting conundrum you have put me in, Queen Azura. I am bound by the old laws, simple and clear, which for millennia have served me right. But for the first time, someone has tangled me in the ancient words of justice. This man, Arthur, must be, has to be punished for the evil that he brought upon the Sentinels and what they have protected for years. But you are right, I cannot punish him with death. Yet."

Saraph inches closer to Azura.

"What punishment do you suggest then, Queen Azura?"

Azura stands up from her kneeling position. "He can be incarcerated for life here on Sentinel Island, under our supervision. Spend the last of his old age repenting for what he has done."

Saraph broods over Azura's suggestion.

"I doubt repentance would come easy." Saraph tightens his grip on Costello, who groans in discomfort. "But what you suggested does give me an idea."

Saraph turns, each of its seven heads facing and hissing at Costello. "Arthur Costello, you are to spend the rest of your days confined to the Garden of Eden."

I gasp. Is it a punishment or a reward?

Saraph continues, "You cannot, for any reason, cross the threshold of Eden to the outside world. One step on the thousand-step staircase and I will eat you alive."

Costello brightens up at the prospect of living in Eden.

"But," says Saraph. "You are forbidden to eat from the apple tree. You take a bite from the apple, and I will eat you alive. So, here you will bide the rest of your days, enchanted and bewitched by the apple tree, knowing a single bite will end it all."

I chortle, realizing the poetic justice in Costello's sentence. The old man had longed for Eden for many years. He now gets to live in it permanently. Except, he cannot eat the fruit that he most desires. He will spend each and every one of his remaining days looking at the fruit he cannot have, unless he wants to die. If old age wouldn't kill him, the dilemma would.

Azura bows her head in deference. "Thank you for the kindness, God Saraph."

"Only time will tell if it's kindness or torture for old Arthur."

Saraph releases Costello from his grip. The old man falls on the ground, the impact cushioned by bushy grass. He grimaces in pain. With utmost effort, he stands up as fast as his doddery bones allow.

"I am leaving now, Arthur," says Saraph. "Do not compel me to come and kill you. Remember, no leaving the Garden. No eating the apple."

"But there is no house, no food here. Where will I stay? What will I eat?"

"Figure it out."

Saraph slithers to the apple tree and into the crack. A moment later the snake God is gone, vanished inside the tree. An unseen hand closes the crack in the apple tree, like shutting a door.

Costello faces Azura. "You are my daughter?"

"The daughter you abandoned? Yes, that's me."

Costello creases his brow. "But Lianna never said anything to me. Not even a word."

"When did you give Maa a chance to say anything? You were so consumed by greed. You tried to steal the dagger, took the bribe of diamonds from my grandmother, who was only too happy to see you out of her daughter's life, and you ran away. Left Maa alone and pregnant."

"I know, I know." Costello's face contorts in pain, not physical pain but something far deeper. "I loved your mother. The only person I have ever truly loved. But there was no other way. I knew she would never betray her people and steal the apples. I had to choose - my love or immortality."

Costello pauses. He bows his head. When he looks up his eyes are red and moist, tears welled up behind his sunken eyes.

"And you chose greed," says Azura.

Costello sighs. "The hardest decision I ever had to make."

A stream of tears flows down his cheeks, like water in a reservoir is suddenly released. He wipes his eyes with his shirt sleeve. He looks straight at Azura.

"Forgive me, my child. I didn't know I had a daughter. Or-"

He turns and looks at Aana. "…or a granddaughter."

"Would you have done anything differently had you known?" Azura asks squarely.

Costello remains quiet, unsure how to respond.

"You killed so many people today, Father. You killed an innocent child at the village center. And you would have killed your own granddaughter if I had not obeyed you."

Costello looks at his feet, doesn't deny it. He had meant to kill Aana if it had come to that.

"You are a monster underneath the garb of a human."

Azura walks away.

Costello staggers after her. "Wait. You have to understand…" he raises his voice, so it reaches his miffed daughter. "I had to do it. I had to follow the purpose that has guided me all these years."

Azura suddenly turns around, faces Costello. "And what's that, huh? What's that purpose which has completely twisted your moral compass? Which gives you the license to kill people, innocent people, as you please."

Costello stays quiet.

"Speak! Tell me, what was your purpose?"

Costello clears his throat, as if getting ready to give a toast at a cocktail party.

"To eradicate the disease of old age."

"And how did you plan to do it?"

"By creating a pill for long life, giving every person the choice and freedom to live as long as they desire."

"And you planned to distribute this pill for free?"

"Of course not," he says.

"Then I am sorry to burst your bubble, father. Your purpose was to make money, not eradicate old age."

"That is not entirely true," Costello retorts.

"And who are you fooling with this noble purpose of yours? You are an old man. What use is money if you are going to die in another fifteen or twenty years? Admit it, Father. First and foremost, you wanted immortality for yourself. Money was a close second."

Costello is perplexed. He starts to say something but stops. He is thinking, not knowing how to respond. His true intentions, naked and ugly, have been uncovered, clear for all to see.

"Yes." He clears his throat. "You are right. And it can all be yours as my only heir. The money, the riches, immortal life - all yours till eternity."

"Are you bribing me, Father?"

"Think about it, Azura. Think about what you can provide for your people. They will become rich and sophisticated, living in mansions, dining on meats from Argentina and wine from Tuscany. A perfect life, an envious life."

"And because we are unsophisticated you think we are not rich?"

"Yes! You have not experienced luxury. You don't know what you don't know. Trust me, you will be doing your people a service. They will love you for it."

"Which people, Father? Your men killed most of my people today."

Costello sighs. "What's done is done, Azura. Let's move forward. Let's think of the future we can build together. Let's think of-"

Costello looks around and scurries to Aana. He puts his heavy, wrinkled hands on Aana's tiny shoulders. "Let's think of Aana and the future she can have."

"Aren't you forgetting something, Father?"

"What?"

"You are not allowed to leave this Garden, or eat from the tree."

"Yes, but you can! You can take these apples and fulfill my purpose. Create the pill for longer life and bring it back for me. I am forbidden to eat the apple, but I can eat a pill infused with the apple's elixir. We can entangle Saraph in a technicality again. Saraph said no apple, not no pill."

Costello beams, giving Azura a broad smile.

"First, you might have forgotten, but it is God Saraph. Show some respect to the God who spared your life."

Costello dismisses her with a wave of his hand.

Azura continues, "Second, I am not interested one bit in doing your dirty work. If material possessions made one truly rich, you would not have come here seeking more of it. So, my answer is no, Father. You are to spend the last of your days as God Saraph commanded."

Costello seethes, his nostrils flare, his teeth grit against each other.

"No!" he shouts. "You have to help me get out of here, Azura. I can't live here like a monk and die like a beggar. Please, help me get out of here."

"I am sorry. I can't."

"No!"

Costello thrusts his hands in his hair. He starts to shake. He coughs and coughs. The cancer in his lungs threatens to burst out through his mouth. His face contorts into an agitated expression.

"No, you can't leave me here to die," he says.

His body starts to tremble, as if death is staring at him in the face. His eyes run amok, as if searching for an answer on the ground. Suddenly, all his movements stop, his eyes focused on something few feet from him.

It's his revolver.

"No, Costello. You don't want to do that," I say, reading his mind.

"Shut up, you moron."

He scrambles for the gun.

"No!" screams Azura.

"No!" I shout, bolting after him.

Costello picks up the gun before we can apprehend him. He grabs Aana. Brings up the revolver and stabs Aana's head with the muzzle.

"Stop right there!" he says. "Or I will kill the kid."

We stop in our tracks.

Azura is baffled. "What are you doing, Father? She is your granddaughter!"

"I don't care. I want out. And you are the only person who can help me, Azura."

"Have you lost your mind? There is no way out of here for you."

"There is! Take the apples to my scientists in London and bring me the pill. You do that, and I promise no harm will come to Aana."

Without a word, Azura starts to walk toward Costello, her gait brisk and firm.

Costello points the gun at Azura.

"Stop! Stop right there!"

"Or what, you are going to kill your own daughter?"

Azura keeps moving forward.

"Stop, Azura."

She doesn't.

"Don't make me do this. I will pull the trigger."

Azura keeps moving forward, now yards from Costello.

Costello pulls the trigger.

Chapter 37
Kill, Kill, Kill

Costello pulls the trigger again. And again. Every time it comes out blank. Doesn't fire.

Azura stops right in front of Costello, the gun barrel thrust into her chest. Costello pulls the trigger again. Doesn't work.

"Such madness, such haste that you forgot you spent every bullet on God Saraph. Remember?"

Sudden realization hits Costello like lightning. His shoulders slump, his eyes close. He thumps his forehead in dismay. When his eyes open, for the first time tonight he looks terrified. He had looked scared, deeply worried in the hands of God Saraph. But now, in front of his incensed daughter, he looks horrified.

"Come here, Aana," says Azura, her voice exuding steely authority.

Aana tries to walk, but Costello's large hand on her shoulder stops her.

Azura's fiery eyes burrow into Costello. With the composure that befits a queen, she says, "Let. Go."

Costello ponders.

Azura stays silent, her raging gaze focused, ready to burst any moment.

Finally, Costello relents. He removes his hand from Aana. "Maa!"

Aana darts to her mother. Azura embraces her daughter, her gaze not leaving Costello once. She doesn't trust him, she doesn't care for him. Not anymore.

"Sweetheart," Azura says to Aana. "Go and wait for me at the base of the Garden stairs. I will be there soon."

"I am scared, Maa. I don't want to go alone."

"You are a big girl now, Aana. You are strong, you are powerful, you are the princess of this land. There is nothing to be afraid of. No one can harm you now. I promise."

Azura casts a spiteful glance at Costello, before returning her focus to her daughter.

"You start first, Aana. Wait for me at the base of the stairs, and I will be there even before you know it."

The little girl bobs her head. She turns around and walks away, her pace slow, her eyes looking straight ahead, no more afraid.

Azura waits till Aana is out of earshot. She straightens up and faces her father.

"You know, for once I thought you had a heart."

"I am sorry, Azura. Forgive me."

Azura ignores him. "For once, I thought I saw the heart that my mother saw in you. But I was wrong. I was gullible. Almost hopeful. Just like my mother. Family means nothing to you. You were ready to kill your own daughter, your own granddaughter without batting an eyelid. No qualms whatsoever."

"Forgive me. Please."

In one swift motion, Azura pulls out the dagger of God Saraph.

Costello jumps away in surprise. "What are you doing, Azura?"

"You never deserved to live, Father. I was wrong to ask God Saraph to grant you leniency. Come to think of it, Grandmother should have killed you on the *Primrose* that fateful night years ago. Nothing that has transpired since would have happened. But we have no control over the past. The present, though, is a different matter. I will do today what Grandmother should have done."

Costello brings up his right hand to punch Azura. But he is slow, with reflexes of a seventy-year-old. Azura grabs his hand before it reaches her.

"Goodbye, Father."

"No! Please, no!" Costello's voice cracks, his appeals falling on deaf ears.

Azura tightens her hand on the dagger and jams it at the base of his chin. It pierces the soft tissue above his Adam's apple, runs through his mouth, cutting his tongue and rams into the bottom of his skull.

Costello's whole body shakes uncontrollably. He makes gurgling sounds. Air runs out of pathways.

Azura twists the dagger inside, tearing away brain matter and arteries alike.

Costello collapses on the ground with a dull thud. Dead.

Chapter 38

Rest in Peace

Blood spills out and creeps into the fleshy grass. Costello lays on the ground, unmoving. His eyes open, still in shock. Within a matter of minutes, Azura went from saving him from the clutches of God Saraph to tearing him apart with a knife. The shock of it both visible and palpable in his eyes.

Azura bends beside the corpse of her father. She brings up her hand and waves it over Costello's face, closing his rigid eyes.

"May God be kind to you in hell," she says to the body.

She cleans the blood off the dagger in the grass and sheathes it.

"What do we do with the body? Do you burn the body or bury it in Sentinel culture?" I ask. I motion to the dead bodies of the soldiers as well.

"Bury." She stands up straight. "But carrying these dead men up a thousand steep stairs would be suicide. We have no choice but to bury them here in the Garden."

I nod along. Climbing down a thousand steps was a punishment when we came to the Garden. Now, climbing up a thousand steps with five bodies in tow would be catastrophic.

"Why don't you go ahead and be with Aana? She must be anxious and panicky. I will take care of the burial," I offer.

"You know what?" she says suddenly. A spark lights up in her eyes. "Let it be. Let them lie here for eternity. Let them be a gruesome reminder to anybody who tries to seize the apple tree with force. If you are unworthy, it will end in nothing else but cold death, the soul forever trapped in limbo."

I shrug. "You are the queen. So be it."

She smiles wryly. "I am the queen," Azura whispers almost to herself. "Time to pick the broken pieces of whatever is left of the Sentinels."

"Wait."

I amble over to a spurned machine gun. I pick it up and check the magazine. Enough bullets remain.

"Need to scare away some helicopters," I explain.

Azura nods once and starts walking to the exit. I fling the machine gun over my shoulder and follow.

After a few paces, I stop. I turn to look at the apple tree one last time. Its charm strong, its attraction bewitching. A part of me wants to run, grab an apple, and bite into its juicy flesh.

"Go take one," says Azura. "You proved yourself worthy of it to God Saraph. You deserve it."

I look at Azura and smile at the generosity. "That was before I became a Sentinel. Now, though, I am a Sentinel and forbidden to eat the fruit."

She chuckles. "Right you are," she says, like it was a trick question and I answered correctly.

I turn away from the tree. "Let's get out of here."

We walk to the staircase and find Aana sitting on the bottom step, her glum face propped between her hands. She jumps in delight on seeing her mother. Azura runs to her and picks her up. She plants a kiss on her daughter's forehead.

"You were so brave today, my sweet little girl."

"No, I was so scared, Maa!"

"It's okay to be scared, baby. Even I was scared," says Azura. "But what's more important is that you overcame the fear with courage. And you became fearless."

Aana's face bursts into a grin.

Azura sets Aana down and holds her hand. "Come, time to go to the village."

We start ascending the thousand-step staircase. It proves more arduous now that the rush of adrenaline has subsided. We plow and slog and lift ourselves, one step at a time, fighting against our weary and sleep-deprived bodies. But none of us complain. We all know, this is the final stretch.

We reach the top, come out of the hole in the tree and collapse on the forest floor, our chests heaving, our breathing heavy.

Suddenly, I hear a rustle in the nearby trees. I sit up with a jerk. Azura leaps to her feet.

"Who goes there? Show yourself," Azura yells, pulling out the dagger and pushing Aana behind her.

I bring up my machine gun.

The rustling comes closer.

I remove the gun safety, my finger on the trigger.

And out comes Skinny with five other Sentinel guards.

"My queen," they all say in unison, lowering their tridents and going to one knee.

Azura heaves a sigh of relief. She puts her dagger away. I put the gun safety on.

"I am so relieved to see you all alive. What's the situation in the village?" asks Azura.

"We killed the enemy soldiers at the village center," Skinny offers flatly. No emotion, remorse or relief, in his voice. "We came here to save you and the princess. Found four enemy soldiers in flying machines by the river."

Skinny pauses.

"Killed them all," he says with vengeful pride.

Azura nods, once, twice, thrice, relief gushing through her veins.

"We can rest in peace, finally."

Chapter 39

What's My Name?

The next few hours pass in a blur. We trek back to the village, exhausted, drowsy, and relieved. Quietude shrouds the village. Or, maybe it's the calm after the storm, which left two-thirds of the Sentinels dead in its wake.

Yoni, the Ayurvaid, receives us at the village center now functioning as a makeshift hospital. She takes me by the hand, like I am a kid who will run away, and tends to my broken nose. She cleans crusted blood and piles a stinky paste all over and inside my nose. It's painful. But I am too tired to flinch.

Meanwhile, Azura goes to each and every Sentinel in the room, commiserating lost lives while encouraging them to see the future they need to rebuild together. Tears are shed, smiles are shared, bonds are strengthened. I think that is the hallmark of a true leader – empathetic and inspirational in the same breath. Someone who understands the present, envisions the future, and energizes her people to want to achieve that future. It's that simple. Or that difficult. But, Azura is a natural.

"How are you feeling?" Azura walks over, showing me the same empathy as the rest of the Sentinels.

"I have been better. I feel like a lemon squeezed between God Saraph's powerful hands." I smile. "How are you feeling?"

She shrugs her shoulders.

"Well, I lost most of my tribe today. I nearly lost Eden, the Garden I have sworn to protect. And I shudder to even think that there was a possibility I would have lost Aana today."

She sighs. And then brightens up.

"But you know what. I feel calm. I feel accomplished. As if I battled a monster and won."

"Well, you did."

"Yes, I did." She does not smile. "My father. And I killed him."

I don't know what to say. I grow quiet, grappling with a flood of memories, sad and horrific.

"Hello?" Azura snaps her fingers. "Hello? Where are you lost?" she asks me.

"Here. Now. I feel lost." I shake my head. "Even without my memory, I had a purpose before. Now, I am lost, without a purpose, without a mission. I am a Sentinel, but I don't know what that means anymore."

"Well, as your queen, I can tell you it means rebuilding what we have lost."

"But, how do you rebuild two-thirds of your population?"

Azura smiles. "Slowly."

I am not convinced. "And who would protect the Garden till then?"

"If you haven't figured it by now, let me tell you a secret. The Garden needs no one for protection except God Saraph. My ancestors created the purpose of protecting the Garden because they felt exactly like you feel right now: lost. Protecting the Garden gave them, and now us, a sense of purpose. So, we became the Sentinels, the guardians. The name says it all."

"Name." I murmur the word to myself, as if dissecting it from every angle.

"What?"

"You know, I just realized." I look into Azura's mesmerizing eyes. "I don't remember my name. And the people who knew - Costello, Shawn, Michelle - are all dead."

"If you ask me, it is the best position to be in. You get to choose your own name."

"Yeah…but…" I let the sentence dangle, my mind trying to search my name in its empty storeroom.

A broad grin sweeps over Azura's face. "But if you want," she says. "I can help you with it."

The Apple

My mouth jumps open in surprise. "You have known my name all along?"

"Wait here." Azura turns and rushes out, leaving me puzzled.

I look around the room sheepishly, knowing many Sentinel eyes are on me. I might have become a Sentinel, but I am still a stranger. A stranger who gets special attention from the queen. That cannot be a good starting point to make friends with my comrades.

Azura returns. She clutches a dirty-brown satchel, torn and in dire need of a wash.

"This was on you when we first found you in the Garden." She hands me the bag.

I remember the satchel from my dreams. Both Michelle and I had one when we came to the island.

I take the bag with hesitant fingers. I inspect all its sides like it's some long-lost antique. There is no brand name. No words marked or embossed or stitched into the leather bag.

I look at Azura questioningly.

"Open it."

I unbuckle the front flap and flip it open. There is a smudged rectangular tag stitched at the top of the inside back panel. It says:

NOT WORTH STEALING. TRUST ME.
PROPERTY OF GOOD BOLT.

"Good Bolt? Good? Bolt?" I murmur the name like a mantra.

"So?" Azura grins. "You know who you are now?"

I look up. Ruminate for a second. And, then, grin back.

"My name is *Good*?" I stress on my first name like it is a rabid street dog.

"Well, if you ask me, it could have been Bad." She laughs out loud. "Good is better than Bad."

"Very funny!"

She regains her composure. "Like I said, it's a good place to start, no pun intended. You can choose whoever you want to be now. Just pick a name. Any name."

"You know what? I am just going to stick with my name. My last name. Bolt."

"Bolt… it does have a nice ring to it."

I smile and nod. "I am Bolt. I am a Sentinel."

Azura's lips break into a soft grin. Her chest rises a little. Her head held high, as if proud.

We look into each other's eyes, unsure of what to say next. We keep smiling, keep gazing, like a game of who-blinks-first. If there was ever a moment when I wanted to lean in and kiss Azura, it is this. Right now. Here.

Azura blinks first, averts her gaze. Her right hand unwittingly moves up and clutches the circular locket around her neck, tied in place with a thick black thread. She rubs the locket with her hand, thinking.

"Sentinel Bolt," she says, her voice teeming with cold professionalism, her eyes lost in oblivion. "Earlier, you told me you are searching for a purpose, a mission." She turns. Stops fidgeting with her locket. Looks at me. "I have a mission for you."

I raise my brows, intrigued.

"Your bag…" She points to my tattered satchel. "… reminds me that you were once a hunter. A worthy hunter who found the Garden of Eden."

She pauses. "I want you to find somebody."

"Who?"

Azura raises her hands behind her neck. Using her fingers, she tries to untangle the knot in the thick thread that holds the locket. After a brief struggle, she gives up unraveling the knot. She grabs the thread with both her hands, flexes her muscles and pulls with all her might. Her face contorts, her knuckles turn pale. And then, without warning, the thread rips apart.

"Him." Azura dangles the locket in front of her, one hand clutching both ends of the torn thread.

I am confused. Puzzled, rather.

"I got this locket made when my husband was going into the outside world. Something to remember him by. Something to hold close on days when longing for him knows no bounds. It was his idea. Two lockets of a kind. One for him, one for me. It seemed quite romantic at the time."

She hands me the locket. "It opens. Go ahead, open it!" she says.

I inspect the locket from all angles. It's circular, made of silver, like a large coin. I rub it between my fingers. It's smooth. Both its sides have been polished to perfection. Her constant caresses have dimmed the shine, but I can still catch a faint reflection. Two tiny notches protrude from the locket, one above another, levers to pry it open. I understand what Azura meant. I pull apart the notches. The locket opens like a book, hinged at the spine.

Two smiling faces gaze at me, one on each side, like two adjacent pages of an open book. They are paintings, black and white, probably hand-drawn with charcoal. But the artistry is mind-boggling. Despite using only charcoal, and drawn on two-dimensional paper, the closeup of the two faces is brimming with life. As if a three-dimensional sculpture, each nook and cranny and contour of the two faces are drawn with utmost care, defined to perfection.

One face is of Azura, happy and confident, a glint in her eyes, a curl in her lips. The other face, haughty, bursting with an air of superiority, almost royalty, with black-gray patches of vitiligo.

I gasp! I know the other face.

"You seem to remember my husband," says Azura.

I nod, intently, slowly, remembering the man in my dream, dressed in all black, standing in the shadows of Costello's office.

"Rana," I mutter. "Costello's associate."

Azura inhales deeply, takes a step back, almost stumbling. Her face is ashen, as if I just confirmed her deepest fear, her most profound sorrow.

She takes a deep breath, again. But this time, she stands tall. She adjusts her headdress. Looks me in the eye.

"I want you to find my husband. Bring him home. Alive… or dead."

Acknowledgements

The Apple took me 4 years to write, and another year to edit and publish. And the only reason you are reading it now and not in 2050 is because of my wife and best friend, Megha Kapoor. She inspired me to take up the pen (figuratively), encouraged me when I had to re-start from scratch after 3 years of writing because nothing made sense, and whipped my lazy bottom to "get the first draft done by 24 Nov 2018 or start sleeping on the couch!" Why I remember that date? It was her birthday. And all she asked as gift was the first draft of my first book.

The Apple wouldn't exist if it weren't for you, Megha. You motivated me to start writing. You read my first draft, and the second, and the third…and the fiftieth. You supported every decision I made, and every penny I spent in making The Apple a professional, quality book. For your unshakeable faith, love, guidance and ideas, I am immensely grateful. Love you, sweetheart!

A big hug to my Mom, Suman, who always told me, "Only if you can imagine, you can write". Not once did she fetter my imagination as a child, no matter how weird. In her household, being imaginative was a compliment, and for me, the highest badge of honor. She still fondly recounts the first line of the first story I ever wrote – "My mom is like a queen." Well, she still is – a compassionate, loving queen – who inspired the character of Liana, Azura's mom in The Apple. Thank you for always being there, Mom! Love you!

Thank you to my dad, Vijay, who introduced me to my first novel (a Hardy Boys mystery) when I was 7, and gave me an advice which completely and entirely shaped my grasp of the English language (not my mother tongue). He used to say, "Listen to the sentence, Dev. Listen to its beat, its rhythm.

Just listen. If it's off key, you'd know you haven't followed grammar rules. But if it sounds like music, go ahead and break grammar rules." Dad, you made me find my writing voice when all else failed. Thank you!

I am much grateful to my big sis, Suvigya, and younger bro, Ashutosh. They were my first friends. My first comrades with whom I went on many adventures (all imaginative!). Considering how shy I was, my childhood would have been a heap of boredom if it weren't for them. My sister is and was like a mamma bear, protecting me at every corner. While my brother showed me the secret ingredients of life: spice and mischief! Hugs to my sis and bro for their undying love and unwavering support.

I like to see myself as a storyteller first (passion), a brand builder second (profession that pays the bills), and writer third (hobby). Much, much gratitude to my first storyteller – my Grandma. She made me fall in love with stories to the point that it became a passion, a profession and an avocation. For all the yarns that were stitched, and the imagination that was stretched, thank you Dadi from the bottom of my heart!

I am deeply indebted to Ashima, Digvijay, Aabha and Udit – my mother, father, sister and brother on my wife's side – my extended family who have always, and I mean always, supported me no matter what. I am glad you came into my life because of Megha, but I am happy you stayed because of the close bond we share. Thank you!

A big shout out to my principal, Carver Sir, and English teachers – Gurmeet Sir, Cheema Ma'am and Bhutalia Ma'am – at St. Stephen's School, Chandigarh (India). You taught me, encouraged me, scolded me (sometimes). If I can write today, it's because of you. I owe you. Everything.

To Patrick Knowles, my book cover designer: you infused life into this book with your artistry. You went above and beyond, and delivered a spectacular cover. You were relentlessly helpful and patient. I cannot thank you enough!

To Matrice, my editor: you chiseled The Apple to perfection when it came to you in tatters. In my opinion, you took the book from good to great. You are a true professional who put aside personal tragedy and delivered on your commitment. Much strength to you sister! Thank you!

And, I'd like to thank you – the reader. You took a chance; you trusted a first-time author. I hope I lived up to the expectations you had of The Apple. If not, please do write in to me at devashish.sardana@gmail.com – I am always open to candid feedback.

Thank you!

Made in the USA
Middletown, DE
29 November 2019